Sudden

An anonymous note to the police, warning of a murder to be committed, precedes the burning to death of an unhappy Andrew Lattimer in his exploded car on the purple slopes of the Great Morte Moor. With Lattimer's whorish and greedy-for-money wife missing, and evidence found suggesting that he had made an appointment to meet his murderer on the moor, pipe-smoking Detective Superintendent George Rogers is burdened with a more than puzzling investigation. It is not helped by the dead Lattimer's aggressively-inclined brother and sisters who are convinced that they know who killed him and are critical of Rogers's competence in doing something about it.

More to the susceptible detective's taste, his passion not all spent on investigating dead bodies, is the murdered Lattimer's attractive neighbour who, while reminding him physically of an admired Queen Nefertiti, raises his suspicions by appearing to know more about Mrs Lattimer's first husband – who died violently of a broken neck – and her present lover than perhaps she should.

When a third man, known to have enjoyed Mrs Lattimer's easily acquired favours, is choked to death after a late-night assignation with an unknown woman, Rogers is able to find a solution in which he is forced to accept that it is possible for the sensibly obvious to be turned inside-out.

This, the fifteenth in Ross's series, shows Rogers at the height of his investigative powers, with the police procedure as absorbing as ever, and a characteristically satisfying denouement.

Also by Jonathan Ross

The blood running cold (1968)
Diminished by death (1968)
Dead at first hand (1969)
The deadest thing you ever saw (1969)
Here lies Nancy Frail (1972)
The burning of Billy Toober (1974)
I know what it's like to die (1976)
A rattling of old bones (1979)
Dark blue and dangerous (1981)
Death's head (1982)
Dead eye (1983)
Dropped dead (1984)
Burial deferred (1985)
Fate accomplished (1987)

Under the name of John Rossiter

The murder makers (1970)
The deadly green (1970)
The victims (1971)
A rope for General Dietz (1972)
The manipulators (1973)
The villains (1974)
The golden virgin (1975)
The man who came back (1978)
Dark flight (1981)

SUDDEN DEPARTURES

Jonathan Ross

Constable London

First published in Great Britain 1988
by Constable & Company Ltd
10 Orange Street, London WC2H 7EG
Copyright © 1988 by Jonathan Ross
Set in Linotron Palatino 10pt by
Rowland Phototypesetting Ltd
Bury St Edmunds, Suffolk
Printed in Great Britain by
St Edmundsbury Press Ltd
Bury St Edmunds, Suffolk

British Library CIP data
Ross, Jonathan
Sudden departures.
I. Title
823'.914[F]   PR6068.0835

ISBN 0 09 468330 1 ✓

1

THE CHIEF OF POLICE, ABBOTSBURN. THIS IS TO INFORM YOU
THAT I HAVE CERTAIN KNOWLEDGE OF A MURDER TO BE COM-
MITTED DURING THE NEXT FEW DAYS. I CANNOT WRITE MORE
BECAUSE IT WOULD MAKE ME KNOWN TO HIM. I AM FRIGHT-
ENED. YOU MUST BELIEVE ME AND TRY TO PREVENT IT.

Minute 1. *To Detective Superintendent Rogers from D. Vandis, Chief
Constable.* Anonymous letter and envelope for your information
and whatever action can be taken on this dubious warning. What
does he/she think we can do?

Minute 2. *To Detective Sergeant Magnus from Geo. Rogers, Det. Supt.*
What does this envelope and note tell us apart from its message?
Record all details. Photocopy and despatch original to laboratory.
Immediate.

Minute 3. *To Detective Superintendent Rogers from R. Magnus,
D/Sergt.* Envelope, white self-seal. Posted p.m. 16 August at
Abbotsburn General Post Office. First-class stamp. Delivered HQ
8.30 a.m. 17 August and opened in Admin. Dept. Note printed on
trimmed A4 script paper. Subject to confirmation by laboratory
examination, text on both envelope and note appears to be by
black felt-tip pen. Fingerprint fragments on paper and envelope
too few characteristics for identification. Photocopies attached.

Minute 4. *To Detective Chief Inspector Lingard from Geo. Rogers, Det.
Supt.* Unless you have a crystal ball in your office which will
identify anonymous letter writers, there seems little we can do
about this uninformative warning. It may be a hoax but needs,

nevertheless, to be borne in mind. All unusual deaths purporting to be natural, accidental or incidental on any violence to be brought to my notice immediately. If somebody does get murdered it is a certainty that we will be criticized by those with more hindsight than we have foresight. Keep file active. All CID personnel to note.

2

Detective Superintendent George Rogers sat with his file of papers in the well of the Abbotsburn Crown Court. The case being tried before judge and jury was deadeningly familiar stuff to him, its facts made anaemic of interest by the drawn-out hours of legal time-wasting and misrepresentation of motives. Rogers felt paralysed to a mental numbness in a suffocating closed-in atmosphere exhausted to staleness by too many lungs.

A woman, the unhappy result of his most recent investigation, stood indicted on charges of murder, attempted murder and manslaughter, and a psychiatrist had been endeavouring to convince the jury that her actions had been provoked in a mind disorganized by a womanizing husband's callousness and corrupted by an addiction to cocaine – both happening to be the truth – presenting a picture of a woman whose intent had been misunderstood and whose brain had been warped to irresponsibility.

Rogers, the victim in the attempted murder charge, had already given his evidence, narrowly overcoming an accusation by defending counsel that his being stabbed in the belly had been due to his own gross carelessness in receiving a kitchen knife being handed to him with a complete lack of malice by the accused. This was a remarkable something that he had foolishly or wickedly misunderstood at the time in the no doubt surprising circumstance of the blade of the knife penetrating its full eight inches into his intestines. Leaning towards sympathizing with her misfortunes, the allegation had neither surprised nor overly offended him, thankful that, in his effort to weaken Rogers's evidence, counsel hadn't also subjected him to the hackneyed accusations of barefaced lying, corrupt practices or having made improper sexual advances to her.

The scarlet-robed judge, inclined to tetchiness with a counsel tediously pursuing legal points he had already made frequently and lengthily throughout the trial, was also inclined to frown at any unexcused departure from the well of his court. Rogers, his need for a smoke becoming desperate, suffered. His inner discomfort was such that the woman prosecuting counsel engaged his attention only peripherally, attractive and shapely though she was beneath her grey-white barrister's wig and black stuff gown. And that was abnormal for Rogers who, with not all his passion spent, and now divorced by virtue of his wife's desertion of him, needed to include attractive and congenial women in his forward thinking were he not to spend the rest of his life making his own bed and, too often, preparing his revolting make-do meals in an empty flat.

An inch or so over six feet tall, he still possessed his own black hair, his full complement of teeth and a flat belly – although, thanks to the woman in the dock, a badly scarred one. His eyes were a deep brown with a policeman's unblinking stare and could darken and be hard at what they saw of inflicted cruelty, of the suffering and death it brought to *Homo sapiens* and those beings unfortunate enough to be born as animals. He had an arrogant wedge of a nose which he disparagingly compared with the beak of a vulture; a nose too often forced to sniff at the noisome flesh of the violently dead. His mouth, showing a reasonable amiability, could still discourage the over-familiarity of unsought mateyness. Working, and at most other times too, he wore charcoal-grey suits, white shirts and muted silk ties with matching breast-pocket handkerchieves, disdaining gaudiness in clothing as flamboyant self-advertising. Despite these impediments – as he chose to consider them – or because of them, women were attracted to him. But even in the solitariness of his bed he had convinced himself that he needed an agreeable rapport with a woman rather more than the availability of her body. And that, he accepted, could be the result of his approaching his thirty-eighth birthday.

His present massive boredom, concealed by a professional impassivity, was interrupted by a uniformed PC approaching him from behind and whispering a moist 'Urgent, sir' in his ear while handing him a folded piece of paper. Written on it was *Mr Lingard waiting on foyer phone. Said sudden departure reported*.

Lingard was his elegant second-in-command, the 'sudden departure' meaning that somebody had died, almost certainly bloodily because no non-criminous death would be the concern of the CID. It seemed a good enough reason for Rogers to stand, give an unnecessary but placating half-bow to His Dreadful Eminence, the judge, and escape the courtroom.

The sergeant in the telephone booth, holding the line open against any pushful member of the public wishing to use it, handed the receiver to Rogers. 'David,' Rogers said into it. 'You've saved my reason. What's happened?'

'I'm about to beetle off to find out.' Lingard's voice drawled, unflurried in what he was saying. 'An emergency call to the Fire Service and then passed over to us. A car on fire, a witness says – a little incoherently, I understand – probably due to an explosion because he heard the bang. A man inside, but chummy couldn't get near enough to drag him out and had to leave him burning. No other details given. Situation, the moor road above Morte-fuot. The communications car and ambulance are on the way, and I imagine that the fire appliance is already attending.'

'See you there, David,' Rogers said, closing down with an unaccustomed feeling of relief at the prospect of an investigation.

He handed his file papers to the waiting sergeant. 'Give these to our solicitor with my profound regrets,' he said, his tongue lodged firmly in his cheek. 'Tell him that I've been called away on a suspected murder.'

Outside, the brazen sun in a clear sky bounced heat from the stonework of the Law Court and from the melting asphalt of its parking area. That seemed unusual in Rogers's experience, accustomed as he was to being called out from his bed at night to somebody's dying in drenching rain, or to an Arctic-like world of freezing snow. Death by criminal violence and Rogers were not good friends. Unlike undertakers and wreath-makers, it laid an unremitting obligation on him to bring death's agent to justice. He filled and lit his pipe on the way to his car, already wondering how a man could get himself blown up in his car on a road that wasn't much more than a second-class goat track. And whether this was the predicted murder he had largely forgotten about during his four days of attendance at court.

3

Mortefuot, once a village meriting inclusion in the Domesday Book, was now, but for its name, an outlying adjunct to Abbotsburn. Only a crumbling grey stone church, the inhabitants of its graveyard outnumbering its Sunday congregation, survived the village it once served. Situated on the lower slopes of Great Morte Moor, Mortefuot's one-time northern road, a neglected inheritance from the Dark Ages, survived as a limestone track. Leaving the built-up area by a lane it rose to the slope of the moor, then doubled back to run along the flank above the village.

Rogers, his pipe necessarily clenched tightly between his teeth, climbed the steep gradient of the track in bottom gear, his forward vision showing a windscreen full of sky, his vision narrowed by banks made higher by giant ferns. Rising above them, he could see a thinning-out column of black smoke. The car's suspension, thumping and rattling over outcrops of limestone, shook the steering wheel in his hands. The interior of the car was only a little less hot than a baker's oven and he felt as though he was sitting on damp flannel. The two tiny flies who had chosen to come along with him, undeterred by a giant slapping hand, made determined and irritating forays against the sweat on his face. Unprofessionally, he considered, he had discarded his jacket and loosened his tie, beginning to doubt that all this was actually a relief from the boredom of a courtroom crawling to a verdict in full drone.

Reaching the turning onto the flank of the moor, he lost the steep gradient and most of the ferns, with climbing slopes of purple heather beneath a lot of blue sky replacing them. A half-mile or more of banging and rattling brought him to the rear of Lingard's green vintage Bentley, the tail-ender behind a police communications car and a white ambulance – each with its crews in shirt-sleeve order standing outside them – and the huge vibrating scarlet and chrome fire appliance that blocked Rogers's view of the smoking car in front of it. Pulling in behind the

Bentley and switching off his overheated engine, he unstuck himself from his seat and climbed out as Lingard approached.

His second-in-command, looking unnecessarily jaunty for the occasion, said, 'If you have tears to shed, George, prepare to shed them now.'

A dandified dresser with stylish mannerisms, Lingard was as much out of place on the rugged moor as would be a peacock. Elegant, blond, blue-eyed and a good-looking bachelor, he could afford to wear bespoke shoes and hand-sewn shirts high in the collar and long in the cuffs; in cooler weather, colourful and often embroidered waistcoats with his beautifully tailored suits. None of which made him less than disconcertingly physically destructive when he needed to be. Addicted to pushing attar of roses snuff into his patrician nose with flourishes adopted from the Regency period, and exemplified by his admired Beau Brummell, he would have preferred to have been born into that age of gallants and the enchanting women who feigned the vapours at their licentiousness. Still in love – so Rogers was convinced – with the memory of a promiscuous woman who had died in another's bed, he now sublimated what affection remained in him on his cherished Bentley.

'Fill me in, David,' Rogers said, putting on his jacket and tightening his tie as they passed by the sides of the parked vehicles baking in the sun. 'It's a killing? Not just a fire?'

'No chance.' Lingard was definite. 'A bomb of some sort planted in the car. The Fire Officer is sure and there're two witnesses, a Mr and Mrs Gullick. They were up here walking when it happened, heard the bang, then saw the car start to blaze. Other than that, I've had no more time than to ask them to stay put.'

Rogers now saw the car and he halted, standing with Lingard near the knot of firemen in their yellow helmets, one of whom was hosing water at its wheels and base. Smoke was coming from beneath it and, where the spray hit metal, it steamed and made a hissing noise like frying bacon. The bonnet lid had been burst from its hinges and flung to hang over the radiator, exposing a ripped apart engine. The rear of the car, although black with carbon, had escaped visible damage, only the tailgate window being shattered. The windscreen glass had been broken out and through its frame Rogers could see the head and shoulders of what had been a man or a woman. Blackened with carbon and hairless, the face had a small box-like object projecting from its jaws.

Rogers said, 'That thing in the face looks a little odd, David. Does anybody know what it is?'

Lingard shook his head. 'No. You can't get near enough and it's covered in soot anyway.'

'I've a feeling the poor devil in there is going to prove to be the subject of that anonymous letter,' Rogers said.

'Me, too.' Then the elegant detective murmured, 'Those know-it-alls you mentioned in your minute are going to say we should have anticipated something like this and had a squad of men up here waiting for it to happen.'

'Won't they just,' Rogers said drily. He moved to speak to Edmunds, the Fire Officer, wearing his identifying white helmet. 'I understand you think it's a planted bomb, Willie?' He had to raise his voice against the engine noise of the fire appliance.

'I wouldn't be here if it wasn't.' Edmunds was the fire Service's equivalent of Rogers; tall and gangling with a bony sardonic face and a man not to be taken too lightly. 'It was an explosion right enough, and not due to the fuel tank going up.' He grinned. 'And if you're going to ask me when you're going to be able to poke your head through the windscreen and have a closer look, it'll be another fifteen minutes at least. Too hot by far, even for a fireproof copper.'

'And hot enough without it.' Doing nothing but looking and shouting made Rogers sweat. 'Where's the smoke coming from?'

'The oil sump mainly. But the tyres as well. And before you ask, we've kept the water away from the body as much as we could.'

'Good for you, Willie. You had the emergency call from a man, I'm told.'

'From chummy up there, waiting with his wife.' Edmunds nodded his helmet in the direction of an outcrop of rock above them. A man and a woman sat on it, visible only from the waist upwards. Both wore red woollen hats and what looked like green shirts.

'He'd be a hell of a long way from a telephone, wouldn't he?'

'That's what I thought, George.'

'I'm going up there. Give me a shout when you've cooled the

car off.' To Lingard, he said, 'Get Sergeant Magnus up here with his camera, David. And I want him to sift through the ashes before the car's moved.' Magnus of the Fingerprint, Photographic and Search Department was a finder of the virtually unfindable, his searching eye meticulous in identifying evidential material in the debris of a crime. 'Then organize a body bag and shell and get the coroner's permission to move the body. While you're at it, notify the Pathology Lab that it's on its way to the mortuary. It'll make Dr Twite's day to have somebody other than a cardiac arrest to chop up.'

'And the Chief Constable?' Lingard suggested.

'Most certainly,' Rogers agreed. 'Make optimistic noises and say that the job's well in hand. We don't want him pressing any panic buttons just yet.'

For Rogers, whose normal habitat was sensibly equipped with flagstones for walking on, the climb through the tangling heather to the limestone boulder at high noon was exhausting. The sun seemed a lot nearer the earth than it should be, and there were myriads of zig-zagging face-flies apparently happy with his company. His two witnesses were sitting on the shadeless boulder, both with the air of placid proprietorship. Both were grey-haired and looked alike, weathered to the colour of varnished wood, stringy and dried out, and almost certainly having been born without sweat pores. Each wore a green tartan shirt with twill shorts and clodhopper climbing boots. Their red woollen headgear, pulled down to their eyebrows, had obviously been hand-knitted, and they both held knobbly walking sticks in their hands. Were they each not at least twice Rogers's age, then he would accept that appearances lied grossly.

He said 'Good-morning' as he joined them, then smiled affably. 'I'm Detective Superintendent Rogers and I'd like to ask you a few questions. You're Mr and Mrs Gullick?'

'How d'you do.' The old man had half-risen from his sitting position and then relaxed again. The woman nodded her head in acknowledgement.

'I understand that you saw what happened down there, Mr Gullick. Could you tell me from the beginning?' He hoped that he was meeting an observant and extremely gabby couple who weren't going to bugger things up by having different opinions about what they had seen.

12

'I'll be glad to,' Gullick said. 'And then we'd want to get on with our walk.'

Mad, Rogers thought, feeling the sun roasting his back. *They have to be.* 'I won't keep you long,' he promised. 'I can see you later for anything I think we've missed.'

'There isn't a lot. My wife and I were up here to do our fell-walking. We do our dozen or so miles every day. Except when it's snowing, of course. It keeps us fit.' He swivelled his body and pointed his stick to a higher reach of the moor behind him. 'We were up there . . .' – he looked at the watch on his bony wrist – '. . . say quarter past ten, about an hour ago. We heard a car coming up Old Morte Walk with the engine being revved something awful.'

'A red one,' his wife amplified. 'The sun was shining in our eyes so we couldn't see properly, and then only its roof.'

'Yes,' Gullick said, as if used to her doing it. 'I was coming to that. Then this car stopped and reversed, I thought to go back from where it came. But it didn't. It came forward again as if the driver'd changed his mind, or didn't know how to get back. Then he did it two or three times more. I thought he was drunk or a bloody idiot – God rest his soul – so we got on with our walk to get away from the noise he was making with his engine. Sounds carry up here, y'know.' His faded blue eyes looked down the slope at the burned-out wreck. 'We couldn't have imagined that was going to happen.'

'I'm sure you couldn't,' Rogers assured him, seeing Mrs Gullick about to interject again. She seemed a nice old lady, though one promising to confuse her husband. And he was fascinated by her fragile-looking skinny legs, but remembering that mountain goats had them as well. 'What happened next, Mr Gullick?' he asked.

'Well, almost at once we heard this bang and there was the car just moving slowly along with the bonnet thing up in the air, and smoke beginning to come from the engine part.'

'It was on fire,' his wife said. She had the expression of a woman who had found it necessary to monitor what she thought her husband to mean.

'That was afterwards,' Gullick said, the slightest trace of irritation in his voice. 'Let me to get it right, m'dear.' He continued with Rogers. 'When the car stopped, there was another bang. Not a loud'n . . . like a sort of whoosh, and flames and smoke covered the car. It really shook me, I tell you, and I told Mary to stay where she was while I saw to what I could do. By the time I reached the car it was impossible to get near it . . .'

'Samuel could never have got him out,' his wife interrupted him. 'Even I could see that from where I was.'

'You keep referring to the driver as "he" and "him", Mr Gullick,' Rogers said. 'Did you know it was a man?'

'Yes, though I couldn't see him very well in the smoke and I don't think I would've recognized him anyway. Not with that thing in front of his face. He was a horrible sight – not moving, of course, and I'm sure he was dead. Please God, I hope so.' He grimaced his distaste, then cocked an eyebrow. 'You don't know who he is?'

'Not yet.' Rogers sensed that Gullick might. 'Do you?'

'I'm not sure, but he could be Mr Lattimer. He's a neighbour of ours and he's got a red-coloured car just like that. When the fire brigade arrived and put water on it, I thought I recognized the number plate. Well, the NHO on it, which was all I could make out. But it could be anybody's, couldn't it?'

'Do you know what the full number is?'

'Only it was an A registration and that there were three figure ones in it.'

'What is Mr Lattimer's address?'

'Penruddock Close. I think his house is called Larches, but I'm not sure.'

'He's married?' Rogers glimpsed a brief warning frown from Mrs Gullick.

'Yes, there is a Mrs Lattimer I believe,' the old man said carefully. 'We don't know either of them that well – you know, keeping themselves to themselves, seeing them occasionally when they leave the house or come back to it.'

'Would you know what he was doing up here in his car? Would being on the track in it be something usual?'

Gullick shook his head. 'It don't make sense to me. It peters out to an even rougher track a mile or so along. It isn't used now and it doesn't go anywhere but towards an outlying farm.'

'We've seen cars up here in the evenings,' his wife said. 'Young people, you know.'

Rogers smiled. 'I don't suppose we should ask why. Did you see anybody up here this morning?'

'Not a soul. Only us and a lizard or two.'

To Gullick, he said, 'You made an emergency call to the fire service. We're a long way from a telephone up here.'

Gullick pointed his stick downwards. 'Penruddock Close is that batch of houses below us. It isn't all that distant.'

Rogers could see the grey slates of roofs amid the green of trees at the bottom of the steep and undulating slope. In terms of a crow flying it, the distance between it and where they themselves were perched was probably not more than half a mile. But only thinking of doing it, of going straight down and then back up again through the heather and rock under a hot sun, made him feel exhausted. 'And I'll bet you weren't even out of breath,' he said admiringly. 'How long would it have been between the explosion and your getting to the phone?'

Gullick thought about that. 'Twenty to twenty-five minutes. Mind, I had to get down to the car and I spent a mite of time wondering if I could get him out.'

A car's horn sounded from below and Rogers saw Lingard waving to him. 'I have to go,' he said. 'I'm sorry we've held you back from your walk, and grateful to you for your help.' Remembering the warning frown given by his wife, he added, 'I'd like to speak to you later if it does happen to be Mr Lattimer in that car.'

'If it is,' Gullick replied, putting meaning into his words, 'I *could* know a thing or two to tell you.'

As Rogers descended, his jacket feeling like a hair shirt on him, he could hear Mrs Gullick wading into her husband with sharpish words. It boded fairly well for the information he would dig out from him were the body in the car to be that of the keeping-to-himself Lattimer.

4

With the three cars having been reversed into the heather to allow the fire appliance and the unneeded ambulance to leave, Rogers joined Lingard in a searching contemplation of the burned-out car. He could now recognize it as a Ford Escort, a model similar to his own car. Close to, he read the number plate as A3111 NHO.

Despite its dousing with water, the car's metal still gave off stored warmth. With the doors locked or jammed and the side windows thickly sooted, the two detectives had to look into its interior through the glassless windscreen, seeing its well awash with the soggy ash of upholstery burned from the skeletal frames of the seats. The melancholy sweet smell of burned flesh augured ill for the lunch Rogers had earlier wished for. The blackened body, sunken in its disintegrated seat, wore the ashy outlines of jacket and trousers, and the ghostly grey traces of a shirt-collar and tie. Where ash had fallen away to leave the flesh exposed, there were bright pink patches of peeled skin. The skull was hairless and a glossy black from water, the eyes melted to a shapeless jelly behind a melted and misshapen spectacle frame from which the lenses had fallen. The metal box-like object, grotesquely impacted in the jaws, showed on one of its panels an empty cable socket and a row of terminals.

Rogers had winced at seeing it. He had met many ways of crossing the grim threshold and this must have been one of the least pleasant. 'Poor devil,' he muttered. 'That must have hurt.'

'It's the car's radio,' Lingard said.

Rogers nodded. 'So I see. It would have been blown out of its compartment like a bullet.'

'You think?' Lingard was doubting it. 'If he was sitting upright when it happened, its trajectory looks wrong to me. It should have shot out about stomach high and gone between the seats, not up into his face.'

'It happened,' Rogers pointed out with indisputable logic, 'whether it's feasible or not. He could have been lying sideways

16

and explosions can do queer things.' He knew, because he could recall attending the wreckage of a naval jet plane that had exploded on impact with its pilot still on board. Near it, side by side on ploughed soil and looking like a pair of transparent gloves, he had seen two tissue-thin skin hands. Unflattened, they had been perfect in detail and shape from wrists to fingertips with only the nails missing. Impossible to imagine and inconceivable even when seen, yet it had happened.

'Something else,' Lingard said, not wholly convinced. 'Have a good look at the engine. There's something there I'm sure shouldn't be.'

The engine, its fitments and mechanisms broken or wrenched off, its bulkhead driven in towards the driver's compartment, had been less affected by the fire, carbonization being only super-ficial. Rogers looked carefully into its chaos, searching for what his second-in-command had found and was not about to tell him. 'Ah!' he exclaimed, reaching behind the exhaust manifold and lifting a rubber hose still attached at one end out of sight beneath the engine's sump. 'You mean this?'

'The thing on it, yes,' Lingard agreed. 'It could be a timing device, only it doesn't look like one to me.'

'No, it doesn't. Nor like anything else I've seen.' Rogers leaned down to examine it closely. Wired to the hose was a slim four-inch long green plastic bar, having connected to it a broken length of cable threaded through a black tapered rubber plug. Rubbing off soot with his fingertip and praying fervently that it wasn't anything that could blow off his hands, he exposed in a tiny recess what appeared to be a miniaturized glass valve and a short length of stiff wire intercepted by a transistor the size of a lighter flint. Screwed to the opposite side of the bar and lying parallel with it was a flat strip of metal, its free end standing proud of a small metal insert in the plastic.

If Rogers had met anything like it before, it now defied recog-nition. Wiping his fingertip clean with his handkerchief, he said, 'It's a new one on me. Any guesses?'

Lingard, charging his nose with snuff, shook his head. 'Only that it's electrical and was probably connected to the battery. You've noticed the wires?'

Rogers hadn't, but said 'Yes' and looked. The casing of the battery, split and deformed, had been crushed against the bulkhead. From its terminals, in addition to its connecting cables, ran two thin wires still taped to the side of the casing. 'The only thing we don't see is what it exploded. Logically, I suppose, we wouldn't.' He straightened his back, feeling sweat trickling down his spine. 'The Forensic Science Laboratory can sort this out, but have Magnus photograph that gadget in detail when he gets here. Have copies made and send out half-a-dozen bodies this afternoon to suppliers of electrical equipment and suchlike. Somebody has to know what it is.'

Turning away from the car that had told him as much as he thought he needed for the moment, Rogers said, 'I don't believe we're going to have any problem in identifying the body. It's almost certainly that of a chap called Lattimer. Whoever he is, he must have been mighty unpopular for somebody to go to such a hell of a lot of trouble in clobbering him.' Telling Lingard what information he had obtained from the Gullicks, he lifted his head and sniffed in the warm heather-smelling air, looking around him at the vast sloping expanse of moor from which the two ancient fell-walkers had already vanished. 'The immediate problem,' he said, 'seems to be, where was he going to up here where only mountain goats and lecherous teenagers seem to come? What was he here for? Was it to meet sombody?'

'I think you once mentioned, George,' Lingard murmured, 'that I hadn't a crystal ball in my office. And I haven't.'

Rogers grunted. 'I was hypothesizing, asking myself the questions I'll need to find the answers to.' He looked around him again. 'You know, David, if he was coming up here to meet someone, that someone could have hidden when he saw the Gullicks trotting up.'

'And even still be up here, unable to move until we've gone?'

'If he is, he'll have to stay hidden,' Rogers replied, not overly impressed with either his own suggestion, or with Lingard's. 'We'd need a helicopter we don't happen to have to find him.'

'Another of our problems is, who's the writer of our anonymous note?' Lingard unnecessarily reminded him. 'Whoever it is apparently knew, or guessed, that Lattimer was for the chop.'

'Agreed. So why warn us and not him?'

'Perhaps he did. Lattimer wouldn't necessarily know how or when.'

'No, but I think he'd have come running to us if he had.' Rogers shook his head decisively. 'Whoever wrote that note was probably close enough to the man who was going to kill Lattimer to know something about it, close enough to be frightened of being clobbered himself for telling tales out of school.' He looked back at the car and its grisly occupant, and pulled a face. 'I'm leaving you here, David. Get through to headquarters and have a policewoman meet me in Penruddock Close without hanging around to powder her nose first. There's a Mrs Lattimer down below who won't know yet and I don't intend doing it on my own. Of one thing I'm certain, and that is she'll know a damn sight more about all this than you or me.'

'And that wouldn't be so very difficult,' Lingard agreed, already on his way to the communications car and knowing that with his senior choosing to be the messenger of doom and disaster, his own would be the softer option.

5

Parking his car in the shadow of a tree at the entrance to Penruddock Close, Rogers waited for the policewoman he had asked for. There were, he counted, eight houses in the close; houses undoubtedly owning to panelled front doors with decorative and unusable brass lion's-head door knockers, large double-glazed windows, severely shaved lawns and two-car garages. Running up a slope with Great Morte Moor a looming purple backcloth, each was separated from its neighbours by an ample space, each possessing its complement of beech trees left standing from the wood that had been despoiled for their building.

After fifteen minutes of impatient finger-tapping on the steering wheel and a rapid and irritable puffing at his pipe, Rogers decided that he would have to brave a woman's grief on his own. It would not be easy for him because he would have no answer to why such a horrible death should have visited her husband, no way of consoling her anguish, helpless as he always was against a woman's desperate weeping.

Leaving his car, he walked up the slope of the road, reading the name plates as he passed each house. He saw nobody other than a black-haired woman in a floppy white hat bending down with her back to him and snipping secateurs at a garden bush. It was only with an unwanted passing thought that he judged the rear view of her an attractively shapely one. The house beyond hers had near its door a thin slab of tree trunk with *Larches* carved on it and he entered its short drive.

Putting his pipe away and forming in his mind what he thought to be suitable phrases from a bearer of bad news – 'Does your husband happen to own a car, registration number A3111 NHO, and is he the only one to drive it?' being necessarily the first one – he pressed the bell-tit at the side of the door. There was no reply to that, nor to his repeated pressings. Trying the door and finding it to be locked, he moved along to the front bay window. Peering through it, he saw a well-furnished sitting-room, satisfying himself that it was unoccupied. Doing it, he noticed a long rectangular lidded glass case on the sill inside. It contained small ferns and mosses placed around African violets, all drooping badly as if unwatered for days. Larger potted ferns at each end of it appeared similarly neglected.

Relieved that he would have no distraught woman on his hands he turned away, then decided that it would be wise to see if there were anyone at the rear of the house, and try the back door. The garden behind was deserted and his knocking on the door with his fist resulted only in silence. Although it could be only a fanciful suspicion, he was anxious that he should not blunder in overlooking the possibility of a dead Mrs Lattimer being inside. He looked through the kitchen window, seeing an accumulation of unwashed china and cutlery on a draining board, then into a room containing not a lot more than a television set, two easy chairs and a glass-fronted case of books.

Leaving, and apart from a guilty relief at not having been able to break his bad news, he felt irritated and frustrated, not yet able to say without question that the body in the car was assuredly the remains of a man named Lattimer. Not that he had any doubt, he told himself, but that wouldn't be nearly good enough for Her Majesty's Coroner, nor for any other legalistically-minded character who hadn't the chore of proving it.

The woman in the floppy white hat he had seen earlier, now dead-heading a tall stand of marguerites with her secateurs, stared at his approach. Looking younger than she probably was, he found it easy to smile at her and stop, her front being even more attractive than her back. The glossy black hair, mostly concealed by the brim of her hat, was chopped to hang below her ears, her eyes blue-black and what he would describe officially as being a full mouth, but recognizing as a man with the normal amount of blood in his veins as unsettlingly sensuous. She wore sandals on bare feet, an olive-green skirt and a thin open-necked shirt. Clearly – and happily for men without murder investigations on their minds – she was bra-less.

'I'm sorry to bother you,' he said from the footpath, 'but I'm looking for a Mrs Lattimer. I'm told that she lives next door.'

She hesitated, then said 'Yes', not having moved towards him and her expression definitely discouraging.

'She's apparently out,' he offered, wondering what the woman saw wrong with him.

'So you would know, wouldn't you?' She was now distinctly hostile. 'I saw you looking through the windows and going around to the back.'

He ignored that, although he guessed that she was a woman who, patently taking in his description, would be dialling the police station number immediately on his departure. 'Do you know when she'll be back?' he asked.

She turned away from him, saying curtly over her shoulder, 'I'm sorry, I'm busy. I have to go.'

'A moment, please,' he said hastily, realizing that he was losing the struggle against suspicious unhelpfulness. 'I'm a police officer.'

That didn't impress her either, but she halted. 'Anybody can say that,' she retorted. 'Any burglar, in fact.'

He took his warrant card from his pocket and held it out. 'Burglars operate at night,' he said affably. 'In the daytime they're housebreakers.'

She stepped across the grass to him and read the card. 'Why didn't you say so in the first place? Is there something wrong?'

Near to him, although she had yet to smile, she was dazzling; a woman he should need dark glasses to look at. 'I'd like a few words with you,' he said. 'I've enquiries to make.'

'If you have, you'll have to tell me about what.'

Which was precisely what he didn't wish to do. 'As much as I'm able,' he assured her, smiling to promote a little friendliness.

'And not out here,' she said, taking off her orange-and-green gardening gloves. 'I don't wish to be seen gossiping in the road with strange men.'

She led him along a path to the back of the house, dropping her gloves onto a side doorstep but not, he noticed, relinquishing her hold on the secateurs. He approved her caution, if not her apparent judgment on his persona.

The patio onto which he followed her was paved with dark-red brick, canopied with bright blue scalloped canvas, and cut off from a long lawn by brick troughs of red geraniums. A wooden bench with yellow slab cushions stood along the house wall next to a plate-glass door, and draped on the wall was a large Turkish-style carpet. Four Van Gogh straw-seated chairs stood around a plain hardwood eating and drinking table. In a corner was a barbecue grill with an angular black iron hood and chimney. He thought it not a bad place to be on a hot afternoon.

She invited him to take one of the uncomfortable-looking chairs and sat herself on the bench, placing her hat and the secateurs at her side, then removing her sunglasses and leaning back against the carpet. 'Now, Mr Rogers,' she said. 'What is it that you wish to ask me?' Her eyes, now revealed as a deep green, were steady on his.

'Your name first.' He was brisk, knowing that he would have to wrest the initiative from this rather forceful woman to get any information.

She smiled for the first time. 'Now I know you're a policeman. Eleanor Caine. Caine with an "i" and an "e".'

'And you know the Lattimers?'

She nodded, only just committing herself to it.

'An odd question, Mrs Caine, but I'll explain it if necessary. Do you know the registration number of Mr Lattimer's car?'

She was surprised, staring at him. 'Yes, it so happens I do. It's A3111 NHO.'

'And does he wear spectacles?'

'Yes, he does.' She wrinkled her forehead. 'Why?'

'Ah!' Rogers now knew that he could forge ahead. 'I'm looking for Mrs Lattimer because I'm afraid I've to break the news of her husband's death.'

Her mouth dropped open and she straightened herself. 'Oh, my God!' she exclaimed. 'How absolutely frightful. Not

Andrew, surely? I saw him leaving this morning. How did it happen?'

Rogers judged her to be more surprised than shocked. 'He's dead, Mrs Caine,' he prevaricated, 'and anything else will have to be for Mrs Lattimer. Can you tell me now where she is, or when she'll be home?'

'I don't know. She isn't . . .' She was obviously trying to take in what he had told her, chewing at her bottom lip. 'Should I be telling you all this?'

'You haven't told me anything yet,' he said as amiably as he could. 'I'm investigating Mr Lattimer's death and obviously you have something to tell me about his wife.'

She thought about that, then said, 'I don't believe she will be coming back.'

'Go on.' He was now sitting in an interrogator's chair, pinning her down with an unblinking stare. 'I still need to know where she is.'

'I don't know,' she said. 'I feel dreadful about telling you this, but she went off in a car about ten days ago. I guessed she was leaving because I saw her loading suitcases into the boot, and she just looked as if she was. You know, angry face and banging things. I haven't seen her since, so I'd call that leaving, wouldn't you?'

'Given some background to it I might. Do you know whose car it was?'

'No, I'd not seen it before. It was a red one; a dark red, more a crimson, I suppose. A sort of big hump-backed saloon. Very shiny, I remember, and it seemed to be low on the ground.'

'You saw the driver?'

'Not really. He didn't get out of the car to help her at all.'

'That sounds like a taxi-driver.'

She shook her head. 'It didn't look like a taxi to me and she was sitting next to the driver when they left.' She bit at her bottom lip again, thinking. 'When the car turned around to leave I saw them through the windscreen. Not clearly because of the reflections on it, but I did have the impression that the man had a quite noticeable moustache. It was a dark one, a very bushy one.'

'Is there any reason you know why she would leave home?'

'Yes, there is.' She looked at him anxiously. 'I can tell you in confidence?'

23

'Of course.' The canopy above them had given her flesh a not unattractive cool blue cast, and Rogers accepted ruefully that his own occasionally blue-ish chin and jowls must now be deepening to something close to indigo.

'There's a . . .' She stopped, sudden comprehension in her eyes. 'You said you were investigating his death. Is there something more to it than that?'

Damn he swore to himself, then realizing that she would know soon enough were she on speaking terms with the Gullicks. But even so, not from him. 'He was found dead in a burning car, Mrs Caine,' he said. 'Which is, I think, reason enough. So please don't ask any more questions about it, but go on. And I'd be grateful if you'd be frank with me about what you know. Women don't usually leave their husbands without cause.'

She thought about that also. 'I think I understand and I hope you'll not mention to anyone else what I tell you. As far as I know, her cause would be another man. She has – or had – a lover.' Her nose wrinkled, whether in distaste or derision Rogers was unable to decide. 'He's what she called a gentleman farmer.'

'You mean somebody who doesn't do the mucking-out himself? Put a name to him, Mrs Caine.' He smiled disarmingly. 'I'm sure you can.'

'According to the telephone directory, he's the Honourable Roger Jervaise of Brigthorpe Hall. She calls him Hodge.'

'The pet name for Roger,' he told her. He knew of him, but wasn't going to say so. 'Presumably unknown to her husband?'

'Possibly, possibly not. Although she was often enough out on her own in the evenings – for all I know nights as well – for him to suspect.'

'That could mean bridge parties or sewing circles,' Rogers pointed out, putting scepticism in his voice.

She smiled gently. 'I'm sure you can't be that naive, Mr Rogers. She told me quite a time ago that he was a friend of hers. She detested Andrew, you know. Her husband, I mean. They were constantly bickering and it became embarrassing. It's why I've had less contact recently with either.' She appeared to have put aside any sadness she might have felt about the death of a neighbour.

'Was he the sort of man to resent his wife going out on her

24

own?' Rogers had the sometimes capricious capability – if capability it was – of running parallel channels of thinking through his brain. At that moment, while his mind was pursuing the fact of Mrs Lattimer, a part of it was regarding admiringly the long slender column of Eleanor Caine's exposed throat; a civilized progression, he considered, from a male's more ordinary captivation with female breasts which could be, after all, designed specifically for babies. Having it, she reminded him of the elegant sculptured head of Queen Nefertiti.

'I don't know,' she said doubtfully, staring at him as though having divined his interest in her throat. 'I'd never given it much thought. He did occasionally go out on his own, usually after she'd already gone out. But that needn't mean anything, need it?'

'So bickering about things domestic?' he suggested.

'Yes. Audrey drank too much and he didn't approve. Or that she smoked. Chain-smoked actually. Quite obviously she thought him wet – which he wasn't – although he hadn't the strongest of characters . . . not really. And he seemed so very unsure of himself.'

Rogers took his notebook and a pen from his jacket pocket. 'Could you give me a description of them, please?'

'Yes, of course . . . No,' she corrected herself, rising in one lithe movement, surprising him into making his own token rising and clumsily tipping back his chair. 'I can do better than that, I've a photograph of them both.' She looked quizzically at him. 'It's a terribly hot day, so will you have a drink? And do please sit down.'

Although tempted, a dried-out Rogers said, 'Thank you, no. It'd be a near-death for me in the afternoon,' regretting it as soon as she had left him and he had, after up-ending the chair, resumed his seat.

Waiting and gazing at the stretch of lawn and flower beds he wasn't actually seeing, he thought that a woman as physically mesmerizing as was Eleanor Caine should have her sensuality concealed beneath a yashmak, for it spelled trouble and its end product, desirable as it might be, wouldn't be worth it. Despite which, despite guessing that her husband would inevitably be huge, muscular and aggressively possessive, he knew that had he been primitive *Pithecanthropus erectus* a million or so years ago, she was the sort of woman he would be now have banged on the head and hefted off to a convenient cave.

When she returned to the patio he was showing, almost excessively, the impassivity and buttoned-downness of a police officer very much on duty. She handed him a postcard-sized coloured photograph. That near to him he smelt that her scent had been augmented by the odour of gin.

She sat, and said, 'That was taken a few months ago in my sitting-room.'

She was on it, sitting side-saddle on the arm of a rose-pink sofa and looking coolly elegant. The Lattimers occupied the sofa's seats, neither appearing to be enjoying the drinks they held; she, a long-haired brunette in a flouncy green dress, her features narrow and sharp planed with what he judged to be a heavily lipsticked and discontented mouth; he, with the appearance of a mild sheep in an undistinguished three-piece brown suit with receding rufous hair, black-rimmed spectacles and looking as if he had just been slapped down and was not prepared to do anything about it. Both appeared to be in their early thirties.

Rogers found it difficult to relate the man pictured in high-coloured gloss with the awfulness of the blackened corpse in the incinerated car. 'May I borrow this?' he asked.

'You may keep it.' Her dark eyes were fixed on his as if he were an intimate, and he found it unsettling.

'Thank you.' He put it in his notebook and returned it to his pocket. 'Do you know of any relatives?'

'Yes. I believe he has two sisters and a brother. I know nothing about them other than that they live locally. She has none that I know of – other than, she once told me, a dead husband.'

Rogers's eyebrows lifted. 'You mean, of course, before this one? Do you know his name? Anything about his death?'

'No, I don't. She mentioned it when we were talking about something quite different, and I wasn't interested enough to ask for more.'

That took some swallowing, Rogers thought, unless she was remarkably different from the commonality of women. 'What did Mr Lattimer do for a living?'

'He's an accountant with the Abbotsburn Finance Group.'

'It's Tuesday today. Shouldn't he have been there scratching away at his ledgers, or something?'

'So far as I could see, he'd been home for over a week.' She was staring calmly at him, liking or not liking – it was difficult to tell which – the hard masculinity of his swarthy features, the arrogant nose and his unblinking policeman's regard of her.

'Since his wife left with her baggage?'

'I didn't happen to sleep with them,' she said drily, 'but I imagine that the two incidents aren't unconnected.'

'You told me that you'd seen him leaving this morning. What time was that?'

Her forehead creased. 'Did I say that? If I did, I meant I heard him leave in his car.' She pouted her lips in thought. 'It was about a quarter to ten. It could have been some time before or after, but not by much.'

'So you didn't actually see him?'

'No. But it couldn't have been anyone else, his is the last house up here.'

'And apart from this morning, he's been out in his car since his wife left?'

'Several times.'

'Yesterday, possibly?' He was trying to pin down when the bomb had been placed in the car.

'Yesterday afternoon – late. I was in the garden when he went out.'

'And coming back?'

'I heard his garage door being banged when he came back at about seven.'

'Have you happened to notice anyone calling on him recently?'

'Once,' she said after a moment's thinking. 'Two nights ago when I came home and was driving into my garage. I saw the back of a small car in his drive; I'm sure a blue Mini.'

'You don't know who drives it?'

'No, I'd never seen it there before. At least, I hadn't noticed it.'

'The time, Mrs Caine?' He thought the visitor could be a woman. They seemed to be in the majority of Mini drivers.

'Elevenish. Round about then.'

'Did you hear it leave?'

She shook her head. 'No. But I'm sure it wasn't there the next morning. I would have noticed that.'

It was almost as if she had been expecting it when he said, 'Perhaps your husband might be able to give me further information about Mr Lattimer? I'd like to see him when it's convenient.'

'I doubt that it would be,' she said, a half-smile on her lips. 'He's not often here and what he knows about our neighbours isn't much.'

'I see.' Rogers thought that he had been rebuffed.

'I don't think you do.' She was mocking him now. 'You'd have to fly to a very lonely oil rig in the North Sea to do it. He's been gone a week and it will be at least another three weeks before he's back again.'

Not sure that he had seen it and, if seen, understood, her mouth had seemed to add a silent 'If then.' He couldn't think of anything to say in answer to the words he had heard, or of anything more he could ask her about the dead man. He said, 'Where in the close do the Gullicks live?'

She looked surprised, but didn't ask him why he wanted to know. 'Down at the entrance. A white house with lace curtains and a large stone dog on the doorstep.'

'You know them?'

'I'd have to, wouldn't I. But only as decidedly eccentrics. They're said to have won a hundred thousand pounds with a Premium Bond some time ago and given most of it away to their children and charities.' She smiled wryly. 'Now they seem not to need a car, and they're said to live on lettuce leaves and carrot juice.'

'I would, too,' Rogers said with an amiable self-deception, 'if it meant that I could go trotting over the moor as they do at their age. And they'll probably live for ever.' He stood from his chair. 'You've been most helpful, Mrs Caine, and I'm grateful.'

She had risen from the bench and was disturbingly near to him again, near enough for him to smell her scent and to wish that he could not. 'You've persuaded me against all my instincts not to gossip, Mr Rogers. I hope I've done the right thing.'

'I'm sure you have,' he said. 'There may be one or two questions that'll crop up later, and if there are I'd be grateful if I can see you again for the answers.' Standing, almost as tall as he was, her slender elegance had the capability of making him feel ponderous and awkward.

'Of course. I'd be pleased to.'

Rogers, walking back to his car – he could see the long-delayed policewoman standing by it – was convinced that Eleanor Caine was a woman to be kept at a distance. She might, he guessed, be one for whom being alone was a boredom, not to be alleviated by snipping off the heads of dying marguerites and knocking back gins on her own. He could be doing her an injustice, but it left him wondering what effect her solitariness might have had on a suddenly wifeless Lattimer.

6

Rogers neither liked the Headquarters building, nor particularly enjoyed working in it. Relatively new, it was still soulless, a bleakness of stone and glass, its interior a contemporary stark-ness of plasterboard, metal and plastics. Although in it there was only one of each, it seemed to Rogers in his darker moments to be overrun by Chief Constables, Deputy Chief Constables, Assist-ant Chief Constables and Administrative Chief Superintendents, all demanding from him, without delay, progress reports, crime statistics and completed Home Office forms of befogging com-plexity. While a delegated Lingard had dealt with the bulk of the paperwork during his four days' absence at court, he had left enough of it needing Rogers's personal attention to haunt him while fulfilling his obligations to the murdered Andrew Lattimer.

In his office, the venetian blinds closed against a too intrusive sun, his jacket hung over the back of his chair and his bared forearms sticking to the surface of the desk, he cursed the un-Englishness of the afternoon's sweltering heat. Even his attendant flies – apparently finding him sweet-tasting that day – moved lethargically, slow to take off from moist skin at the menace of his flapping hand.

Armed with an opened telephone directory, he was patiently dialling through its listing of fifteen Lattimers for the brother and sisters of the dead man. The ninth, *Lattimer P., 17 Saxon Park Road, Abbotsburn*, proved to be the brother. His initially strong voice, eager to tell whoever it was calling that he was, indeed, Philip Lattimer, broke to a gasped 'Oh, no!' on Rogers's telling him as painlessly as he could that his brother had died in a burned-out car. When it seemed that he had recovered, Rogers asked him if he knew the whereabouts of his sister-in-law. His 'I certainly do not' sounded as if that were the last thing he wanted to know. Rogers, explaining that in her absence he appeared to be the most available next-of-kin, suggested that they should meet at the unoccupied house to see what happened to be what. In answer to Rogers's question, he said that his sisters' names were Drusilla and Kirstin Lattimer and that he would inform them of Andrew's death.

Closing down, Rogers checked the directory's listing, finding no Lattimer D., but a Lattimer K. with an address at 31 Love Lane, Abbotsburn, who he guessed could be the second sister. That item of routine checking recorded, he composed the not very revelatory formula for the retrieval of a missing or mislaid woman from somewhere in a 750,000 acre shire of about 800,000-odd citizens.

WHEREABOUTS SOUGHT: Mrs Audrey Lattimer, approx. 30 yrs, slim build, narrow features, shoulder-length dark-brown hair, wears make-up, cigarette smoker. Left home at Penruddock Close on/about 10 August in unidentified dark-red car; male driver with heavy moustache, unknown destination. If traced do not, repeat not, interview but inform urgently D/Superintendent Rogers. Photograph to follow in Crime Intelligence Bulletin.

Lingard, his customary immaculateness marred by a sweat-stained shirt and smudges of soot on his trousers, came into his office in the middle of Rogers's jotting down the more interesting facts of his interview with Eleanor Caine. Flopping inelegantly into the visitors' chair, he complained, 'There's something to be said in favour of freezing to death in the Arctic, George. I'm cooked.'

'There are,' Rogers said unsympathetically, 'a lot of mad buggers outside who actually like it hot.' He laid aside his pen. 'You're stuffed with more useful information than I am, I hope?'

'I wouldn't think so.' Lingard took out his snuff box, sniffed tobacco into his nostrils, then dabbed a blue silk handkerchief at a few uninhaled grains. There weren't many for, following Beau Brummell's precedent, he moistened it after buying with cold tea.

'Mostly routine bits and pieces. The body's out of the car and on its way to the mortuary. Sergeant Magnus is still knee-deep in ash and he's found some pieces of what he and I believe to be the remains of a metal tube. I'd lay my best shirt on its being the container of whatever explosive was used. That's guesswork, of course,' he qualified cautiously, 'considering the load of junk that was blown from the engine.'

'If you're proved right,' Rogers said, 'it sounds a mite old hat to me. A pipe bomb, in fact. Nothing else?'

'From the car?' Lingard pulled a disappointed face. 'Only what you'd expect, I'm afraid. The ashes of a leather wallet, a few coins, a melted ball-pen, a couple of spectacle lenses and a metal comb. A watch on his wrist – too far gone to tell us what time it happened – and a signet ring on his left middle finger with an L engraved on it.'

Rogers frowned. 'We didn't find a house key?'

'Not while I was there, and as it'd have probably been with the other things in the driving seat, I don't imagine we shall.'

'A pity,' Rogers replied sardonically. 'I'm about to live up to somebody's misguided opinion of me as a scruffy housebreaker.'

After giving Lingard the meat of his interview with Eleanor Caine, he said, 'Things to do, David. It seems probable that the bomb was wired to Lattimer's car last night. Detail a small squad to do house-to-house enquiries in the close and immediate vicinity, excluding the Gullicks and a Mrs Caine who I've already seen, for any significant sightings in the area. And any of Lattimer's own movements, of course. So far as the Gullicks are concerned, I want you to see them personally when they get back from their mountain climbing. Gullick told me that he had something interesting to tell us about Lattimer, possibly more interesting if you can detach him from his wife for a word or two. So far as Mrs Caine is concerned, if it's necessary for her to be seen again it had better be by someone armoured by virtue against a *femme fatale*. Me,' he added with a grin.

With Lingard gone, Rogers retrieved from his notebook the photograph of the Lattimers and Eleanor Caine, frowning at it thoughtfully, not being able to dispel the nagging feeling that, despite the lack of evidence for it, Mrs Caine had been a lot closer to Andrew Lattimer than she had admitted.

7

When Rogers braked to a halt outside the house, the police-woman he had instructed to mount guard, and had rather overlooked, was sitting in her Panda car and failing to conceal the tedium she had suffered. Before being sent away, she told him that she had seen nobody who could remotely be connected with the house, but had, she believed, heard a telephone ringing at short intervals from one of the rooms.

With Philip Lattimer still to arrive, Rogers used his waiting time by going to the rear of the house on what he would call a sniffing around for information. The grass on the small lawn there had been neglected, being tall enough to hide a stalking cat and brown from the sun and a lack of watering. Shrubs and flowers in the narrow borders showed the same neglect. Still with the illogical but nagging fear that he would miss out on finding a dead Mrs Lattimer, he searched the garden for signs of a burial and wasted his time. For a less permanent concealment, he searched a cedar-wood shed at the end of the garden. It contained nothing but a motorized lawn mower, gardening tools and lots of dusty spiders' webs.

Returning to the front of the house, he was conscious of unseen watching eyes, accepting that curtained windows could be the auditoriums to a neighbour's drama. And Eleanor Caine, not now in her garden, would, unless she was knocking back long cooling gins on the patio, be one of the audience. Contemplating the doors to the garage, he considered the normal man's impatience with closing and locking them after his leaving and tried them. The first door was locked, the second not. Twisting the lever, he swung it up and over to the loud sound of clanging metal. Empty, the garage contained only the faint smell of exhaust fumes, a shelf of the different oils and greases needed to keep a car from grinding to a halt, a clear glass window and an inner door obviously leading into the house. Turning its handle, he found it locked. Tyre marks on the cement floor and an oil drip tray showed that only one car used the garage. At the side of the tray was a cigarette stub, screwed flat by the sole of a shoe. Crouching down to it, he teased the paper partially loose, seeing nothing of a brand name or logo on it, then leaving it there to be photographed later.

To one part of Rogers's thinking, there had to be some significance in Lattimer's being a non-smoker and in a cigarette stub being discarded near his car, possibly by whoever attached the bomb to it. Were that so, Rogers considered it to have been an act of stupefying foolhardiness while an explosive was being carried or handled. His other thinking was that it could easily have been dropped there by the chain-smoking Mrs Lattimer before she fled bag and baggage from her unhappy husband.

When a small yellow Spitfire two-seater drew up behind the tail of his own car, he stepped outside and closed the garage door. The man who climbed from the car and came towards him was nothing like his dead brother. Stocky and athletic looking, he had dark copper-coloured hair and what Rogers would call a rat's nest beard and moustache that seemed to cover everything of his face but his eyes, nose and mouth. He wore a lightweight casual jacket and narrow blue trousers. His unbuttoned shirt showed an excessively thick neck, around which was hung a thin gold chain.

They shook hands formally, and Rogers said, 'Sorry about all this, Mr Lattimer.' Ever ready to read a man's character from his face, he saw behind its gravity, in the small grey eyes, an overly pugnacious masculinity promising to raise his hackles.

'Yes.' Lattimer wasn't apparently one for the niceties of another's response to bereavement. 'Why didn't you tell me what happened?' he demanded, almost as though Rogers were responsible for it.

'I thought I did. What in particular didn't I?' Rogers could sense his strong hostility.

'You didn't tell me he was killed by a bomb.'

'Only because we don't know that he was,' Rogers answered him, keeping his voice level. 'And not wishing to upset you further by what may prove to be only a bad guess. Who said he was?'

'Mr Edmunds,' he retorted accusingly. 'He attended and he should know. I rang him to find out exactly what had happened and he told me.'

'Why should he tell you? He's a fire officer, not an information bureau.'

'Because I happen to be a sub-officer who works with him and entitled to know.'

Rogers couldn't remember ever seeing him but then, his attendances at fires were happily rare. 'I wouldn't lean too heavily on the bomb theory were I you,' he said. 'It's by no means certain, as Mr Edmunds must have told you.'

'Don't you know who did it?' Lattimer made it sound as though he should.

'Given time,' Rogers said, walking him to the rear of the house, now more than certain that his self-willed hackles would be raised. 'And given the co-operation of those who knew him best. The house is locked and it might help if I can get in. By force, if necessary.'

'Is that right?' The edge of hostility in his voice was still there. 'Shouldn't you have a search warrant?'

It was the way he said it that nettled Rogers. 'To serve on your brother? On his missing wife?' His eyebrows were down, his expression clearly saying *You bloody idiot*. 'I'm not looking for stolen property in a villain's house, Mr Lattimer. Which is what you usually want search warrants for. I'm trying to find out who killed your brother and why. It's why I asked you to meet me here.' He was, Rogers considered, one of those odd characters whose mother must have been bitten pre-natally by a policeman, leaving him with an inherited dislike of them. It hadn't been a very good start.

'I'm looking after my brother's interests.' He had blinked at Rogers's unintended flak, but there was nothing apologetic in his answer.

'Good,' Rogers said, unmollified. The sweltering heat, itching underwear and another's obstructiveness didn't make for a placid temper. 'And so am I. You can do that by getting me into the house.' He pointed a finger at an open casement window in the white plastered wall above the flat roof of the garage. 'I'll bunk you up and you can climb through that window. It's either that or I'll be forcing the door and damaging it.' He had long attained the professional *gravitas* that avoided straining muscle and sinew when there was somebody else to do it for him.

Lattimer's eyes showed objection, but he shrugged and said, 'If you say so.'

Rogers, with his back against the wall, cupped his hands together and Lattimer put a gritty shoe on them. Grunting against his unexpected weight, the detective heaved him upwards to where he could lodge his elbows on the roof's edge and lift himself. Although he showed no enthusiasm for it, he did it effortlessly and not, so far as was visible, bothering to sweat. Standing away from the wall, Rogers looked up at him as he swung the window further open and put a leg through it. 'When you're in, come straight down and open the door for me,' he called out.

While the back door was painted a nice glossy blue that brought pleasurable thoughts of a cool swimming pool to Rogers, he didn't appreciate looking at it for a longer time than he considered Lattimer needed to trot down a flight of stairs to open it. When it was unbolted and Lattimer stood aside for him to enter, apart from giving him a hard long look, he decided only to remember it. Taking the lead, he strode along a short passage to the sitting-room he had seen into from its window, Lattimer following behind and giving him the feeling that he would be closely monitored.

With the furniture and furnishings largely in primary colours and without much evidence of good taste, the room revealed clearly a womanless man's approach to house-cleaning; which was to leave well alone and hope that it wasn't as bad as it looked. Too, there was a quiet heaviness of confined air in it, although without the smell of stale tobacco smoke, as if the windows had not been opened for days. It felt like a house in which somebody was lying newly dead, the echoes of speech and movement gone from its atmosphere for good. A small escritoire attracted Rogers's first attention and he went to it. 'Do you know of any reason why anybody'd want to kill your brother?' he asked Lattimer as he flipped through the few documents in its pigeon-holes.

Lattimer scowled, possibly at what the detective was doing. 'Absolutely not,' he said. 'Why should they?'

'Somebody had.' He wasn't finding anything of immediate interest and he bent to open the drawer below. 'I understand he was Mrs Lattimer's second husband. Is that so?'

'Yes. What are you looking for?'

'I don't know. Whatever it is I'm not finding it yet,' he said tersely, grunting as he stood upright. 'What was her name? Tell me something about her.'

Lattimer scowled again, this time apparently at the thought of doing it. 'Her name was Conway. Andrew met her in Chaddersley after her husband died.' He was suddenly red in the face, his eyes creased in anger. 'The bitch!' he burst out. 'The bloody money-grabbing bitch! She's at the back of it and now she'll get all this! I'll see her in hell first!'

'I take it you don't like her?' Rogers said drily, deciding to ignore but not forget what he had said. 'Were they married in Chaddersley?' He moved to the fireplace where a large clay bowl of dried flowers and grasses had been moved to one side of the aperture.

Spittle had flecked Lattimer's beard and he wiped at it with the back of his hand, his outburst over as suddenly as it had started. 'Yes. None of us liked her even then. Christ knows why he ever married the bitch. She grabbed him, you know, it was obvious. He's my brother, but he was a damned fool to do it, although he knew it later, too.'

'He told you?' The fire grate contained paper ash, too thoroughly pulverized to offer any hope of exposing what writing or printing had been on it, indicating only a desire for the concealment of the contents. On the hearth itself stood an empty brandy bottle and two drink-smeared glasses.

'No.' Lattimer looked irresolute. 'If you have to know, we weren't all that close. My sister told me.'

'The one in Love Lane?'

'Yes.' He looked surprised and annoyed. 'How'd you know that? I didn't tell you.'

'No, you didn't.' Rogers stepped to one of the fireside chairs, a puffed-up and bloated eyesore in jazzy stripes. Lying on the carpet beside it was a tipped over sherry glass, further evidence of the dead man's disinclination to wash things up. And, he guessed, of a woman's visit. 'Did she also tell you that Mrs Lattimer had gone away on her own about ten days ago?' he asked.

'Yes, and a damned good riddance.' He was impressing the detective as a man with more prejudices in him than intelligence.

'That doesn't exactly sound as if she were money-grabbing, does it?' Rogers observed. 'How long had they been married?'

Lattimer scowled again as he thought. 'Four years. Sometime in February.'

A telephone bell rang from behind the door near to the front window, and Rogers said, 'I'll answer it.'

The door opened into the entrance hall with a flight of stairs at its far end. The telephone stood on a leather-topped table with a couple of directories, a pad of scratch-paper with N'OUBLIEZ PAS! printed as a heading, and a small tagged brass key that had been well-polished by long carrying in a pocket. With the still monitoring Lattimer not far from breathing down his neck, he lifted the receiver and pressed it tightly to his ear against whatever was said over it being overheard.

'Abbotsburn 620404,' he said, reading the number from the dial. In the silence that followed he could hear light breathing and, more remote, the muffled sound of metronomic thudding; then a soft exclamation and the click of the line being disconnected.

'Who was that?' Lattimer demanded as Rogers replaced the receiver, narrowing his eyes even smaller with suspicion.

'I don't know,' Rogers replied. 'Probably the wrong number.' He picked up the key from the table and went to the front door, releasing the lock and opening it. Inserting the key from the outside, he manipulated it in operating the tumblers. Leaving the door open and returning inside, he dangled the key in front of Lattimer and said, 'I'll take charge of this.'

'No you won't,' Lattimer growled, reaching out for it. 'You're a bit bloody heavy handed aren't you? I should have that, and I shall.'

Rogers put it in his pocket. Other than his face seeming more swarthy, he showed nothing of his irritation, swallowing it because this man had lost a brother. But his words were brusque and definite, Lattimer's continued antagonism not going down well with him. 'Under normal circumstances you might. They aren't normal now, and Mrs Lattimer remains the legal owner of the house whether you approve of her or not.' He retrieved the scratch-pad from the table, having seen the shadowed indentations of writing on it in the oblique lighting from the sun. 'I shall take this, too,' he said, challenging objections and getting none.

He moved to the end of the hall and mounted the stairs, followed by his dogged shadow. Two of the bedrooms were obviously unused, the bath and shower room suburban ordinary other than the full-length mirror that had been fitted at the foot of the bath. It seemed that one of the Lattimers had obtained a sort of satisfaction from a viewing of his or her naked body, and Rogers was already betting on its being Mrs Lattimer. There was a glass shelf of things needed to make a man's exterior acceptable at breakfast time, but only two items of what might be a woman's cosmetics.

The third bedroom contained two single beds united by a long stridently pink velvet-covered headboard, one remaining un-made with male green pyjamas thrown carelessly down on it. The dressing-table had on it a few jars and tubes which were defi-nitely for a woman's use. The built-in four-door wardrobe was more interesting. Inside, at one end, a short row of a woman's dresses and blouses, together with parts of the wall behind them, had been sprayed lavishly with red paint. The aerosol of a car's touch-up enamel from which it had come lay on the floor below them. Rogers knew that it could only be a vicious expression of hatred, that the dead Lattimer hadn't exactly approved of his wife's leaving him.

'I don't imagine that his wife did that herself?' he said to Lattimer, putting a finger on the paint on one of the dresses and feeling it tacky. 'Not doing it and leaving *his* clothing untouched?'

Lattimer didn't intend accepting that. 'That's not my brother's doing. Somebody else could have got in here and done it when he was out.'

'True, if that somebody else had a key,' Rogers agreed, almost affably for the sake of some sort of harmony. 'Would you say another woman?' By an unwanted twist of his mind the thought of the conveniently next-door Eleanor Caine came to it, but he dismissed it almost guiltily.

The dull flush of rising blood came from behind Lattimer's beard. 'My brother,' he said grittily, 'wasn't that sort of a man.'

Rogers closed the wardrobe's doors. 'Do you know whether Mrs Lattimer is the sort of woman to associate with other men?'

'I'm damned sure she is,' he said vehemently. 'She's a cow if ever I met one.'

'Do you *know*?' Rogers held Lattimer's eyes in a steady stare. 'And if you do, with whom?'

'No,' he said contemptuously, 'I don't. She'd be unlikely to tell *me*, wouldn't she? But I'm going to find out.'

On the way down the stairs, satisfied that his pessimistic anticipation of finding a dead Mrs Lattimer had been unjustified, Rogers said, 'I've finished now, Mr Lattimer, and I'm grateful for the help you've given me.' Holding that the most necessary social courtesies were duplicitous, his was no exception, being his commitment to a constabulary civility.

Lattimer obviously accepted it as such, for he answered with a scornful grunt, waiting while Rogers re-bolted the back door and slammed shut the front door after them. Then he climbed into his car, did a manifestly irritated three-point turn and accelerated down the slope to the main road.

Rogers, getting into his own car, didn't believe that he could ever grow to like the hairy cross-grained badger of a man; not, anyway, being about to grieve over it.

8

Lingard's fear of his Bentley being vandalized was paranoiac, and he parked her outside the Gullicks' house where he might keep her in view, ready to savage any lout daring to lay impious hands on her, even to lean on her. She was elderly, drank too much in her six cylinders and was his surrogate mistress; elegant in her racing green, her long strapped-down bonnet from which sprouted stainless steel exhaust tubes, wire spoked wheels and the baby-skin soft leather upholstery on which he disliked other people sitting. Because it fitted in with his self-acknowledged panache, her black canvas hood spent more time folded back than not. Climbing from her, his blond hair tangled from his wind-swept driving, he closed the door without slamming it and gave her flank an affectionate pat.

The ancient man outstretched on a padded lounger in the middle of the sun-baked lawn could, in the detective's eyes, have passed for a living and breathing grey-haired Egyptian mummy.

With a dilapidated straw hat covering his face, he wore only a string singlet that showed prominent rib bones, and a pair of brief khaki shorts supported loosely over a sunken-in stomach. On Lingard's approach across the grass, he lifted the hat and blinked his faded blue eyes at him. 'I knew it was you,' he said. 'I heard your car making that noise on the fell.'

'Superintendent Rogers said you had something to tell him when Mr Lattimer had been identified,' Lingard told him, a little offended at the harmonious throbbing exhaust of his car being called a noise. 'He has been, and I'm here to see you about it.'

Gullick had moved no more than to lift his hat, and he said, 'The sun doesn't come out often enough that I'm going to waste it. You mind?'

'No, I'm all for it myself,' Lingard assured him, although preferring to be other than standing in it. 'What was it you had?'

'His wife,' he said. 'I haven't seen her for more'n a week, but she was carrying on before that. I used to see her.' He scratched at one of his thighs, both of which looked as if they had been subjected to famine conditions for several years.

'That's interesting, Mr Gullick. Please go on.'

'You know she was a flighty bit of stuff? Well, we used to call 'em flappers, only . . .' He snorted laughter from between his dentures. '. . . only they didn't seem to have much of 'em in those days.' He must have sensed Lingard's incomprehension. 'Flappers. Because what you saw of 'em they weren't much bigger than envelope flaps.' He laughed again, then sobered. 'I shouldn't be joking about it, should I? I used to see her pass here in the evenings. The garden looks out on the main road and I saw her being picked up in a taxi more'n one time. And a big shooting brake kind of car once. Mud-coloured it was, like the ones you see climbing rocks on telly.'

'You saw the driver?' Lingard thought that Gullick had in him the makings of a dirty old man.

He shook his head vigorously. 'It was getting dark and he was just a shape. Like she was when she was brought back late at night. Or not at all unless I didn't hear the car, and I think I would've.'

'I'm sure you would, too,' Lingard murmured to himself.

Aloud, he said, 'Didn't her husband go around raising hell about it? Go chasing after her? Wait down here for her to come back? No yelling blue murder or any argy-bargying?'

'No, none of 'em. I don't know that he ever did. God save him being laid out in his box, but he was a soft 'un. And a miserable sod as well.' His already wrinkled face creased further into an expression suggesting perplexity. 'You being here asking me questions, your mate and a policewoman being in the house and cars coming up here, that means he was murdered, don't it?'

'More or less,' Lingard admitted. 'Why?'

'I don't know. Only lately when I saw him, he looked as if he knew it was coming. I've seen it before when I was soldiering, so I know. Have you ever seen that in anybody?'

'I only seem to see them after it's happened.' Lingard withdrew his tiny ivory box and inhaled snuff, wondering what else of consequence he could ask this old man who spent so much time spectating on his neighbours.

Watching him flap his handkerchief at his nose with disapproval showing in his creases, Gullick said, 'You'll get polyps in your nose as big as golf balls using that stuff.'

'So I've been told before,' Lingard said indifferently, 'but they're a long time coming. Who were his particular friends around here?'

'I don't think he had any if you ask me, other than that Mrs Caine next door.' His face was expressing innuendo. 'Her husband's more away than he's home.'

'You think they were having an affair?' God save us from our neighbours was the thought in Lingard's mind.

'I don't think anything.' Gullick was now attempting to look pious. 'That'd be slander, wouldn't it.'

'What about Mrs Gullick? Would she know anything?'

'She knows about what I do, and she's out.' He creased his face again. 'No, there's a bit more. She told me that Mrs Lattimer wore some pretty fancy bits of jewellery. The real stuff too and my wife'd know, she saw it up close. And we don't think the poor chap would be in the sort of job that'd pay for them.' He rapped a bent finger against his skull in annoyance. 'Damnation, I'm forgetting things. Something else, too. My wife screws money out of everybody hereabouts for the anti-vivisection people. He

41

came to the door one afternoon last week when she was doing her collecting. She said he hadn't shaved, he stunk of drink and had a dirty shirt on. In her book that was worse than having leprosy and she nearly had kittens when he gave her a ten pound note, because that's generous around here. It's usually a quid just to get you off the doorstep. That's what she said he wanted and I guess she was right, being the chatty sort and wanting to find out why he was looking like a dog's dinner.' He turned on his side, lifting himself on one elbow and looking up at Lingard. 'She's really gone then?' he asked.

'It could be.' Lingard was almost as close in giving out information as was Rogers. 'Has your wife mentioned anything else about either of them?'

'A couple of days ago there was a fat man she'd never seen before. He was knocking at the door and spying in the window, but he couldn't have got any answer because she saw him drive away a few minutes later.'

'Did she describe him to you?' Lingard was interested. Most of the fat men he knew and had heard of carried, beneath their blubber, an unexpected ruthlessness in dealing with other people.

'Only that he was very fat and togged up in a business suit. And also, she said his car was a big black one. A Jag from how she told me.' He was beginning to lose interest in what Lingard wanted. 'You'll have to see her yourself if you want more than that, and she won't be back until late.'

'Did you or Mrs Gullick hear any movements at all during last night? Noises of footsteps, or a car's engine?'

'*I* didn't. Anything less than the Last Trump I wouldn't. I'm in bed and asleep.' He relaxed back on the lounger and showed his teeth. 'And if my wife had, she'd have been telling me about it from here to breakfast time. So she didn't.'

That was his lot and Lingard left him with his hat back over his face, apparently oblivious to his saying 'Goodbye, Mr Gullick, and thank you' in a sudden return to the sleep from which the detective had disturbed him.

Cranking the starting handle of his Bentley to fire her engine, sweating even from that minor exertion, Lingard thought without any pleasure about his coming interview with a dead Lattimer. His being dead would be no bar to giving out information, albeit through the medium of a scalpel wielded by Dr Wilfred Twite, graduate in, and practitioner of, morbid pathology.

9

Driving out of town for the twelve miles to Brigthorpe Hall with only a part of his mind on the mechanics of doing it, Rogers found difficulty in convincing himself that he had gained much information he could regard as useful. Nor, he thought, were the characters he had so far interviewed or heard about particularly promising as informants of workable facts. A possibly cuckolded man, blown up and incinerated to speechlessness in his own car by an amateur's bomb; his chain-smoking wife, still apparently in the flesh despite his fears, and now believed to have scuttled off with an unidentified male; a too-attractive neighbour who had told him things, but leaving him wondering whether to believe them or not; a boorish, aggressively-inclined brother of the dead man who hadn't even asked whether he could view the body; and, finally, a telephone caller who had closed down when he heard a voice that had patently been neither the dead man's nor his wife's. The more he thought about it all, the less sense it made; the more certain he was that he might be suffering the onset of investigator's myopia.

The notepad headed N'OUBLIEZ PAS! – Rogers's almost forgotten French made it 'Don't Forget!' or something similar – had been dusted with black graphite fingerprint powder, revealing a heavy impression *Meet 10.00* amongst a scribble of angular and meaningless doodlings, the latter suggesting to him an unquiet mind.

Having just had a bellyful of the unpleasant Philip Lattimer, he felt no eager anticipation towards the bearding of local bigwiggery over the delicate matter of his fornicating with another's wife, a man who might consider offensive his private peccadilloes being questioned by the common clay of a policeman. For which, he reminded himself, he had only a woman's word at second-hand. Nevertheless, he had used his telephone to arrange an appointment, answering Jervaise's 'About what?' by replying that it was for nothing either of them would care to discuss over it. 'Make it now,' Jervaise had said as if it were going to be a damned nuisance. 'I shall be going out soon.'

Rogers knew the Honourable Roger Loring Jervaise only by reputation and by virtue of his local eminence. A few years back he had sat as a magistrate on the Petty Sessions Bench, dispensing justice to the sinning *hoi polloi* of the county. From this he had retired on grounds not disclosed publicly – and therefore to be presumed discreditable – by his brother magistrates. He had always been known as a man to be treated with prudence, a man who reputably would, given a free hand, hang poachers. Dredging in his memory for the criminally inconsequential, Rogers brought up from five or six years back something about a much younger wife reputed by rumour and her sudden absence to have left him, and this coincident with the departure of the then farm manager.

The entrance to the Brigthorpe estate was guarded by a gateless arch not a lot smaller than the Arc de Triomphe. Skirted by overgrown shrubbery, its two huge piers held in their house-sized pedestals cobwebbed windows and painted flaking doors, both manifestly unoccupied and obviously having served earlier as lodges. Rattling his car over a cattle grid beneath the arch and onto the sunken road that twisted and then lost itself in the far wood of closely-packed trees, Rogers found himself under the mild scrutiny of sheep feeding on the grassy slopes. Black-faced, meek and thick in the head as they undoubtedly were, he had an odd affection for them, not caring overmuch for eating them as mutton. Exploited down to the last tuft of wool on their backs, whoever it was said that the meek would inherit the earth had, in his not too humble opinion, somehow got it all wrong.

Not until he had passed through the trees into the open space they surrounded did he see Brigthorpe Hall. A massive building, squatting rather than standing, it was built of the same dark-grey stone he had seen in the arch, its skin decaying in leprous patches with ash-grey lichen complementing its age-worn shabbiness. Two turreted towers, each with three stages of lofty mullioned windows, flanked a broad façade of more windows. Parapeted steps rose to a doorway between pillars and, carved in the stone above it, was a just-discernible armorial bearing and the date

1587. Although bright with sunshine, it looked an appropriate place for a haunting.

Rogers braked his car to a halt behind a tan-coloured Range Rover parked at the foot of the steps. Passing it, he saw its interior to be equipped with a six-place shotgun rack and a floor-to-roof dog guard grille. The double door to the house was weather-beaten and aged beneath its varnish, tall enough for a mounted horse to enter without its rider banging his head on the lintel. He tugged at the iron bell-pull at its side, heard a remote jangle of metal, and waited.

The portly man who opened the door wore black trousers and a light-grey nylon jacket. A smoothly shaved character with plastered-down grey hair and a long lugubrious chin, he re-garded the detective as though he had deliberately chosen to disturb his afternoon's siesta. Which, Rogers considered, giving him as cold a stare as he could in the heat, probably made him a butler of sorts. 'My name is Rogers,' he said, 'and I've an appointment with Mr Jervaise.'

'Yes,' the man acknowledged, adding a reluctant 'Sir' after a pause, standing aside for him to enter and smell as he did so the ripe odour of sweet wine. Led past a wide sweep of stone stairway at the foot of which stood an unburnished suit of black armour, Rogers was shown into the cool shadowed gloom of a large room where he was left waiting. Standing in front of a fireplace probably built for roasting whole oxen, he could sense the echoes of generations of past voices in what was evidently a sitting-room should one not mind large open spaces around the antique armchairs, chaise longues and small tables occupying it. As if to remind him that he was dealing with no ordinary sheep farmer, there were rows of large gold-framed paintings on the dark panelled walls; perpetuated likenesses of generally unhand-some Jervaises; male and female ruffed and periwigged, farthing-aled and bustled, frock-coated and garbed in fox-hunting pink.

Jervaise kept him waiting, possibly deliberately, and, when he did come in and head for the fireplace, made it clear from the way he said 'Good afternoon, superintendent. Please sit down,' that the interview was a concession.

Rogers, by no means regarding it as such, returned his greeting and moved to give him the right to his own fireplace, though remaining standing.

Jervaise, a thick-set meaty man, his very mass impressive, was inches taller than the detective, putting the summer's heat at nought by wearing a deep-green Norfolk jacket, knee breeches with woollen stockings and half-boots. As were his painted forebears, he was unhandsome with tow-coloured hair, wide-set and protuberant pale-green eyes that gave a suggestively un-human cast to his face, a large fleshy nose and a small mouth he kept partly open as if either adenoidal or about to say something. He emanated a refined brutishness and the hard masculinity to which women were reputed to surrender with indecent eager-ness. Rogers, occasionally biased in his assessments of his fellow men, saw in him the type who, back in feudal times, exercised envied seigneurial rights on the dairy maids and the wives of his house servants, intriguing him as a possibly endangered social species.

'Well, superintendent,' Jervaise said, his hands behind his back and his legs astride, 'what is it you wish to see me about?'

With no inclination to do any eggshell walking, Rogers replied, 'I've been given to understand that you know, and have an association with, a Mrs Audrey Lattimer.'

'So?' He hadn't denied it, hadn't reacted angrily, but certainly had given the detective a hard stare. 'What would that have to do with you?'

'She's been missing from her home for some ten days.' Rogers tried hard not to be too interrogative.

'And you're asking me if I know where she is?' He couldn't have liked that, but was keeping hidden what he felt.

'I thought you might. Do you?'

'No, I don't. If I did I would, of course, tell you.' That, surprisingly, quite agreeably.

'It's necessary that I find her, Mr Jervaise,' Rogers said. 'Her husband's been killed.'

'Good God!' That had astonished him, but clearly by nothing of thunderbolt proportions. 'Was it an accident?'

'No.' Rogers was prepared to be unusually forthcoming. He had, after all, been a magistrate. 'It's more serious than that. He was killed in his car this morning under circumstances that would certainly lead to a charge of murder.'

'Which rather explains your personal questions, yes?' He re-garded Rogers thoughtfully. 'But you're not going to tell me more, eh? In case I might be involved through his wife? That, superintendent, is right and proper.' His attitude had changed to one of mild amusement, as though he now had the detective taped and his enquiry evaluated. He took from his pocket a flat leather case and withdrew from it what appeared to be a piece of twisted black twig, putting it between his teeth and lighting it with a match. Its smoke smelled of warm creosote.

Rogers side-stepped the question and said, 'At the moment, I'm interested only in finding Mrs Lattimer. It seems obvious to me that whatever the extent of your association with her, it could help.'

Jervaise smiled with the impregnability of his pedigreed bigwiggery, none of its amusement reaching his pale-green eyes. 'It wasn't such that I would kill her husband for the sake of it.'

Rogers smiled back at him as if any such thought was insanely preposterous and had never entered his head. 'I meant you might know where she could be,' he said. 'Where, perhaps, you might have taken her on occasions.' He was thinking of the small and discreet hotels used by large numbers of misnamed couples with either illegible or untraceable home addresses.

'You've got it wrong, superintendent, and I'll make it short because I have an appointment in town in twenty minutes.' His expression showed that this was going to be man-to-understanding-man stuff. 'The lady you are looking for was one of the more gross errors of judgment one can put up with for only short periods. I don't know for certain where she is but, wherever it is, I hope it's far enough from here for her not to bother me. I last saw her two weeks ago, and I gave her money to stay away.' Whatever it was he chose to read in what Rogers thought was an impersonal expression, he said, 'She was, I'm afraid, that sort of a woman. She'd told me that she was leaving her husband and demanded quite outrageously that she should move in here until she found somewhere else she could go.' Staring at Rogers as if he were one with him, he added, 'She was not a woman one would care to introduce to friends. One wouldn't, would one?'

'I've never met her,' Rogers equivocated. 'You don't mind my asking how much you gave her?'

'I do, but I shall tell you.' He looked intently at the cheroot, made tiny held between his thick finger and thumb, and

47

grimaced. 'Five hundred pounds and the address of a suitable hotel I'm not at all certain she'll go to.'

'I'd like it in case she has,' Rogers said.

'The Continental at Thurnholme Bay, if you'd care to enquire there.' Then he said carefully, 'You may possibly believe there to be a certain amount of squalidness in all this, superintendent. So be it, but in view of the importance of your investigation I've been unusually frank with you. Naturally, I would prefer my name not to be mentioned, and I rely on you for that.'

Rogers made no reply to that. It depended too much on imponderables. 'Do I understand that she visited you here?' he asked. He sensed that behind the urbanity there was a repressed intolerance and dislike for him and his questions about his personal affairs.

'Where else?' Jervaise said. 'Being who you are you obviously know that my wife isn't here, that she ran off to France with her hairdresser who, I'm sure, will fail to attract her affections for much longer.' There had been bitterness in his words.

Rogers thought that there was a hell of a difference between a cuckolding ladies' hairdresser and a farm manager, but accepted that rumour could often get things wrong and that it might just be a question of with which of them Jervaise would prefer his wife to run away. 'I'm told that Mrs Lattimer doesn't drive. How did she get here?' he asked.

'She came here by taxi, for which I always paid, and left the same way.' He looked at his cheroot again. 'Could I ask who mentioned my name to you?'

'I'm afraid not.' Rogers tried to look regretful. 'Did she speak of her husband at all?'

'I didn't have her here for a discussion of her domestic problems, superintendent,' Jervaise said, touchiness in his voice. 'She did complain once that her marriage had been a mistake, that the poor fellow kept her short of money, never took her out for what she called a good time, was beastly to her – that sort of nonsense. I didn't necessarily believe her, but it was no concern of mine and it suited both our books to act as if it were so.'

'How did you come to know her?' Rogers asked. He couldn't believe that she was a woman to be picked up from under a lamp-post, nor that Jervaise was a man to do it.

'You'll forgive me, superintendent,' he said in a brusque

mind-made-up voice, 'but I believe I've given you everything I'm able to.' He tossed the stub of the cheroot against the iron fireback behind him with a gesture of finality, looked at his wristwatch and moved towards the door. 'I'm sure you have other people to see, as I have, and I won't detain you further.'

Getting into his car, a more or less satisfied Rogers guessed that for all Jervaise's civilized urbanity, had their interview taken place back when Brigthorpe Hall had been built, he would by now have had molten lead poured into his ears to give him more weight for his hanging. Outside on the public road, he wasted a quarter of an hour in watching vainly for Jervaise and his Range Rover to leave for the appointment he hadn't believed existed anyway.

10

In his office, Rogers received a telephone call from Detective Superintendent Baggerly, his opposite number in the adjoining county force and not one, he considered, who added lustre to his profession.

'George,' Baggerly said. 'That missing Lattimer woman you asked us about. You're born lucky because I had dealings with her myself in a roundabout way. To be brief, because I've got the Chief buzzing for me, she lived at Chaddersley Green with her husband, a chap called Norman Conway, way back four years or so. He was a chemist of sorts with a local agricultural company – pesticides and so forth – and a pretty weak sister by all accounts. She was one of those hardcore fluffy pieces with come hither boobs; a shirt-lifter with a reputation for having it off on the side with the milkman, the paper-boy and any floating voters happening to knock on her door when her husband was out at work. He was daft enough to fall out from his bedroom window when he was standing on a kitchen stool to weed his hanging flower baskets, or whatever it was he was doing up there. It couldn't have been more than fifteen feet, but the bloody idiot had to fall on his head and break his neck. She was downstairs in the kitchen and heard him yell and ran out to find him on the flagstones. So far, so good. Naturally, my department wasn't called in to what was obviously an accidental death, but I was involved later because of the coroner's officer.'

Baggerly sounded as if he had suddenly tasted green bile. 'He was a married sergeant with kids and the silly sod met her again after the inquest – which made it death by misadventure, by the way – and was conned into giving her some in-bed comforting. He later admitted it and said he considered it had been a one-off public relations exercise in his own time. That is, until she started chasing after him and ringing his home and office, making a nuisance of herself and him the laughing stock of the force.

'Jealousy, Herbert; just jealousy,' Rogers said. 'Was she serious?'

'God knows. Myself, I think she was touched in the head. But whatever, I landed up with the job of Complaints Investigating Officer – as if I didn't have anything else to bloody well do – and having to sort out both of them. She told me during her interview that God had put the finger on her husband for the way the mean bastard – her words, George, not mine – had treated her. So far as the sergeant was concerned, she said that she had only permitted the invasion of her body . . .' – he snorted his humour – '. . . because she hadn't known he was a married man. To cut it short, chummy finished up by being posted to another division as a beat sergeant, and the last I heard of her was that she'd sold the house and had tied herself up with another bloody idiot. That was your Lattimer, I suppose?'

'It was. You're happy it was an accident?'

'I'm never happy about anything,' Baggerly growled, 'but nobody here, including the coroner, had any provable reason to suspect otherwise. And,' he added with a touch of finality in his words, 'I don't want to now.'

That was it and, for Rogers, Audrey Lattimer's matrimonial curriculum vitae was becoming interesting; a woman who, putting aside any thoughts about the enticements of her breasts, he was growing more and more eager to interview.

Not taking his car, but feeling the need to breathe out what tobacco smoke had accumulated in his lungs, he decided to walk the few hundred yards of hot pavement to the Abbotsburn Finance Group's offices. Unlike his widow, the dead Lattimer remained much of a nonentity, needing not a relative's sentimental appraisement but a somebody who had been close to him, able to tell an enquiring detective, voluntarily or under persuasion, illuminating facts about him. His apparently neglected employers could be just the people to do it. For Rogers, it was a basic tenet that to know what had made a victim tick was to discover who had stopped the ticking.

Negotiating his way through the High Street's swarm of shoppers – too many, he thought, with oddly acquisitive noses, furtive eyes and dragged along screaming children – he caught an unexpected glimpse of Lingard's yellow hair and the side panels and exhaust pipes of his Bentley in a line of slow-moving traffic approaching him. Stepping into the road and waving his second-in-command to a halt, he said, 'Permission to come aboard, David,' already climbing in and closing the door, gently because ever mindful of Lingard's diktat against passengers slamming it. 'Find a parking place,' he instructed. 'We need to talk.'

Lingard turned the Bentley into the kerb and braked to a halt on double yellow lines. 'I hope you swing some useful clout with traffic wardens,' he said. 'There's nowhere else.'

It wasn't the coolest place Rogers would have liked. Heat waves rippled up from the Bentley's long green bonnet and her polished brass fitments dazzled. With the canvas hood folded back he felt exposed, the sun already beginning to barbecue him on hot leather upholstery, his dark-grey suit doing its best to keep the heat in at sweating flesh level. Even in an atmosphere heavy with exhaust fumes he could smell the mortuary's formalin on the elegant Lingard's clothing. 'Tell me what our respected pathologist has diagnosed from his chopping up of Lattimer,' he said.

'Apart from my having found it extremely vomit-making,' Lingard answered, a grimace on his narrow features, 'there was nothing that'll help us much. Wilfred said he could have died instantly when the radio hit him in the face, but rather doubted that it did because he found what he thinks might on later examination prove to be carbon particles in his nose. Which could mean that he may have breathed through it during the burning of the car.' He grimaced again. 'On the other hand, boxing clever, he couldn't be sure of that either, because it seems that the radio was completely blocking the windpipe and he could have been asphyxiated. That is, if he wasn't already dead.' He shook his head as though despairing. 'The saving mercy is that he

51

would have been dead or unconscious by the time the fire started. Wilfred said we could choose which we preferred and, personally, I'd go for the sudden death.'

'You could be right.' Rogers was noncommittal. 'Nothing else?'

'Yes. He'd had a recent breakfast of eggs and toasted bread and, Wilfred's certain, a noggin or two of whisky or brandy on top of it.' Lingard's face expressed his revulsion. 'God Almighty! He almost stuck his nose in the stomach to smell it.'

'He probably found that more agreeable than the stuff you poke up yours.' Rogers smiled his words. 'You've seen the Gullicks?' He was filling and lighting his pipe, intending to charge his system with nicotine before entering an office which could possibly be an unfriendly No Smoking Zone.

'I saw *him*.' Lingard recounted the gist of his interview with Gullick. 'The fat man with the Jaguar interests me as much as anybody. He seemed anxious to have words with Lattimer, so I'll put out a circulation to see if he can be identified.'

In his turn, giving Lingard a summary of his talk with Jervaise, Rogers said, 'It has to be him picking up Mrs Lattimer in his Range Rover. Something he forgot to mention, and which doesn't surprise me.'

'What might though,' Lingard replied, 'is what DC Garwood told me when I met him in the road doing his door-knocking. He said that the man in the house opposite Lattimer's saw a Range Rover outside it last night. Just before nine o'clock and too dark to have a good look at the character getting out of it; but, he says, a big tall man. No lights were showing in the house, the man got no answer to his knocking. He did a bit of window-peeping and left after a few minutes in what our informant thought to be a rare old paddy. Jervaise?' There was mocking humour in his eyes.

Rogers's swarthy face showed a momentary irritation as if wanting to bite hard on something. 'Dammit, David! I wish I'd known that before I spoke to the lying sod. He wouldn't call there to see her, that's for sure. So why would he want to see Lattimer? The night before he was killed, too.'

'I take it that you've considered that she might never have left his place?' Lingard suggested.

'In depth, and at length.' Having reconsidered, Rogers was happier, realizing that he was, in fact, now with a future advantage in not having known of Jervaise's visit beforehand. '*And* trying not to work out how many men it'd need to dig up God knows how many acres of sheep grazing land to find her if she hadn't.' He had shifted his gaze from Lingard to the end of the street. 'I hope you've a good excuse ready, David,' he said smiling. 'There's a warden heading for us and I'm about to abandon ship.' He unlatched the door and climbed out. Before moving away, he said, 'I've a lot to do so see Kirstin Lattimer for me. She seems to know more about our dead friend and his marriage than his brother does. And find out where the other sister lives. Apart from which,' he added hurriedly, 'when I see you next remind me to tell you something about our gallivanting Mrs Lattimer who seems to be very careless in the way she loses a couple of husbands.'

11

The narrow office with the discreet black nameplate identifying *The Abbotsburn Finance Group* in gold leaf at the side of its door was squashed between the office of an estate agent and the Olde World Tea Shoppe. On its screened windows was the red and not so discreet lettering *Homeowner Loans*, *Personal Loans* and *Remortgaging Consultants*.

Rogers entered the reception cubicle and stood at its counter. Behind it was a large room with five desks, each equipped with a girl, a typewriter and supporting books and documents. Against a wall heavy with shelves of red box files, an unattended photocopier churned out paper sheets with a repetitive thumping noise that nudged recollection in his mind. At the back end of the room were three small offices, their interiors obscured from inquisitive borrowers by fluted glass partitions. As much as Rogers could see through them, only two were occupied.

One of the girls came to the counter and gave him a glossy lipsticked smile. He smiled back, hoping that he didn't look as though he needed money, and gave her one of his cards. Asking to speak to whoever it was in charge – she told him it could be either a Mr Chaffer or a Mr Mullet – she left him. When she returned she led him to one of the small offices. It had on the glass door in more gold leaf the name *Hamish Chaffer C.F.I.* and she opened it for him.

The man who was Chaffer stood from behind his desk as Rogers entered and said 'Please take a seat,' holding out his hand to be shaken.

Rogers shook it, feeling it distastefully and warmly damp, and sat in a leather chair opposite him. 'Thank you for seeing me,' he said affably. 'I wanted to talk to someone about your Mr Lattimer.'

He was looking at a fat simulcrum of himself had he been an unlikely five stone or so heavier. Filling his extra large chair comfortably, he had the detective's wedge of a nose, similar dark-brown eyes that contained a foxiness that Rogers hoped wasn't in his own, and a mouth that his different genes had apparently shaped to advertise a meanness of spirit. His skin, paled by the strip lighting overhead, was lard-coloured, his black hair longer and manifestly trimmed and fashioned in a more expensive salon than a policeman might convince himself he could afford. In his dress the imagined resemblance ended, for with his outsize navy-blue suit he wore a white shirt striped boldly in ultramarine and an electric-blue silk tie. Despite the blubber he carried, he looked hollow, an inflated balloon of a prosperous business man. Rogers, who would always admit he could be wrong, already had him docketed as likely to be a smooth pettifogger, and one not entirely at his ease with a policeman.

If Chaffer hadn't flinched at Rogers's words, he had only been just short of doing so. 'Yes,' he said. 'What a shocking tragedy. How did such a dreadful thing happen?' Despite the emotive words, his was a damped-down reaction.

Rogers, his bad news preempted, stared at him curiously, his eyebrows lifted. 'You know? So soon?'

'Yes, I was told.' His fat fingers, beautifully manicured, were twirling a pen while he looked down at his blotting pad. 'Somebody told me.'

'Oh? Could I ask who?' Chaffer's attitude was already puzzling the detective.

'I'd prefer not to if you don't mind.' He paused, his eyes hunting away from Rogers's steady stare. 'She may have been talking out of turn. In fact, I'm not at all now sure who it was.'

'Think about it, Mr Chaffer,' Rogers pressed him, not troubling to hide his disbelief. 'I'm sure it'll come if you do.' When Chaffer shook his head, he said, 'All right. I won't bother discussing with you what you already know, so perhaps you'll tell me something about Mr Lattimer and his background. He was your accountant, wasn't he?'

'Yes, he was. We shall miss him.'

He wasn't what Rogers would consider forthcoming and he appeared to be accepting the role of a suspect under interrogation, of which the detective was about to take advantage. 'I understand,' he said, 'that he wasn't working when he died. That he hadn't been for some time.'

'No, he hadn't. He wasn't at all well and we agreed he should spend a few days at home to get over it.' He reached for the telephone on his desk. 'Do you mind if I have my partner, Mr Mullet, in? He'll know more about this than I do.' He tapped a button and waited, then said, 'Gerald, I have Detective Superintendent Rogers with me, asking about Andrew's employment with us. Could you step in for a moment?'

Mullet, apparently occupying the adjacent office, came in almost on the heels of having been asked. He wasn't a physically impressive man, being scrawny and angular with pinched features under a bulging forehead that Rogers thought must be crammed with mind-numbing interest percentages and accruements. His sandy hair was plastered flat to a scalp that showed through it and he had apparently forgotten to remove the depressed cleric spectacles from his nose. His brown suit was nondescript as if it didn't matter. When Rogers – who was sure that he wouldn't like to owe him money – shook hands with him, he held dry skin and bony knuckles.

As Mullet sat, much as a man might lower himself onto broken glass, Chaffer said, 'Superintendent Rogers is asking about poor Andrew's background and his illness, Gerald. I'm sure you'll be able to help.'

Although Mullet had yet to speak, having only forced a thinnish smile when shaking hands, Rogers could sense in them a shared nervous tension, see it reflected in the stiffness of features that tried to conceal the uneasiness. Because he had no idea why it was there, he adopted a straight-faced attitude of unawareness

55

of its existence. 'Exactly what was wrong with Mr Lattimer?' he asked. 'Had he to see a doctor?'

'We don't know,' Chaffer replied. 'He was complaining of migraines and not sleeping. He was certainly in no condition to have the pressures of the office on him, for which he had complete responsibility. He was forgetting things, making unusual mistakes in his paperwork, even getting material lost from the computer. That's so, Gerald, isn't it?'

Mullet nodded vigorously. 'I had to watch his work so carefully lately. It was most embarrassing to have to reprimand him.'

'Have either of you been in touch with him since he went sick?' Rogers asked.

'No,' Chaffer said, then adding, 'He did phone us once or twice, saying he hoped to be back soon.' He lifted the lid of an embossed silver box on the desk and, without offering around, took from it a cigarette, put it between his lips and snapped a lighter at it.

'But not your calling him? Or ringing his house and trying to?'

Chaffer hesitated. 'No, I'm sure not. Did you, Gerald?' he asked his partner.

'No, I didn't,' Mullet disclaimed hastily. 'I had no need, having been told how he was progressing.'

Knowing that he was being lied to – though neither of them doing it very well – Rogers held a finger up and said, 'Is that the photocopier I can hear?'

Chaffer, surprised, said, 'Yes, it is.'

'It's quite loud, isn't it? Loud enough to be heard over a telephone.' He looked pointedly at the instrument on the desk. 'I mean, you could have been calling Mrs Lattimer this afternoon. You know, to give your condolences to her. The wife of an employee and all that.' He smiled disarmingly, now certain that he had stumbled onto a situation about which he wished to God he had some inkling.

'No, not at all,' Chaffer blurted out, which Mullet echoed by shaking his head. Then Chaffer said, 'We were going to later today, or perhaps tomorrow. Not right on top of his death.' He tried to look compassionate. 'She wouldn't have appreciated that, would she?'

Rogers simulated mild astonishment. 'I thought you were

56

going to tell me that you knew she'd left home about ten days ago. Probably about the time he went sick. Didn't you know?'

The fat man wagged his head as if plagued by gnats. 'We didn't know,' he muttered, apparently to his blotting pad. 'We didn't damn well know. But I'm not surprised.'

'He told *me*,' Mullet interposed. 'Not that, though. I mean he told me that his marriage wasn't working out. I didn't ask him why and he didn't tell me. We just can't afford to be involved in an employee's domestic troubles. Only in so far as they affect his work, of course.'

Rogers, growing impatient with the largely unmeaning answers he was getting, said, 'I believe you drive a black Jaguar, Mr Chaffer.'

The foxy brown eyes blinked. 'I do,' he agreed. 'Why do you ask?'

'It and you were seen outside Mr Lattimer's house a couple of days ago,' Rogers said with an unambiguous positiveness. 'You got no answer to your knocking and you looked in his window for reasons best known to yourself. And, no doubt, to Mr Mullet as well.'

Mullet had glanced sharply at Chaffer who had tightened his lips and was frowning.

'Well?' Rogers said tersely. 'I do need an answer to that.'

Chaffer screwed his cigarette into an ashtray and sighed. 'Yes, I did and I was hoping I wouldn't have to tell you. Not now that he's dead. *De mortuis nil nisi bonum*, you understand?' he said, revealing some of his academic window-dressing. 'We were getting serious problems in not having him in the office and we'd decided that what he'd said about being ill might not be the truth. In fact, we were sure of it, suspecting that he'd been drinking heavily. *And* one of the girls had seen him out in his car when he was supposed to be at home. I went to speak to him to give him a warning, an ultimatum if you like, that if he couldn't return immediately in a proper condition to work we would be forced to get a permanent replacement.' He had been watching Rogers's face closely as he spoke, but if he sought for understanding in his expression he was disappointed. 'That sounds callous to you, doesn't it? Especially as he'd been with us for seven years. But I'm afraid that a business such as ours has to come first, personal

57

feelings notwithstanding. As I say, we weren't happy at all about him supposedly being ill.'

'We accepted that he was worried about something,' Mullet said, his head thrust emphatically forward like a hurrying tortoise, 'but it didn't excuse his coming to the office smelling of drink, or letting it affect his work.' He was obviously Number Two in the partnership and, as obviously, loyally backing up whatever Chaffer was caring to say.

'In fact,' Chaffer continued as if he had not been interrupted, 'as a result of our finding him out that day, we've already taken steps to get a replacement.'

'You'd naturally considered he might have been unwell and in bed when you called?' Rogers said drily.

'Of course I did. And I'm sure he wasn't. His garage was open and empty.' Chaffer took another cigarette and lit it.

'So you looked in the house window to make sure?'

'So far as I knew then, Mrs Lattimer might have been in and not heard me.'

Rogers couldn't argue against that, although he had decided that neither of the two men was wholly believable. 'Was your visit to his house the only one?' he asked, trying to look as though he knew it wasn't.

'Most certainly.' Chaffer sounded truthful about that. 'There has been no occasion for either of us to do so.'

'Had either of you met his wife? Or spoken to her on the phone?'

'Neither of us,' Chaffer said firmly, shaking his head as if doing so would have been a mortal sin.

Somehow, the current of unease Rogers had thought he sensed earlier had gone. If it had existed, it had now been replaced by a new-found assurance, possibly because he had failed to touch on a matter they had feared to be the object of his visit. With neither of them – at the moment – could he consider too seriously an involvement with Lattimer's murder. Mullet seemed a nonentity who would be palsied at the mere contemplation of it. Chaffer, on the other hand, gave him only the impression of having been the archetypal fat boy, probably bullied at school for being one and who would, now adult, exact any revenge on his fellow men he felt necessary through the trouble-making curse of money borrowed.

Rogers stood. 'Thank you for giving me your time and help,' he said. 'I take it there isn't anything more you think you should tell me?'

Both Chaffer and Mullet were on their feet, not very successful in holding back their relief at his going, and this time without any proffered hand-shaking. 'I'm pleased we've been of assistance,' Chaffer said, his words as insincere as had been the detective's gratitude. 'If we hear of anything we shall certainly pass it on.'

Back in the street and threading his way through the thinning out citizens whose servant he theoretically was and whose often dirty work he was often employed to do, Rogers could think of no reason for altering his earlier view of the two men as being distinctly devious and unlovable. His sixth sense – a not always reliable counsellor even were he actually equipped with it – was insisting that they had something pretty serious to hide and that he hadn't got within light years of even suspecting what it was. He had learned little about Lattimer, his only certainty being that Chaffer and Mullet were destined to be the subjects of some immediate and probing enquiries.

On his return to his office he was given two telephone message forms. The first, from DC Lewis at Thurnholme Bay, reported that he had questioned the manager of the Continental Hotel and examined the visitors' register. Mrs Audrey Lattimer had not registered as a guest there during the past two months checked, nor had any of the staff available recognized her from the description given.

The second, from the liaison officer at the Forensic Science Laboratory, said that burnt powder scrapings from the seat of the explosion in the Escort car had been provisionally identified as the residue of smokeless nitro-powder as used in shotgun cartridges; that fragments of metal not originating from the engine had possibly formed part of a short length of aluminium tubing.

12

Lingard had, with an excessively friendly smile and a new-found glibness, convinced the traffic warden that his Bentley was an official Q-car and that in following a suspect vehicle the ancient engine had overheated, requiring a period of cooling to get it started again. His colleague, he said, had decided to walk back to Headquarters to report their failure but would, if asked, undoubtedly confirm his no option in committing a no-waiting offence. That he had kept two of his fingers crossed went unnoticed by the normally unbending warden who must have had an imprudent liking for elegant men with blond hair and blue eyes.

Returning to his office because he wished to check Rogers's notes on the Philip Lattimer interview, he found on his desk a report from one of the detectives dealing with the identification of the electrical device found in the engine compartment of the dead Lattimer's car. From its photograph it had been identified as the core of a fish tank thermostat. Normally enclosed in a watertight glass tube, its bi-metallic strip was designed to bend inwards and make an electrical contact with a heater when the temperature in a tank fell to a predetermined low. On an examination of the actual device it was found to have been crudely modified, its metal strip removed, reversed and replaced on the opposite side so that contact and the effecting of an electrical circuit was made when a higher temperature than normal was obtained.

It wasn't difficult for Lingard to work out the thinking applied to that. Fixed close to the exhaust manifold as he had seen it to be, the increasing heat from a running engine would, at some stage, bend the metal strip to make contact, close the electrical circuit through the car's battery and explode the bomb wired to it. It could never be an accurate timing device, he decided, but efficient enough for the purpose of the sick and evil mind contriving it.

Because he felt grubby, he was not prepared to interview a

possibly delicate-nosed woman while still smelling of burned flesh and the mortuary's formalin, and he drove first to his lodgings for a scrub, a change of clothing and a refilling of his snuff box. It was shortly after six o'clock when he parked his Bentley outside Love Lane which, irritatingly, was blocked from traffic by a bollard at each end of it, and searched for number thirty-one. He knew the lane, its present more decorous address changed a couple of centuries earlier from the Old English name of Hores Alley, and its history had interested him. Hidden behind the town's museum it had, no doubt in the opinion of lusty and hedonistic male citizens, deteriorated sadly from being the site of seventeenth-century stews that were later Victorian brothels, then still later to working-class cottages until developed recently into upmarket town houses, shoulder to shoulder like books on a shelf and back-dated with neo-Regency doors and bull's-eye window glass.

The house Lingard sought was one such, the window curtains drawn in its mauve-coloured plastered front. He pressed the door's bell-push, waiting long enough to think about pressing it again when a woman's voice said 'Yes? What do you want?' through a small grilled microphone set in the doorpost. He saw too that he was being scrutinized through a tiny viewing lens in the door's centre. He held his warrant card in front of it and said, 'Chief Inspector Lingard. Are you Miss Kirstin Lattimer?'

When she conceded that she was, he said, 'If it's convenient, I'd like to speak to you about the death of your brother.' After the rattling of a security chain the door opened and he stepped directly into a twilit sittingroom.

Slenderly built, Kirstin Lattimer was young and mahogany-haired with a Mediterranean olive skin, and, in Lingard's quasi-misogynous opinion, possessing very passable heart-shaped features. While her freshly lipsticked and sad mouth was generous, her eyebrows were heavy and wilful, the eyelids pink-tinged as if she had been weeping. She wore a yellow tunic dress over narrow black trousers and was bare-footed. Although the detective towered over her, he considered her a woman he would not particularly care to cross. He also considered her a woman who, if she even only half-tried, could arouse a man's baser instincts with just a tiny flick of her eyelashes.

'Please sit down,' she said, passing him and seating herself in one of the two wooden-armed elbow-bruising chairs facing, in the absence of a fireplace, a television set, an elaborate music centre and skeletal metal shelving containing books.

Sitting – the upholstery of the chair was warm as though only recently vacated – Lingard thought it an odd room, being very narrow and running from the front door to the windowed rear of the house. The opened window, shaded with partially closed vertical parchment louvres, looked out into what he could just make out as a small walled courtyard with white garden furniture in it. Close by the window was a shut door and, next to that, iron spiral steps, apparently designed for thin midgets, leading to the floor above.

'I'm sorry about your brother's death, Miss Lattimer,' he started formally, 'and sorry I have to intrude in your bereavement. However, in view of the circumstances of it, we do have to seek information about him.'

She was holding herself stiffly upright, her hands with their highly-polished fingernails folded on her lap, her unblinking dark eyes fixed on him. 'Don't you know who did it?' she asked.

'Not yet, but we will.' Lingard, wearing his solemn-in-the-presence-of-death expression – it made him feel like a professional mourner – wanted to smile confidently at her, but thought he had better not. 'We're only in the preliminary stages. You know, digging into things.'

'I see. He was killed with a bomb, wasn't he? My brother Philip thought that is what happened.'

'I'm afraid so.'

'I thought you had come to tell me who did it.' She made it sound like a reproof.

'No,' he said, wanting to avoid discussing the means of her brother's dying. 'I've come to see if you are able to suggest where Mrs Lattimer might be found. You know she's missing, of course?'

Her lips thinned. 'I don't know where she is, but you should. That woman killed Andrew.'

As she spoke, Lingard had seen between the window louvres the quick movement of blue fabric, possibly that of a dress. He showed nothing of what he had seen. 'You mean you think she did? Or you know she did?' he said. He had heard these emotion-evoked accusations so many times before.

62

Her eyes momentarily slid away from his. 'I mean she killed him indirectly by what she did to him. She married him and then acted like a whore – which I'm certain she was before she fooled him into marrying her. Poor Andrew couldn't cope with her rottenness at all and he should have thrown her out. But he didn't. He was much too kind, too generous and he had given her everything she wanted.' Her voice became impassioned. 'She's cheap and common and nasty, a horrible woman who should be punished for what she did to him.'

While Lingard accepted that he was listening to the wormwood and gall of bereavement, he still thought that some of it could be true. 'How did you know about this?' he asked.

'He told us, naturally he would. We're his family.' Her eyes brimmed with tears. 'He felt so wretched . . . so upset. He had to tell someone.'

'Did he know who the men were she was, er, being unfaithful with?' He had heard a deep-throated whine coming from the courtyard; a dog's whining for certain.

'And you believe that one of them might have killed him?' She made it an accusation that he did and that he was keeping it from her.

'I've no reason to,' he replied, searching her face. 'Have you?'

'I don't see why not if one of them wanted her badly enough.'

'It's happened before,' Lingard admitted, 'but from what you've said, don't you think they've already had what they wanted from her? Satisfaction and all that being its own reward?'

'No, I don't,' she said, her expression lowering them to the same level of promiscuity as her sister-in-law. 'And from what I've read, it never was.'

'Apart from Mrs Lattimer's lovers, could there be anyone else disliking him?' he prodded gently. 'Or, perhaps, fearing him for what he might know about them to kill him?'

She hadn't liked that and showed her resentment. 'Why should they?' she demanded. 'He was the most gentle, kindly and inoffensive man you could ever know.' Her eyes brimmed again.

Lingard had expected that; the newly dead always eulogized, and elevated by sorrowing relatives for entry to the Calendar of Saints. 'Of course,' he said hastily. 'I didn't suggest that he wasn't.' When he saw that she had unclenched her hands and

63

that they lay resting on her lap, he said carefully, 'Imagine for a moment that somebody knew, or guessed, that he was going to be killed, and wrote an anonymous note to that effect. Could you put a name to anybody close enough to him to know and to wish to give a warning without disclosing their identity? I mean, he or she would have to care, wouldn't they?'

That surprised her and she frowned. 'Was there a note? To Andrew?'

'Not to him,' he equivocated, knowing that if he said to whom she would hold the police responsible for not preventing it. 'I'm sorry I can't tell you more. Is there anybody?'

'If there is, I don't know who. He didn't have any close friends. She saw to that.'

'What about her? Didn't she ever mention any friends of hers to you?'

'None of us saw her after the wedding, so she couldn't.'

Lingard raised his eyebrows. 'Instant dislike? Or did she see to that also?'

'Both.' She wasn't liking that if her tightened mouth was an indication.

Lingard left it. 'You didn't say whether you were told the names of any of her lovers,' he reminded her. 'I'd like to know.'

'If I did I'd tell you. I'm sure Andrew never knew who they were. I don't believe he would wish to know.'

Peculiar fella, Lingard said to himself. Aloud, he queried, 'Why wouldn't he?' While listening to her he had been trying to assess her personality. Fiercely loyal to her dead brother without a doubt, and behind the grieving a sturdy self-possession and a thrusting will that could make most easygoing men cringe.

'He was obsessed with her, although he hated what she was doing to him,' she replied. 'He said once that it was a terrible thing to love somebody.'

'I agree with him there,' Lingard murmured, almost inaudibly, then asked, 'Was his wife leaving him the reason he wasn't at work?'

'No, I'm sure not. He was probably unwell, as well as depressed about it. But he did tell us that it was probably the best thing that could have happened, that he would get over it in time. It wasn't as if she looked after him – she didn't. He often had to get his own meals when he came home and she was out. And . . .

well, she wasn't a proper wife to him in any sense of the word.' Bitterness had made her voice hard.

'But more to it than that?' Lingard suggested, as though joining with her in a disparagement of Audrey Lattimer. Close to the window this time, he had glimpsed in the courtyard a movement of blue dress and the flesh of an arm.

'Yes, if you mean the dreadful quarrels they had for which she was totally responsible.' She looked away for a moment, her eyebrows down. 'She was vicious – threw things at him and hit him, scratched him. I know she did. We saw them on his face.'

'We?' he queried, thinking the dead Lattimer a great one for unburdening his troubles on her and making her unhappy also.

'My sister,' she said shortly, as if displeased he had asked.

'Is she Drusilla?' he persisted.

'Yes.' It was a reluctant admission.

'She lives with you?'

'Yes.'

Her lips had tightened again after that begrudged word and Lingard wondered whether he was inadvertently rattling an embarrassing family skeleton. 'I would,' he said, 'like to speak to her. Now, if it's convenient. You know? First-hand information and all that.'

She was weighing him up with her dark eyes while she thought that out. Then she said, 'It wouldn't be convenient and I'm sure my sister cannot tell you any more than I already have.' She hesitated, then went on. 'She had a very serious accident some time ago, before she came to live with me. She was badly hurt . . . disfigured in her face and is still having surgical treatment. Naturally, she doesn't wish to see anyone other than her immediate family, apart from having taken our brother's death very badly.'

'I understand, of course I do,' Lingard said, 'and I'm sorry. Would it help if I were to phone her from my office?'

'No,' she said firmly. 'I'm sure not.' She rose from her chair with Lingard, recognizing his dismissal, standing. 'Now if you'll excuse me . . .'

Sharp raps on the window glass interrupted her and Lingard, turning his head, had a blink of an eyelid's glimpse through the louvres of a woman with one side of her face grotesquely feature-less before she moved quickly out of his view.

'My sister,' Kirstin Lattimer said curtly, her eyebrows down and visibly annoyed. 'Please stay here.' She went to the window and pulled the louvres closed with a draw cord, then left through the door.

Standing deserted in semi-darkness, Lingard took the opportunity of looking around and for recharging snuff-denied nostrils hungry for attar of roses. There was nothing chintzy about the room, its furniture being what he called Contemporary Uncomfortable – as his chair had been – and gracelessly functional. The pictures covering too little of the white-painted walls were black and orange abstracts in thin aluminium frames, the wall lights – which had not been switched on – black tubes aimed mostly at the pictures. The shelved books looked new in their immaculate dust jackets and a few general interest magazines overlapped tidily on a stripped pine sideboard. Any ambience the house might have inherited from its lustful past had been effectively deodorized by respectability, and if anything in it gave psychological insights about Kirstin Lattimer, they escaped the detective.

Coming from the courtyard and barely reaching his ears, he heard the low-pitched voices of the two women, though not what was being said. One voice – he thought Kirstin Lattimer's – sounded angry and was followed by urgent whispering.

When she returned, she looked no happier. 'My sister,' she said, 'has no objection to seeing you, although not now. If you will come back at half-past eight exactly she will.' She was twisting her fingers together. 'I possibly shan't be here. I can't, so you won't . . . you understand?'

He didn't know what he was supposed to understand, whether she had a fear he might bully her sister, look too hard at what disfigured her, or even rape her. Though slightly miffed at her thinking him capable of whatever it was, he said pleasantly, 'I promise I won't embarrass her, or whatever else it is you're worried about.'

As she walked him to the door he knew, for all her feminine attractiveness, that he didn't much like her, even accepting that having just lost a brother she might not give a damn whether he or anybody else did or not.

Climbing into his Bentley after having walked around her to ensure that no unspeakable hooligan had stolen the spare wheel, or scored lines with a coin along her paintwork – his haunting fear – he took more snuff. It would, he supposed, help him in his thinking of what significance he should attach to Kirstin Lattimer's retracted remark that Mrs Lattimer had killed her husband. That was difficult to believe in her ten days' absence from her home and in view of the means employed, but it was not historically uncommon for an unhappily married woman – and Kirstin Lattimer had suggested it might be so – to incite an insatiable and possessive lover to a similar deed of savagery.

13

With a cooling sun beginning to drop down to the moors and a nearly invisible paperwhite moon rising from a not-too-distant sea shut from his view by intervening terrain, Rogers drove his car from the Headquarters forecourt. Not having telephoned Gervaise to advise of his coming, he was intent on bearding him unalerted, to catch him cold before he had time to dream up more of his dissembling evasions. He was not yet classified as a suspect for Lattimer's murder, but he had certainly lied by omission, which meant held-back information, some involvement – probably at its periphery – that Rogers was determined to chisel from him.

After nine hours of what he considered a largely unproductive investigation, Rogers was as far from touching on a motive for Lattimer's death – and there had to be one – as he had been when eating his breakfast that morning. And that reminded him. Not normally too concerned with eating, he had missed his lunch and was now likely to miss also his hoped-for meal at the early-closing restaurant he usually favoured. That he had a chin stubble – fashionable now and called a designer beard – needed a shower and a change from a sweat-stained shirt, wasn't doing his *amour propre* much good either.

Passing through what had once been an open market place, but which was now a complex and confusing system of cross-overs, one-way streets and traffic signs, he was held up at a red light. The few seconds waiting he had were long enough for him to see and recognize Eleanor Caine opening the door of a green Volkswagen outside the General Post Office; too short to note anything other than that she was hatless, cool-looking in a white short-sleeved dress, wearing saucer-sized sunglasses and holding a letter in her hand. She hadn't seen him, for which he was thankful, and, driving away, realizing that he had experienced the absurd and unwelcome lurching sensation in his chest that was one of nature's signals of a strong sexual attraction. It wasn't anything he wanted with a woman who was a source of information and a potential witness, and a married one at that.

Leaving the town with the setting sun in his eyes, the road climbed and dipped steeply between dark plantations of regimented fir trees, then curved and twisted through fern and purple heather and massive outgrowths of grey limestone. Within a mile or two of Brigthorpe Hall and negotiating a blind bend, he was frighteningly confronted by a tan-coloured Range Rover using the centre of the road in what to his momentarily startled mind was a get-out-of-my-bloody-way driving. Braking hard, his tyres screeching on the tarmac, he pulled his nearside wheels on to the grass verge inconveniently spaced with trees, and jolted to a halt with his radiator just short of nuzzling the trunk of a silver birch. Cursing the arrogant Jervaise both for his manic driving and for not being where he was expected to be, he turned in the road and accelerated after the now vanished Range Rover.

He was nearing the outskirts of Abbotsburn before he sighted it and drew in behind, identifying Jervaise's bulky figure through its rear window and wondering if he were coincidentally intending to call on him at Headquarters to unburden himself of whatever might be lying heavily on his conscience. It was a lightly held naivety soon lost when the Range Rover was turned through the creeper-hung arch leading to the enclosed courtyard of the Minster Hotel.

Rogers, following in, waited until it was parked against one of the high stone walls, then pulled up beside it. He climbed out as Jervaise, clearly recognizing him but not acknowledging he knew him or wished to, slammed the door shut and started to walk away. 'A moment, Mr Jervaise,' Rogers said sharply. Though still simmering about being run off the road, he was not prepared to make an issue of it. 'I was coming out to see you.'

Jervaise, clad in cavalry twill trousers and a Donegal tweed jacket, appeared less Edwardian than he had before. He was also a lot less civil. 'As you can see,' he pointed out with an officer to an other rank attitude, and with the psychological advantage of being taller than the detective, 'I am not in and I have an engagement. I see no necessity for missing it.'

'I'm sure you'll find what I've to say to you more important.' Rogers was hard and authoritative, intending not to be pushed off the road a second time, and in a mood to be irritated by eyelids blinking too noisily. 'I've questions to ask you about any connection you may have had with the death of Mr Lattimer. Either here and now, or otherwise at my office.'

Jervaise, his small mouth tightening, his pale-green eyes angry, knew clearly what Rogers was threatening. 'I hope for your sake, superintendent, that you are very sure of your grounds.'

'If knowing that you were at Lattimer's house last evening about the time a bomb that killed him was planted in his car can be called reasonable grounds, then I am sure.'

This time Jervaise's mouth dropped open. 'A bomb!' he exclaimed. 'You didn't tell me.'

'No, I didn't.' Rogers saw that resistance had gone, the bloody-mindedness about to be shelved. 'No more than you told me you were there. Where shall we talk?'

Jervaise stared at him for long moments and what he saw in the detective's face must have given him little comfort. 'All right,' he said at last. 'There's the Lord Kitchener Suite. It isn't used in the evenings.' He turned and stalked across the yard towards the door of the hotel.

Walking along the corridor leading to the suite with Rogers close at his heels – he trusted no one not legless or arthritically octogenarian not to make a run for it should their guilt weigh heavily enough – Jervaise said crisply, 'I trust that you aren't about to suggest that I'm the sort of man to kill anyone, least of all with a bomb.' It was a warning to Rogers to be careful with whom he was dealing.

'I'm sure you're going to tell me if you're not,' Rogers said drily. They were passing the open door of the Wellington Bar into which he looked enviously, seeing the white-haired waiters serving drinks and bar snacks to carefree citizens not having to worry about anything so inhibiting to drinking and eating as digging out a murderous villain from among their fellows.

The suite was half-panelled in wood with cream turned gravy-brown walls and ceiling, its four tall velvet-curtained windows looking out onto a grassed square of corporation landscaping where past malefactors were once publicly hanged. The room's centre was occupied by a long wax-polished and elderly conference table with a dozen linen-seated mahogany chairs around it and, near the huge marble fireplace, four antiquated leather club chairs fitted with white antimaccassars. Above the fireplace hung an oil painting of a life-sized stern-faced and heavily moustached Lord Kitchener as a much bemedalled Field Marshal. The room, full of the shadows of the centuries it had lived through, was a microcosm of a hotel that had largely, and sensibly, ignored as much of change as it could since the death of Edward the Seventh.

Rogers closed the door and sat at the table, while Jervaise stood beneath the painting, his hands behind his back. He was mistaken if he thought he was about to control the interview on his feet, or at all. 'I'd prefer you to sit,' Rogers told him, indicating the chair opposite him.

When the unwilling Jervaise, frowning his displeasure, had seated himself, Rogers said, 'To the point. I'm not satisfied with what you told me this afternoon. When a woman with whom you've been associating with sexually vanishes after being allegedly paid off by you and isn't to be found, I have to question the truth of what you said . . .'

When Jervaise started to say something, his expression thunderous, Rogers flapped an imperative hand at him. 'No. Let me finish. When you deliberately avoid telling me that you visited her house long after you were supposed to have ended your affair and, coincidentally, on the evening the bomb that killed him was wired to her husband's car, it suggests to me that you've a lot you wish to hide.'

Jervaise was pulling with finger and thumb at his fleshy nose, his eyes narrowed in staring at the glossy surface of the table. If Rogers could read anything in his expression, it was not guilt but more a matter of how cautiously little he should disclose. 'I told you as much as I considered necessary under the circumstances, superintendent,' he said, challenging him with a hard look. 'Had you asked specifically, not been so secretive, I would have told you. Nor,' he added scowling, 'did I, or do now, care for your attitude.'

'I don't like yours at all.' Rogers gave him a tight-lipped smile, certain that it would irritate him as an indifference to his comment. 'Why did you visit Lattimer's house last night? At nine o'clock if that's slipped your mind too.'

That had gone home, but wasn't denting his stubbornness. He said, 'Having had nothing to do with Lattimer's death, I can't think why my private affairs should concern you or anybody else. My word should be enough.'

Rogers stood, scraping his chair back. 'I made a mistake in not arresting you straight away on suspicion of being concerned with his murder,' he said sternly. 'I can find the answers I want the better for your being in custody.'

That shook Jervaise as it had been intended to; although his hostility remained after resistance had fled. He clearly worked hard at the problem facing him as Rogers waited. 'I won't forget this,' he choked out angrily. 'Sit down, man, and ask your damned questions for all the good it'll do you.'

Rogers hesitated as if in doubt about his willingness to do it, then slowly resumed his seat. 'That's sensible of you,' he said. 'So now tell me why you went to Lattimer's house.'

'To beat him silly – to get him off my back. Does that satisfy you?'

'It interests me,' Rogers answered, one part of his thinking acknowledging the improbability of Jervaise having killed Lattimer; another part, accepting that most witnesses were cursed with an imperfect recollection of events, insisting that he certainly might have. 'You had a reason, of course?'

'Of course.' He pulled at his nose again, peering down its length at Rogers as if over the sights of a shotgun. 'You've heard of the saying that if you act like a sheep you'll be eaten by wolves? That's it; my philosophy. He telephoned me yesterday morning out of the blue. I'd never spoken to the fellow before, leave alone met him or set eyes on him. He said he was "Mr Lattimer" . . .' – there was derision in his voice – '. . . that he knew all about me and his wife and could prove we had had an adulterous affair. He said he could kick up a hell of a stink I wouldn't forget, sue his wife for a divorce and name me as the co-respondant. I should have cut him off. He had one of those oily voices that made my flesh creep and reminded me of prissy little unimportant men, frightened of their wives and everybody else. Instead, I told him I didn't know what he was babbling about and why he was saying all this to me.' Jervaise sounded gritty, not conversational, and he was recounting this without the slightest sign that he cared one way or another what Rogers thought of it.

Rogers said, 'You're saying that Lattimer is one of the wolves?' He said it as if it surprised him.

'You know what I mean, so please don't interrupt. Following that he said that his wife had gone missing and he was about to report it to your people, but wasn't at all certain yet whether he would mention my name as someone knowing where she would be. I told him to damned well go ahead, but to remember very carefully the law against criminal defamation of character for which I would certainly sue for heavy damages. I must admit that that didn't seem to worry him, for he surprised me by saying that we should talk about it man to man, that he also had something of mine – which he refused to disclose – that his wife had taken and that I wouldn't wish anybody else to see. I could, apparently, have it back and my name kept out of his divorce proceedings if I'd agree to help him. That I knew was nonsense; he was threatening to blackmail me if I didn't.' Jervaise's features showed briefly the latent savagery in him. 'I asked him how much was this help going to cost me and he said not much, but thought we should talk about it, though not on the telephone. I knew then that I had to deal with him and I pretended it suited me also, telling him yes, I would prefer that. He asked me to call on him because his car was in for servicing, and that he would be on his own. That suited me too, so we agreed I'd be there at nine o'clock.' He paused, then demanded, 'How did you know about the time?'

Through the windows the dying sun shone rectangles of dull pink light into the room, Jervaise squinting his eyes against it, his face glowing as if from an inner fire. With his back to it, Rogers's face was shadowed. 'Tell me what happened when you called,' he said, ignoring the demand.

Keeping the detective waiting, his stare never leaving him, Jervaise took a cheroot from its leather holder and scratched a match at it with deliberate slowness, allowing the smoke to trickle from his mouth. 'Nothing,' he said flatly, having stretched the waiting for as long as he could. 'He was out. Or too damned frightened to answer the door.'

72

'But he wouldn't have known you intended beating him, would he? And were you?' Looking at Jervaise's thick arms and his meaty hands with their hard knuckles, the brutishness in the contours of his face, he knew that in the event he would have felt sorry for Lattimer.

'I was,' Jervaise assured him grimly. 'Believe me I was, and you should know. It's the only way to deal with blackmailers, the only justice they'd understand.'

'Not the only way,' Rogers observed, his face expressionless. 'Sometimes they've been killed.'

Jervaise snorted. 'The meanest intelligence would understand that I'd hardly be telling you this if I had.' He made that an insult.

'If you say so,' Rogers said equably. He wasn't about to explain that the meanest intelligence could know from experience that it was by no means uncommon for a suspect linked unarguably to a major crime to admit to an intent to commit, or admit to having actually committed, a lesser offence of a different character if he thought his apparent frankness would divert suspicion from him. 'Was there a light on in the house?'

'No.'

'But you still thought it necessary to look in the windows?'

'We do unconventional things when we're angry, don't we? Nor is there a law against it.'

'No, there isn't and I've done it myself,' Rogers conceded. 'But not with the beating up of someone in mind. You should know that Lattimer lied to you if he told you that his car was being serviced. Did you see it?'

'I did. I saw it in the garage. Through the window, if that doesn't displease you,' he said with heavy sarcasm.

'Didn't you ring him later to find out why he'd not been in?' Rogers was thinking between the lines of what Jervaise had said and not finding much he could dispute.

'Why should I? He was the one who wanted to meet me. Not I him.'

'So could he have called *you*? Say, to make an arrangement for a meeting the following morning? This morning, in fact.' Rogers, watching closely for the flicker of awareness in his eyes, saw nothing he could read.

'No he damned well didn't,' Jervaise barked at him. 'Don't talk bloody nonsense, man.' He tapped an inch of ash from his

73

cheroot to the floor, scrubbing it in with his shoe. 'If you're satisfied and haven't any more stupid questions to ask, I'd like to go.'

He had half-risen from his chair before Rogers stopped him. 'No, I'm definitely not satisfied, and I haven't finished yet anyway.' Waiting until Jervaise, scowling and with a definite reluctance, had lowered himself back, he said, 'There's the matter of Mrs Lattimer. There's more to tell, isn't there?'

'Is there? Not that I'm aware of.' His wide-set eyes were curiously unsettling in their reflection of the antagonism projected through them.

'I want to know more about her, and who better to ask?' Rogers thought out his words, wanting badly the help of his tobacco but deciding against what could be taken as a softening of his approach. 'For a start, I'm not satisfied that you've told me the full facts about your association with her. You told me that she invariably came to you by taxi. That wasn't so, was it?'

'No.' That, obviously, wasn't bringing him out in a sweat. 'Had I considered it important, or any of your business, I would have mentioned it. I picked her up near her home on two or three occasions when I intended taking her out for a meal. Is that all you're concerned about?'

'Not all. When you last saw her, when you gave her the money to stay away, what was her reaction?'

Jervaise shrugged his indifference. 'What one would expect from a woman like her. When I told her that in no circumstances could she stay at my place, that I thought anyway we'd better part company, she put on an act of being heart-broken, which I knew damned well she wouldn't be. It was all rather tiresome and when she realized that tears weren't working she started screaming at me, telling me that her husband knew and that she was being forced to leave her home – altogether an embarrassing scene. That was in the drawing-room and I left her to it while I collected the money from my safe. When I returned she'd calmed down considerably – she was putting her face back in order actually – and she accepted my suggestion that I should subsidize a hotel bill until she found somewhere else. But I left her in no doubt that she wasn't to return to the Hall.'

'Did she suggest that you give her the money?' Rogers, not in the business of wholly accepting explanations, thought that

Jervaise was being altogether too expansive for somebody objecting to being interrogated. He knew, though, that arrogance cared nothing for the opinions or sensibilities of others.

Jervaise tilted back his head and stared balefully down his nose at him. 'Certainly not. I offered it to her. I've already told you, she had become a nuisance.'

'So you have, but it seems to me that anyone less acquainted with what you've said to be the facts could consider that she'd threatened you with some kind of exposure to get it. You know?' he said pointedly. 'Being the same sort of nuisance to you that her husband was later on?'

'Are you doubting my word?' Jervaise's temper flared.

Rogers smiled, he hoped disarmingly. 'I'm presenting a hypothesis. Obviously you don't agree and I'll accept it.' For the moment, he told himself. 'Do I take it that you've neither met nor communicated with her since you paid her off?'

'You *will* take it, and I didn't pay her off as you put it.' He was stiff with furious resentment. 'I gave it to her to tide her over with her accommodation.'

'She never booked in at the hotel you recommended.'

'That's too bad. I only suggested it when she said she'd prefer Thurnholme. I didn't really give a damn where she went.'

Rogers tapped his forefinger softly on the surface of the table, musing aloud as if to himself and shaking his head. 'It's odd . . . odd to say the least. Nobody that I've spoken to has seen her or heard from her since she left her husband . . . she just seems to have vanished.'

Jervaise said nothing to that and Rogers left it hanging in the air. The room had grown gloomy, seemingly isolated from warm-blooded humanity. He heard the dusty rustlings of what were certainly mice or giant-sized death-watch beetles behind the wainscoting. He could think of nothing further he could usefully ask and he was tired of talking and listening. He pushed back his chair and stood. 'I won't keep you any longer, Mr Jervaise,' he said, 'but I shall certainly be speaking to you again.'

Jervaise rose. Whatever complexities were present in his make-up, faint-hearted apprehensiveness appeared not to be among them. He bared his teeth. 'I meant it, superintendent, when I said I wouldn't forget this. You've exceeded your authority and I shall be taking it up with your Chief Constable.' Disdainfully, he tossed the stub of his cheeroot towards the fireplace. It didn't reach and if he noticed it smoking on the floorboards he didn't care. Pushing his chair roughly aside, he strode from the room.

With the door banging behind him, Rogers laughed. He said mockingly to nobody in particular, 'Thank you for nothing, you overbearing sod. And it's decent of you to allow me to prevent your setting fire to this insignificant old hotel.' He picked up the still smoking stub and dropped it on to the stone hearth, screwing it to extinction with his shoe. Were he not disposed to give Jervaise the benefit of a doubt or two, it need not, he surmised, be too far different from how he had dismissed a screaming and troublesome Audrey Lattimer. That she had not been found was increasingly disruptive to his thinking, leaving a large gap he was unable to bridge.

14

Rogers, the creases in his forehead showing that something not too pleasing was going on behind it, sat at his desk and jotted down the notes of his interview with Jervaise, trying hard not to colour them with the man's intractability and his possibly understandable truculence. He was feeling the necessity of finding uninterrupted time to sort out the ragbag of information he possessed into logical order. There had been something said by somebody, or a hitherto insignificant fact revealed, that had, without his having analysed its meaning, lodged into his brain. There it rested, a skulking irritant, refusing stubbornly to stand up and be named.

On a less professional note he was wishing that he had been in his office an hour or so earlier, for Eleanor Caine had called to speak to him, apparently a short time after·he had seen her outside the post office. She would, he thought ruefully, have been an uplifting antidote against the largely unpleasant and unlovable characters he had been meeting. A Caller's Message form recording her visit had been placed on his desk.

For the information of D/Supt. Rogers. Mrs E. Caine, Charter-house, Penruddock Close, called at 18.50 and left the following message in your absence. Reference the car in which Mrs Lattimer left, Mrs Caine has since recalled further details and wishes to add to the description she gave you. The car was fitted with a bow radio aerial and she believes that there were more than two headlights. There was a square red sticker on the bottom left-hand corner of the windscreen. Mrs Caine will be back home after 23.00 if wanted.

Despite his earlier and happier thoughts about her, Rogers felt a spasm of annoyance for the wasted time caused by her delayed recall, sending an amended description of the car to the Information Room for immediate circulation to the divisions.

As well as discussing with Lingard – who was now visiting the Traffic Department's record office – his interview with Kirstin Lattimer and his own skirmish with Jervaise, he had also read the report on the identification of the thermostatic device. A report from Detective Sergeant Magnus whom he had instructed to examine the Lattimers' house and garage had produced an oddity for him to chew over. In Magnus's listing of the contents of the escritoire, he had noticed the absence of cheque book stubs, bank statements, or any documents at all relating to the Lattimers' financial status. Those, he guessed, could be the source of the pulverized ash he had seen in the fire grate. Matters were, he admitted to himself, becoming confused. All added together, they still remained disparate bits and pieces mainly illustrating the obvious, adding nothing so far as he could see to help point an accusing constabulary finger at a suspect.

When Lingard returned, be brought with him a manila folder. 'In full, George,' he said, reseating himself in the visitors' chair and sliding the folder across the desk. 'But in brief from me. Drusilla Jean Lattimer, aged twenty-six years, unmarried and a film processor, whatever that may be. Owner and driver of an old soft-top sports car and, back in April when the accident happened, accompanied by a James McManus, a bank employee and believed to be her boyfriend. Returning to Abbotsburn on the dreaded motorway – eleven at night, peeing with rain and generally murky – she had a burst from a defective front tyre which flipped the car onto its side against the central barrier. That took

77

away the windscreen pillar and her side window, scraped her face along the barrier, and finally landed the car upside-down.' Lingard grimaced. 'Horrible, really. McManus got away with cuts and bruises, but poor Drusilla lost her right eye, bits of her ear, and most of the skin from that side of her face. I only caught a glimpse of it through a window, but I saw she was wearing an eyepatch. Even so, I'm surprised that she's agreed to see me.'

'It's enough for me,' Rogers said, dropping the file into his pending tray. 'I'll read this later. You're for court tomorrow, aren't you? Is there still not a guilty plea?'

Most working detectives loathed the paralysis of inactivity in courtrooms. Lingard was no exception and his expression showed it. 'It doesn't look like it, no.'

'I'd better see her myself, then. You knock out your report before going off and dig out Inspector Hagbourne from whatever he's doing. Give him my interview notes on Chaffer – he's your fat man, by the way – and his partner Mullet. Tell him I want a hard check on their backgrounds, they both had something on their minds they didn't want to share with me.'

'You think they're involved?'

Rogers was sardonic. 'Who knows? But if blowing up unsatisfactory employees with pipe-bombs is a common business practice, I suppose I do.'

'Mrs Gullick's the one who actually saw our fat character,' Lingard reminded him. 'She might have a bit more than she gave her husband and I was to see her later this evening.'

'I'll detail someone else. They'll probably be out cantering over the moor anyway, and . . .' He stopped, frowning, then said, 'I'm getting bloody senile, David. I meant to check it and forgot. Gullick said something about the track leading to an outlying farm and that might be Jervaise's.'

He rose from his chair and strode to the chart boards hinged to the wall, swinging them open to the Ordnance Survey map covering Abbotsburn and the Great Morte Moor. With Lingard at his shoulder he studied the area in which Lattimer had died, poking the stem of his pipe at it. The track, graded as unsuitable for motor vehicles, ran from Mortefuet along the lower contour lines of the moor and entered the B-class road he had travelled at a point six miles short of Brigthorpe village.

'Not what I'd call significantly near Jervaise's place,' Rogers muttered heavily, 'but near enough for me to wish I'd remembered it before we had our little tête-à-tête.' With Lingard diplomatically close-mouthed, he said, 'I see no difficulty in negotiating it with a four-wheel drive, but why should he? Assuming that he's the villain who planted the bomb – which I don't yet – why should he want to be anywhere near it when it went off?' He was arguing with himself.

'I don't know the chappie as you do, but mightn't he want to assure himself that it had worked?' Lingard suggested. 'From a safe distance, naturally.'

'I've a theory that seems a mite more subtle than that,' Rogers replied, thinking it out as he spoke. 'Forget Jervaise being the character who planted the bomb for a moment. We know – or believe we do – that Lattimer was attempting to blackmail the arrogant bugger over his association with his wife and wanted to meet him to talk about it.' He shook his head, almost despairingly. 'Christ! Meet him! We must live in different worlds. So Jervaise says he went to Lattimer's house – which we know he did – to beat him up. Getting no answer to his knocking – we know that too – he left, and tells me rather definitely that he had no further contact with him. But say he had. Say that they'd agreed to meet on the moor – remember the note for ten o'clock? – Jervaise would know that he could easily do it from Brigthorpe in his Range Rover and, most likely, without being seen by anyone. What better place than an empty moor to put the boot in on a blackmailer?' That sounded good to him; too good, in fact, to be the answer.

'Excepting the odd rock-climbing Gullick or two,' Lingard pointed out.

'Exactly. So he saw them on the moor before Lattimer got there, or even after he'd arrived, and possibly from a distance. Operation cancelled, or postponed, and he retreats back home, frustrated again. He could have heard the bomb going off behind him, but he need not. Rattling over that track could drown out an overhead clap of thunder.'

'You're working hard at whitewashing him, George,' Lingard smiled.

'Like hell I am,' Rogers grunted. 'I don't like the bugger and he's a lout, but at the moment I can't see him killing anybody other than by stamping on his face or suchlike.'

'It would make the bomb and their arranged meet an unlikely coincidence,' Lingard said with unconcealed scepticism. 'Needing somebody else who didn't like Lattimer to plant it?'

'It's all a theory, David, and a thin one at that.' Rogers spoke around the stem of his pipe as he re-lit it. 'I'll see Jervaise tomorrow morning and see how it fits. He mightn't have so much fire in his belly by then.' He bared his wrist and checked the time. 'A lovely name, Drusilla,' he said. 'I hope she won't chew my ear for being a few minutes late.'

But it wasn't Drusilla Lattimer he was thinking about on the way to his car. Should his newly-thought-out theory prove to be a fact, he would be back to wondering who of those seen and interviewed could know enough about a threat to Lattimer's life to write that warning note to the police. And knowing of it, not coming forward when the warning had failed in its purpose.

15

Night had fallen when Rogers parked his car near the entrance to Love Lane. The air, cooler but still warm, smelt scented and the full moon, high in the dark-blue sky, cast dense shadows and made mysterious the short length of lane. Away from the centre of the town, it was quiet enough for Rogers to hear a cricket rasping its legs in its call for a mate and the dry rustling of leaves from the cement containers of flowering shrubs. An old-fashioned iron street lamp cast a small pool of light midway along the lane, moths and beetles banging themselves to insensibility against its glass panels. Nothing else stirred, not even the motionless black cat who stared yellow-eyed at him from a doorstep.

The door Rogers sought was near enough to the lamp for him to see its brass numerals. Seconds after he had pushed a thumb at the bell-tit, the hair's-breadth of light showing between the window curtains went out. A woman's voice asked 'Who is it?' through the door-post microphone he hadn't yet noticed.

'Detective Superintendent Rogers,' he answered. 'Chief Inspector Lingard is unable to keep the appointment you made.'

There was a short silence before she said, 'Why can't he?'

'He's been called away on another matter,' he explained patiently. 'It does happen.' Lingard had mentioned a viewing lens and he took out his warrant card, holding it close to the button-sized fitment he could see in the door panel. 'My card,' he said, thinking that he must look villainous in the shadowed light.

'I can't read that,' the disembodied voice said, 'but come in when I call out to you. And please sit on the chair inside.'

He heard the rattling of a safety chain and, waiting, saw a light again shining through the curtains. Supposing the oddness of the occasion to be only the precautions of a woman not wishing her mutilations to be seen by a stranger, he accepted it philosophically enough.

When at last he heard 'You can come in' called out well back from the door he opened it and stepped into the room. At first he couldn't see her, his eyes blinking in the brightness of a single wall light shining onto a chair at the side of the room. She was at the unlit darker end of the room, sitting in an armchair facing a louvred window through which moonlight shone, with only the back of her head and her narrow shoulders visible to him. A large and very hairy dog, upright on his haunches, sat at her side with one of her hands holding his collar.

She said, 'Would you take the chair, and please don't move from it.' Only the dog had looked around, and then only at his entry.

Rogers sat, deciding that one of his unfavourite occupations was talking to the back of somebody's unturnable head while he himself was illuminated in a narrow and discomfiting cone of light from above. Were he asked to describe her, he could say only that what he could see of her suggested frailness, that her short-cropped hair had a glossy tinge of copper in it, that she was wearing what appeared to be a cornflower-blue dress, and that the one arm visible was slender and shapely with a tiny watch strapped to its wrist.

He couldn't believe it would be appreciated should he express sorrow at the death of her brother and her own suffering from the car accident, so he ignored both. 'Miss Lattimer,' he started, 'I wouldn't have had either you or your sister bothered had it not been necessary to our investigation, and I hope that you'll bear with me if I ask questions which might be painful to you.'

81

'If you must.' Her voice was attractively modulated, although a little short of being friendly. 'Tell me first, and tell me truthfully – did my brother suffer?'

Whether he had, or had not, Rogers knew that a painful truth was never a kindness. 'I am a hundred per cent certain that he felt nothing,' he told her firmly, putting earnestness in his words. 'And that is the quite definite opinion of the very experienced medical specialist who examined him.'

'Thank you,' she said formally. 'That is what I had to know. Please ask your questions.'

Leaning forward to avoid in part the discomfort to his eyes from the light above him, Rogers realized that he could see her, silver-sheened by moonlight, reflected in the glass of the window. Only partially obstructed by the opened vertical louvres over it, the luminescent ghost of her showed clearly a face that, unmarked, must have been extraordinarily good looking. Its skin was pale, almost pallid, the flesh-coloured patch over where her right eye had been noticeable only by its contrasting shininess. The skin of the cheek below it was scarred with dark striations running through areas of discoloration. Her only eye glistened in its small pool of orbital shadow and her mouth, unscarred, showed sadness and suffering.

'I'd like to touch on the matter of Mrs Lattimer first,' Rogers said. 'I know your sister's opinion of her; is it yours?'

'It is. She's an evil woman, and I *mean* evil. Which is why, I'm sure, she left him.' The bitterness in her words was plain.

'Evil in what way?' he asked. He knew that if he could see her reflection, she could certainly see his, and her eye had seemed to be watching him when he spoke.

'In the way she treated Andrew. She bled him of everything – his love for her, his money and his self-respect.' Her eye was blinking back tears. 'In the end, although he still seemed to be obsessed with her, he hated her for what she had done to him. He wanted her to go, to get out of his life, and she went. But she didn't have to kill him, did she?'

'I don't know that she did. Why do you?' What he thought of as his well-educated nostrils were beginning to detect the smell of dog, overlaid by a very nice perfume.

'Because she's evil. Because she had taken everything she could from him and wanted to be free of him. Because, also, she

82

can be the only one who could have any wish to. When you find her, you'll see.' When Rogers remained silent, allowing her to unburden herself of the unhappiness she held inside – he guessed that she had had it all ready for the interview – she continued. 'I loved my brother. We were very close and what she did to him hurt me as much as it did him. I knew from the day she fooled him into marrying her that she would be no good for him. She was sly and secretive about who she had been, and none of us liked or trusted her from the time we first met her. I'm sure she felt that, for we were never invited to her house and if I wanted to see Andrew I went there when she was out. Or sometimes he would come to me. She never did and she wouldn't have been welcome anyway. Not even when I was in hospital, though God knows I wouldn't have wanted her to. My sister told you – no, I mean the other one, that she was money-mad, and she was. It doesn't matter now, but Andrew did confide to me that he had had to obtain a quite large loan from his company to pay some debts she had incurred without his knowledge. One, he told me, for jewellery he thought she already had when they married.' She had been fondling the head of her dog as she spoke, as if he were a surrogate for the brother she had lost; noticeable to the watching Rogers that she had not when speaking of his hated wife.

'Did he also confide in you about her going with other men? I mean, you knew she was, didn't you? And names would be useful.'

'I did know, yes, but he never mentioned who with and I can't believe he knew or he would have told me. I'd tell you if I knew, for I'm certain she will be with one of them. Do *you* know?' she demanded.

'I'll bear your suggestion in mind,' Rogers said, disregarding her demand. 'I ask this because I have to, and I mean no offence. Either before or after his wife left him, was Andrew associating socially or sexually with another woman?'

She took that calmly enough. 'I wish he had been, but I'm sure not. He would have told me and, anyway, he would have been so much happier than he was.'

Rogers thought that might clear his concern about Eleanor Caine and was something achieved. 'Going back to your visiting Andrew at his home,' he said, 'were you using a blue Mini?'

83

'Yes, I was. It belongs to my sister and I borrow it when I go out. I don't have my own now.'

'Then you saw him the night before last?'

'Yes . . . Oh God,' she whispered. Her features creased with the anguish of her remembering and her head drooped for long silent moments. Then she took a deep breath and said, 'That was the last time I saw him.'

'I'm sorry.' His voice was gentle. 'I know it must hurt, but how was he? I imagine still concerned about his wife leaving him?' The dog, suddenly lowering himself to the floor, had caused her to involuntarily turn her head to look at him. Undamaged in the profile she had so briefly presented to him, she appeared as sadly a beautiful woman as he could remember seeing.

'He was quite wretched, miserably so, but not, I feel, wholly about her. She was no loss to him and he accepted that. He said he had picked up a virus of some kind and wasn't feeling at all well. He had apparently been told by his employer – Mr Chaffer, I think he said – to go home and rest.'

'I saw a sherry glass that somebody had left on the floor. Was that yours?'

'It must have been. I certainly had a drink while I was there. Is that important?' There was an edge of resentment in her voice.

'Not in the slightest,' Rogers said. 'It's merely clearing up a loose end. Was anything mentioned by him about somebody, anybody, visiting him? Particularly expected on the following day?'

'Definitely not. He had shut himself away from everybody but me.' Her reflection showed the one eyebrow down in a frown. 'I've just remembered – there was something. Not that, but what he did. Two or three times while I was there he got up from his chair and looked out of the window through the curtains. He did say that he thought he had heard a noise, footsteps or something, but then said that he must be imagining it. He was definitely on edge, although I didn't take much notice of it at the time and I didn't hear anything myself.' She frowned again. 'Might that have been her . . . or whoever it was you think was visiting him?'

'Almost certainly his imagination, or he heard Mrs Caine next door arriving home,' Rogers assured her, though he wasn't yet believing so. 'What time was it?'

'Very late. Some time between midnight and when I left,

because I had cooked him a meal and he'd eaten it before we went into the sitting-room.'

'And what time was it when you left?'

For a moment there was surprise, or something very like it, in her face. 'I believe about three,' she said, then sharply and almost defensively, 'I can only go out at night.' Her chin came up. 'Had you thought of that, Mr Rogers? That's the only time I can and not be stared at as if I'm some horrible freak. I did once. Just once, and I heard a little boy telling his mother that I should wear a bag over my head. I'm not exactly a dead woman – although sometimes I wish I was – but I'm close to being one. Why do you think I'm talking to you in the dark?' She spoke fast and jerkily, sounding as if she needed to stop him interrupting her. 'There's no end to it. There never will be. They keep trying . . . on and on in little bits . . . such painful little bits, and no promise that I shall ever be the same again.' A trace of hysteria came into her voice and Rogers could see tears sparkling in her eye's shadow. 'I'm beginning to hate them and I shouldn't do that, but why can't they . . . ? I had nobody but my brothers and sister after the accident. Nobody wants to know you when you are like this . . . nobody . . .' Her face suddenly crumpled and she covered it with her hands, weeping quietly.

Rogers stood from his chair, silent and deeply pitying; disconcerted that his routine questioning had provoked such anguish, defeated by her weeping. He could think of no single word he could say that wouldn't be banal, wounding or falsely reassuring. In her possibly exaggerated unsightliness she had probably been deserted by a no longer so loving boyfriend, or she herself had forestalled an anticipated rejection of her and released him from his attachment. In either event, she would have a psychological scarring that, deforming her personality as it must, might never heal. He could visualize clearly her and the soon-to-die brother each sadly comforting the other in their shared misery: she, desperately wounded both physically and mentally, and he – with whatever camouflaging mask he chose to hide behind – sick from his wife's desertion of him and from whatever sense of personal inadequacy he had suffered.

'I'm sorry I've upset you,' he said, 'and I think it's better I should go.'

'It's not your fault,' she answered him, her words barely

85

audible from behind her hands. 'But please do. I'm tired and I don't wish to talk about it any more.'

Out in the deeply shadowed lane – grey rain should have been falling – he closed the door quietly, taking with him her forlorn despair and grief, their sad echoes promising to disturb and haunt him for what was left of the night. Believing unwillingly in the fact of reincarnation and not, he could admit modestly, yet having attained perfection, he hoped that should he be endorsed post-mortem *Try Again* and returned, it would not be as an entity destined to be a police officer. Nothing of which could stop him wondering why – and Lingard had been explicit about this – she had insisted on being interviewed very much against the wishes of her sister.

16

An off-duty, eardrum-aching and starving Rogers, freshly showered and shaved in pyjamas and dressing gown, suffered no inclination at shortly after midnight to graze on the long grass of deep thinking necessary for the untangling of mental knots. He preferred instead to concentrate on the complexities of grilling a thick gammon steak on a – to him – still strange electronic cooker.

Required as a now divorced member of the force to leave his Police Authority-owned house, he had rented lukewarmly a small three-roomed town flat sandwiched between two others. A secretive eccentric he had not yet seen lived above him and, were sounds reflecting fact, he occasionally exercised a large horse in his sitting-room while playing his piano fortissimo. When not doing that, the silence was so complete that Rogers had difficulty in convincing himself that he hadn't died during the preceding night.

The flat below was occupied by an ageing actress, mid-European accented, over-lipsticked and still youthfully vivacious, who had already alarmed him by demanding that he called her Nanoushka. She, having earlier found out Rogers's occupation, waylaid him at different times on the stairs for his help with an apparently berserker mouse in her bedroom, a malfunctioning television set she had forgotten to plug in, and a dear nephew in the Arabian section of the Foreign Office who, she was utterly convinced, having not written to her for several weeks, had been kidnapped or murdered by the Syrian Secret Service.

In his kitchen, which he was prone to describe derisively as being only a little bigger than two upright coffins joined together, Rogers was thinking while waiting for his steak to turn brownish that the flat needed badly an elegant woman to grace it, to add to it a much desired femininity. As importantly, if selfishly, a woman to also cook a decent meal for them both and to occasionally flick a duster at things. He was comparing his uncomfortable and spartan lot with that he had seen of the earlier alive and wifeless Lattimer – anything that would take his mind away from the tragic Drusilla Lattimer – when the telephone rang in the sitting-room.

Swearing under his breath because he knew that with his being on an unlisted number a caller could never mean anything but trouble, he went to answer it. 'Rogers here,' he growled, not remotely welcoming.

'Sir.' The voice sounded wary. 'DC Collins speaking. I'm about to leave on a suspected break-in and I thought you'd better be told about it. Information Room received a 999 from a Mrs Caine in Penruddock Close who said she'd heard a noise and someone was shining a torch inside the house next door. PC Goater on car patrol was contacted and attended and reported back that he'd found an unconscious man with a head injury behind the house. It's the one belonging to the man Lattimer you're dealing with and I knew you'd want to know. PC Goater asked for an ambulance and it's on the way. He's standing by for instructions.'

'Who is he? The man, I mean.' This sounded too good to be true for Rogers, although too much of a coincidence to be a disassociated housebreaking. In his mind he was already halfway there.

'He didn't say, sir.'

'His description?'

'Not that either, sir.' Collins sounded as if he had been weighed and found inadequate.

'Right,' Rogers said brusquely. 'Call up Goater and tell him to stall the ambulance people. I don't want the man taken away before I get there. That is, not unless he's in so bad a way that he needs medical attention. Then you get up there . . .' His nose had caught the harsh smell of burning meat and he swore. 'Not you,' he said irritably to a surprised and apologizing Collins. 'My bloody supper's on fire. You get on and I'll see you there.'

The kitchen was thick with a fog of blue smoke and his one and only gammon steak, shrivelled and blackened with small flames coming from it, hissed fiercely when he dumped it in the sink and turned a tap on it. Opening the window and switching off the grill, he accepted fatalistically that God had decided for no good reason he could think of against his ever eating a full meal again.

Having dressed quickly while snatching bites at a cube of cheese and a water biscuit, he crept silent-footed down the stairs past Nanoushka's door and out into the night to his car. With little late-night traffic to impede him, he turned into Penruddock Close and pulled in behind the CID Utility even as Collins was disappearing into the drive of Lattimer's house. Parked there, each with its blue roof lamp still flashing, was an ambulance and a police patrol car; needing, Rogers considered, only a fire appliance to give the close the appearance of a minor disaster area, and an even more interesting spectacle for the watchers he could see behind the neighbouring windows.

He found Collins with PC Goater and the ambulance crew grouped at the rear of the house. Nobody spoke until one of the ambulance men whispered 'He's shamming' and Rogers, looking at the man on the flagstones a few feet away, wagged a cautionary finger for silence.

He lay below an open ground-floor window, face upwards on a stretcher, his body covered by a bright red blanket, his head resting on a plastic pillow. Illuminated in the cold glare of the moon, his features and closed eyelids were chalky-white, his bulging forehead disfigured by a small slab of padding taped to it. He looked dead, only a fluttering of movement in his stringy throat showing that he wasn't.

Rogers bent his knees and crouched at his side, his face a forbidding nearness to the eyelids he guessed were shut against the consciousness of a dreadful reality. He waited, allowing his presence to be felt, then said tersely, 'You can open your eyes, Mr Mullet, it's too late at night for you to be playing games.'

It had to be the mention of his name that did it, for he opened them and looked up at Rogers. 'My leg,' he groaned. 'I fell . . . it's broken.' He lolled his head sideways on the pillow, away from the detective. 'Please, I want a doctor.'

'I'll send you off to hospital in a moment,' Rogers said. 'Before you go, though, perhaps you'd like to tell me why you've decided on taking up burglary.'

Mullet shook his head feebly, squeezing his eyes shut as if in an anguish of pain.

'Just as you like.' Rogers wanted, anyway, a medical man's confirmation that he wasn't *in extremis* or suffering before he got down to serious questioning. 'Bear this in mind,' he said sternly. 'As you are now under arrest, I'll be needing an answer to this later on tonight.' In the ensuing silence, he added, 'And being under arrest means that I shall have to search you.' He pulled down the hospital-smelling blanket, seeing that he wore gloves and that his wrists had been handcuffed together. He felt in the pockets of Mullet's jacket and trousers, finding no more than a handkerchief, a mortice lock key and his depressed cleric spectacles, one lens having been cracked and the frame twisted.

He straightened his aching legs, beckoning to the ambulance man who had whispered to him. Around the corner of the garage, he asked, 'Is there anything seriously wrong with him? You said he was shamming.'

'I meant he was shamming being unconscious,' the man corrected him. 'Though that's not to say he didn't concuss himself when he fell out of the window – he's got a nasty lump on his head. He's complained his leg is broken and while we'll handle him as if it is, I'm positive it's nothing more than a bad sprain. Or, at the worst, a torn ligament.'

'No more than he deserved,' Rogers said. 'You can take him now, and thanks for waiting. As he's under arrest, I'm having DC Collins follow along and stay with him.'

With the ambulance and its escort taking away the now unhandcuffed and unlikeliest housebreaker Rogers had dealt with for some years, he turned to the uniformed patrol car driver. Reasonably amiable because things appeared to be going well, he said, 'Good for you, Goater. You must have got here commendably fast. What's the story?'

'We were lucky, sir,' replied Goater, a grey-haired veteran

without enough ambition to be self-seeking. 'I wasn't too far away when Control called me up, and he wasn't going anywhere when I got here. He seemed to have knocked himself out, so I reported back for an ambulance. I had to handcuff him because I thought he'd come round while I was doing it and scarper. He did sort of come to after a bit, but shut his eyes and refused to answer when I asked him who he was. There's a torch and screwdriver inside on the window ledge which I found on the ground outside. I had a quick look around and there doesn't seem to be anybody in the house unless they're hidden away.'

'Of course, they could be in there murdered,' Rogers suggested drily, then seeing Goater's expression change to a sudden realization, said, 'It's all right, I was joking. It's unoccupied. Didn't they tell you that this is where the man lived who was killed this morning?'

Goater looked at Rogers reproachfully. 'No, sir. I knew he was, but I didn't know where he lived.'

'Well, he did and it makes your arrest the more important.' Rogers was working his brain at it, filling his pipe and lighting it while he did. 'He must have heard you coming and panicked, then fell when he scrambled out of the window. He wouldn't be very good at it, being that he's a finance adviser of sorts.' He blew out smoke, a small cloud of silvery floss in the moonlight. 'Have you thought about how he got here? There's no spare car parked in the close that I've noticed, and certainly not one out on the main road. Nor did he have any car keys on him. I don't think he'd walk here, do you?'

Goater thought about that, then muttered 'Bugger it,' under his breath. He said, 'I think I've boobed there, although I don't think I had much choice. When I was getting near the turn-off into the close I saw a car moving off further along the road. It did cross my mind that it could've been him taking off, but not enough to chase after it and find it wasn't. And he was too far away for me to see the colour or make, leave alone the index number. When I found our bloke still on the premises I never thought of it again.' He looked at Rogers anxiously. 'That was his pick-up mate, wasn't it?'

'I imagine it was,' Rogers agreed. 'But there's no boob, no need to feel you're at fault. I'd have done the same myself. It's no matter anyway; I think I know who it was and he's just the man to leave our chap dangling on his own when he was in trouble. You've checked the doors?'

'All secure, sir. He got in by forcing the window.'

Rogers used the torch dropped by Mullet to examine the window's framework. There had been a vigorous but unskilful bruising and splintering of the white-painted wood that must have made noises in the quiet night like an exploding fire cracker, forcing the fastening handle inside from its seating. It was a narrow window with a latching stay stop at its base that might well have tripped the panic-stricken foot of a man used more to endorsing incoming cheques than jumping from somebody else's house.

Normally, Rogers would have climbed through the window – the door key being back in his office – but, satisfied that Mullet had not got to the point of taking whatever he had come for, decided against it. He was already beginning to miss Lingard to whom he could always delegate. 'Get on to Information Room,' he instructed Goater, 'and tell them to send Sergeant Magnus out to do an examination of whatever happened here. Also, a spare PC up here to hold the fort. You can go as soon as either gets here, so do your report tonight and leave it on my desk.'

That, he thought as he left Goater, seemed to be as much as he could do at the house. Chaffer – if Chaffer it was – could wait until he had some sort of confirmation of his pusillanimous desertion from Mullet. For entirely different reasons, he didn't believe that Eleanor Caine could. Not now that he had so fortuitously showered and shaved himself to a presentable seemliness.

17

It was an inappropriate night for rummaging into the squalidness of murder, for Rogers to have to fret about its connection with a moneylender turned inept housebreaker who must have things to tell him. With the night's dissipation of the day's brassy heat there was still a warm languor in the air, a night in which he should be sitting on a terrace and watching pipistrelle bats flying in the moonlight, having nothing more arduous on his mind than the chores of refilling an emptied whisky glass and relighting a gone-cold pipe.

He could see no light in the windows of Eleanor Caine's house and he now hesitated at her gate, fumbling for his car keys, indecisive about what he was insisting to himself was a proper reluctance to disturb her so late at night for information he seemed already to have. That overlaid an inner recognition of his sexual attraction for her and the possibility of a future dangerous embroilment.

His indecision went for nothing when a crack of light appeared between the window curtains. The door opened and she was there, a shadowed silhouette in the light reflected from behind her. 'I've been waiting for you,' she called to him. 'Aren't you coming in?'

He unlatched the gate and went to her. 'It's late,' he said, realizing how obvious and wet that must sound. 'I thought you'd gone to bed.'

'With all that noise going on and lights flashing?' she asked mockingly. 'I've been watching you all. Why was he taken out on a stretcher? And what happened?' She closed the door and he followed in the wake of her heady scent into a sitting-room.

'He fell out of a window and banged his head on concrete,' he explained, not about to tell her too much. 'We're grateful for your call, we really are; although I don't imagine that he is.'

Although he did recognize the rose-pink sofa from the photograph of the Lattimers she had shown him, he saw only vaguely as a three-dimensional collage the rest of the room's furniture and furnishings, his awareness of any of it peripheral to the visual impact she was making on him. It was all incomparably there: the long slender throat, now set off by a gold snake chain, the glossy black hair and her darkly luminous green eyes; the smoothly tanned flesh of her bare arms and legs, and the mouth so shaped that it was inconceivable that it could utter anything but pleasant words. The plain white dress she wore emphasized her slim elegance. Dear God, his inner self was telling him, she's so beautiful. Why hadn't he noticed it so breathtakingly before? Her husband must be imbecilic to leave her for a day, let alone for the three weeks he was spending on some godforsaken oil rig.

'Please sit,' she said, certainly aware of his almost hypnotic

92

scrutiny of her. 'Tell me about it, but first let me get you a drink. I'm sorry, but there's only gin or vodka.'

'Vodka, please, with some mixer.' Rarely touching the stuff, he thought that at least it would be some reparation for his lost supper. He settled himself in the softly-stuffed depths of an easy chair near the brass-canopied fireplace. While she poured the drinks at the lowered flap of a wall unit cabinet, he said, 'There's little I can tell you about your housebreaker, I'm afraid, certainly not his identity. All I can say is that he's not a professional villain and not in the least dangerous.'

'Isn't he the man who murdered Andrew?' she asked without turning her head. She was dribbling what looked like diluted blood into a more than generous amount of vodka.

'You should never ask a policeman that sort of question,' he said smilingly. 'He'd be cashiered and sued down to his last shirt if he answered it and was later proved wrong.'

'And I wouldn't want that to happen, would I.' She crossed the room and handed him his pink-stained vodka, her unsettling nearness and her scent doing his savoir-faire no good at all.

When she sat in the chair opposite him, placing her gin-and-tonic carefully on its fat arm and crossing her legs, he said, 'You'll possibly be called to give evidence in court about what you saw and your emergency call, so perhaps you'd better tell me what led to it. *Gesundheit!*' he added, drinking from his glass, his eyes watering at its unexpected strength.

'And good health to you.' She smiled nicely and sipped at hers. 'There isn't much to tell that I didn't say over the phone. I came back from my friends down the road and was getting ready for bed when I heard a quite loud noise coming from next door, as if something was being broken. I thought from their garden, although I wasn't sure; it could have been from mine. It made me look out from my window upstairs but I couldn't see anything, although I think I would have in the moonlight. It worried me a little being here on my own, and I had to make myself go out into the garden to see what it was.' She quirked her lips. 'I was nervous enough to take a poker with me, but thank heavens it wasn't necessary. I saw a light moving about through the back windows next door, so I crept back indoors and dialled 999 as fast as I could. The policeman was here in minutes and when I heard him talking to somebody in the garden I knew that he'd caught him and that I could stop shaking. I'm not very brave about things like that.'

'I'd have been nervous myself,' he exaggerated. 'You didn't see him at all? To see that he was on his own?'

'Only when one was being carried in the stretcher. Were there two?'

'Probably not if you hadn't seen them.' During her talking she had not deviated in her fixed regard of his face and he was beginning to feel uncomfortable, that being usually his own tactic with suspect witnesses. 'Which reminds me. I'm grateful for the additional information about the red car, and sorry I wasn't in when you called.'

'You haven't found Audrey, have you?' She sipped more of her gin and he followed suit with what he considered rather more fire-water than vodka.

'No,' he admitted, 'and I'm beginning to doubt that she ever existed outside my imagination.' He was approaching the question he didn't wish to ask, a difficult one to put to a woman, and sooner than he had anticipated. He fumbled for something else to say. 'Did you like her?' he asked.

'No more nor less than one would somebody living next door.' She was silent for a moment. 'No. I have to be honest and say that I didn't. Not after . . . well, you know how trivial a matter can lead to it.'

'Would the reason for it be of interest to me?'

'I'm sure not,' she said with positiveness.

'Had you spoken to Mr Lattimer since she left him?' His mind wasn't wholly on the unfortunate Lattimer, for while he could ignore her bare legs and the gentle mounds of her breasts beneath the white dress with a fair degree of equanimity, it was still her slender throat and the pleasantness of her mouth that intruded upon his questioning. He could, he thought fancifully, almost groan his feelings aloud.

'Several times. We do live next door to each other,' she reminded him drily. 'He never mentioned her going away to me if that's what you want to know. The few times we spoke we said interesting things such as "Good-morning" and "How are you?"' Amusement showed in her eyes.

'So how was he when you asked him that?'

'Though he obviously never said anything about it to me, I

could see that he was letting himself go about shaving and wearing clean shirts, that he definitely had something on his mind that was bothering him. That, I assumed, must have been Audrey's leaving him.'

'This morning,' he said, 'you mentioned hearing the garage door being closed at seven the previous evening. Would you have heard had it been used afterwards?'

'I'm sure it wasn't. That is, I'm sure up until about twelve when I went to bed. It does make a frightful noise, especially then. Not quite so often, I have heard it very late at night and it's woken me up.'

He drank the remainder of his vodka, the moment of a potentially angry resentment upon him. 'I have to ask you this, Mrs Caine, because of what another person insinuated when being questioned about Mr Lattimer.' He was straight-faced with no expression in his voice. 'Has there been anything more between you and him than what you've told me?'

Had she thrown what was left of her gin in his face – elegantly, of course – he would have been neither surprised nor offended. Instead, after staring hard at him, she laughed easily. 'You are a delicate soul, Mr Rogers, aren't you. Do you mean that I let him into my bed? That we made love together?'

He had already read the answer in her eyes, foolishly relieved for a man whose attention was supposed to be focussed on murder. He cleared his throat. 'Yes, I do,' he said simply.

'No,' she told him with nothing in her voice suggesting that she was either angry or disturbed. 'Had you known poor Andrew, you wouldn't have had to ask. I may be quite mistaken, but I'd say that he was negative minus when any woman but Audrey was concerned. And then again,' she added calmly, 'your question does rather suggest that I'm the kind of woman who would allow it.'

'It was what somebody else insinuated,' he defended himself, having sudden misgivings about her attitude. 'Never anything I believed.'

She must have recognized the discomfiture in his face, for she smiled engagingly and said, 'I'm not offended by you, only with whomever it was who lied about me. And then not enough to ask you who it was.'

Rising from her chair, she reached for his glass and went to the drinks cabinet. Had he not been searching for relevant questions enough to postpone his departure for a little longer he would have refused another vodka. The alcohol in a virtually empty stomach was already having its effect on his brain, and that urging his tongue to wag crass and imprudent utterances about her attractiveness to him.

She gave him his drink and sank gracefully back in her chair, kicking off her shoes and folding her legs under her without putting down her own refilled glass. She said, 'When you were here this morning you asked me about my husband and whether he would know anything about the Lattimers. Have you done anything about having him seen?'

'No, I haven't. I'm happy to wait until he comes back.' So far as he could see it wasn't going to be necessary at all, but he needed to keep his options open.

She drank at her gin, bit briefly at her lip and gave him a conciliatory smile. 'It was foolish of me, but I'm afraid I told you a lie this morning.'

'You mean he isn't on an oil rig at all?' Rogers, case-hardened against lying as he was, still felt disappointment that his earlier fears were about to be justified.

'Oh, but he is.' She hesitated and bit at her lip again. 'When I told you he was coming back, it wasn't the truth. He isn't.'

'I see,' he said, although he didn't. 'Not at all?'

'I think not. If you do wish to see him you'll have to fly out to Oil Rig Fisherwick offshore from the Orkneys.'

'Don't scream at me if I'm putting my foot in it,' he said warily, 'but would this have anything to do with Mrs Lattimer?'

She stared at him long enough for him to think he was about to receive some female flak. 'Not that I'm sure enough to say yes,' she said at last, 'but as he was lately making a habit of going to bed with her kind I thought it a probability. He had every opportunity when he was here.'

'I'm sorry that you . . .'

She chopped him short, her voice angry. 'Damn you! Don't you ever say that to me! If you have to sympathize with somebody, sympathize with him. He was the one who had to leave and I made him.' While Rogers was wondering ruefully where the hell he could go from there, she whispered something to herself, then said gently, 'And now *I'm* sorry. You weren't to know and I shouldn't have spoken to you like that.'

Because they were so rarely offered, he was always disarmed by a woman's apologies. 'It's no great matter,' he told her wryly. 'My back's broad and I'm already scarred from saying the wrong things at the wrong time.'

'I'm forgiven then?' she asked cajolingly.

Her eyes were soft on his in a way, he made believe, that no woman should look at a man trying to keep his mind on his job. 'Of course,' he said. 'It's forgotten. And now I have to go. Your housebreaker is probably waiting anxiously for my personal attention.' He pushed up reluctantly from his chair and stood. Though he hadn't finished the second vodka, he suspected that what he had had already might be too much with Mullet yet to be interrogated. Apart from which, there were dangerously compelling attractions in getting pleasantly spiffed and allowing the brake to be released on an inhibition or two with this remarkably attractive woman who, if the message in her eyes was to be believed, might see in him an acceptable palliative against her disposal of a philandering husband.

'Oh.' There was disappointment in her face looking up at him. 'Do you have to? Now – now that you know about it, I do so want your advice on what I can do about my husband should he come back here.'

'Is he likely to?' Funny that, he thought. His tongue was feeling thick and stiff and he had only just got that out in one piece.

'That's what I don't know.' Her fingers were pulling at her throat chain. 'If he does . . . it's what's worrying me.'

'I'm sorry,' he said, careful with his articulation. 'I really am, but I can't. Your problem's a civil one and not one in which I can get involved. Not even for advice such as keeping your doors and windows locked. All I can suggest is that you should see a solicitor as soon as you can.' With his mind telling himself to get unstuffed, he added, 'But anything else, call on me. I'd want you to.'

She stood unsmiling, eye to eye with him, close enough for her scent to make his pulses race. For a moment, he thought that he had shot himself in the foot, then she held out her hand to be taken. 'I do understand and I shall look forward very much to seeing you again,' she said gravely. 'Really.'

While there had been no message-sending pressure from her fingers, he was certain that an understanding, a strong rapport, had been achieved, and he was content with that.

Being let out into the still brilliant moonlight, he knew that he had somehow to clear his head of the effects of the vodka he had drunk and to recover some of the impetus towards investigating the death of Lattimer he seemed to have mislaid temporarily in a woman's eyes. Not for the first time, he believed – without actually wishing it to have happened – that he should have been neutered at birth, the built-in needs of an entire male being always a paradoxically prayed-for doorway to inevitable trouble.

18

There was a Walpurgis night emptiness in the town's streets at two o'clock on a moonlit morning, suggesting even more vividly to Rogers's imagery that the so far unsatisfied and unquiet ghost of the dead Lattimer dogged his every move. It was his whimsy that the murder victims with whom his job saddled him invariably did, and he was never quite sure whether he believed it or not. He parked his car outside the Casualty Department and, before entering it, took several deep breaths of the night air, feeling that a soberness of demeanour was back with him.

The antiseptic-smelling surgery was empty of its duty doctor and its customary late-night bleeding and drunken patients. A nurse he knew only as Judy, sitting at a desk as he entered, hurriedly hid a cigarette she had been smoking. 'Don't panic, Judy,' he said cheerfully. 'It's only me. You've a customer of mine still here?'

'Hi!' she greeted him, showing teeth as white as her nurse's cap. 'He's in Cubicle Two and waiting to be hanged, or whatever it is you're going to do with him.'

'Commuted to transportation,' he said. 'He's fit to travel?'

'Doctor McAllister says he is. A slight concussion that's given him a headache and a lesion of a ligament in his leg is his all. Nothing serious enough for an admission, although he asked for it.' She pulled a face. 'He's quite a booby, isn't he?'

'Coming in here, we all are,' he assured her.

Cubicle Two was in an off-set corridor and he pulled its plastic curtain aside to enter. Almost filled by a skeletal steel examination table on which Mullet lay propped by a pillow, there was otherwise a hand wash-basin, a plastic bin Rogers presumed was used for bloody bandages and the unwanted bits of tissue taken from casualty patients, a pile of red blankets on a shelf and two uncomfortable looking metal chairs; one occupied by DC Collins who leapt surprised to his feet at Rogers's appearance.

'I'm sure by now our friend must have told you all about it?' he said to Collins, although looking at Mullet as if including him in the question. But that a neat patch of tape had replaced the padding on his forehead and his sandy hair combed, he seemed as much untouched by hospital treatment as when seen earlier lying on flagstones. Other than, Rogers considered, seeming a little less agonized.

Collins said, 'Only that he thinks he should be taken home, sir. He says his wife will be worried, and he feels unwell.'

'Go and keep the nurse company until I want you,' Rogers told him. 'I'm sure Mr Mullet would prefer to speak to me privately.'

With Collins gone, he moved Mullet's shoeless feet to one side and sat on the table's plastic-sheeted mattress. He took out his pipe and filled and lit it while smiling without amiability at the unhappy man who manifestly regarded, and who was intended to regard, the smile as wolfish rather than friendly. 'As it appears that you are now going to survive your accident,' he said, 'perhaps you feel well enough to tell me why you've suddenly turned housebreaker? Or, to be precise, turned burglar? And before you do, I have to tell you that you are not obliged to say anything unless you wish to do so, but what you say may be taken down in writing and given in evidence.'

Rogers's official caution against self-incriminating gabbiness and therefore unlikely to liberate any pent-up need to confess, seemed thankfully not to have taken effect. Mullet licked his lips, moving his eyes from the detective and staring down the length of his smeared and dusty trousers. 'It has all been a most unfortunate mistake,' he started, his voice straining to earnestness. 'It really has. After you had left our office, Mr Chaffer and I were worried about Mrs Lattimer. About her financial situation, I mean, her husband being so tragically dead, and he having been an employee of ours. We were certain she would be back home and it was decided that I should call on her without delay and offer to help her. When I knocked at the door – several times actually – and got no answer, I went to knock at the backdoor. I thought that she might have some difficulty in hearing me,' he explained, licking at his lips again and still taking an obsessive interest in his trouser legs. 'That was when I saw the window was open with marks on the side of it. I also saw a torch and a screwdriver on the sill as if I had disturbed someone trying to get in. I honestly didn't know what to do, but in the end I climbed up on to the window-sill and used the torch to see if there was anyone inside. There wasn't as far as I could see so I decided the best idea was for me to inform the police. When I was getting down the heel of my shoe caught on something and I don't really remember anything after that. Not until I came to with a police-man slapping my cheek.' He cleared his throat and then, putting a hand to his mouth, coughed delicately. 'I tried to tell him what had happened, but I was dazed and my leg hurt me dreadfully, so I can't remember much about that either. I apologize for there being so much trouble over a complete misunderstanding . . .' His voice trailed to silence and he looked anxiously at Rogers, his forehead now noticeably glistening.

Rogers took the pipe from between his teeth. Though there hadn't been anything remotely humorous in the explanation Mullet had given him, he felt an almost irresistible need to laugh at its absurdity. 'Very gripping, but not a good effort at all,' he said, shaking his head sadly. 'Burglary's too serious a crime to joke about. It's indictable, which means you'll be up in front of a judge and jury. And also, I've no doubt, a rather inquisitive prosecuting counsel who won't be so naive as you apparently believe I am. He'll certainly be inquisitive enough to ask you why you didn't telephone first to find out whether Mrs Lattimer had returned or not, where was your means of transport, and why you should make such an unannounced call anyway at well after midnight and not expect her to be in bed. And, having come for the ostensible purpose of helping her financially, very peculiarly not having in your possession a cheque book or money to be able to do so.' He paused for a few moments to allow the implications to sink in and reach muddy bottom. He was smelling fear in the man and, though he hated being the cause of it, had to push it along to a disclosure of the truth. He said, 'I should tell you also that he will certainly ask you why a neighbour happened to see the light from a torch bobbing about from inside the house – inside, mark you; not from the window-sill – only a few minutes before the arrival of the police officer who found you.'

Mullet looked as if in the dumb anguish of despair, his jaw muscles working hard as he wagged his head from side to side, his bony hands clenching and unclenching.

'I know that Chaffer drove you there,' Rogers pressed on. 'And you've probably guessed that he left you to it when he saw the police car arriving. When he's arrested, are you so sure he's going to support you in the ridiculous story you've given me?'

Mullet had already, only too patently, considered that. 'He made me do it,' he got out, his eyes back on Rogers. 'I wanted no part of it.'

'No part of what? That which you were looking for?' Fragmented paper ash in a fireplace was in his mind, and he guessed. 'Documents you didn't want anybody else to get hold of?'

It was a palpable hit, the dismay in Mullet's expression showing it. 'You've found them? You know?'

'It's your telling me I'm interested in,' Rogers said, becoming stern and pointing the stem of his pipe at him. 'Not my telling you. So you'd better start again, hadn't you? With a little less fiction and a lot more fact.'

Unprofessional as Mullet might be at breaking into houses, he was no fool and now surely thinking out what he was to say, how much he could hold back on. Rogers waited patiently, looking with feigned interest at an assembly of small glass containers, two gauges and green rubber tubing attached to the wall near Mullet's head, but wondering nevertheless for what fearful purposes they were used.

When he spoke he seemed composed and resigned, the fear he had diminished. 'I apologize for having lied to you,' he said with none of his earlier lip-licking. 'I was trying as well as I could to protect my partner. In a sense I believe I may justify what I was stupid enough to do.' He put his fingers to his forehead as if smoothing away pain. 'I have to tell you now what we didn't wish to say to you this afternoon. Lattimer was dishonest, a thief, and totally so. He was responsible for the general administration of loan issues, although of course they had to be approved and authorized by myself. In that position he contrived to obtain a loan of twenty thousand pounds for himself under a fictitious name with falsified collateral from a genuine account. I regret to admit that it deceived me completely and, naturally, I am rightly held responsible for it having been done. This happened last . . .'

He stopped, startled, and apprehensive, when a woman's muffled shrieking came from further down the corridor. 'What was that?' he asked.

Rogers, not happy himself about the interruption but accepting that not every patient took medication with mute suffering, said, 'It's only somebody having a needle stuck into her arm.' For him, that was nearly the worst thing he could think of. 'You were about to say when it happened.'

'Yes, last December. Since when there had been regular monthly repayments by building society cheques drawn under the fictitious name we had accepted in such good faith. We discovered later that he had opened the account with only two thousand pounds of the money stolen, obviously to be able to continue the deception. I must say that all this was discovered by a most unlikely chance and, when it was, he was immediately discharged.'

'After returning what was left of the money, I assume,' Rogers suggested helpfully. This, certainly, was the so-called loan mentioned by Drusilla Lattimer.

'He refused to tell us what he had done with the remainder.' That had come out reluctantly. 'Up until his death we were negotiating with him about its return, but after it we agreed that we had no recourse but to sue his estate. Which is why, regrettably, we decided to see if in Mrs Lattimer's absence we could find documents implicating him without any doubt in defrauding us.'

Mullet had been showing small signs of uneasiness and they had not been missed by Rogers. He stood from his seat on the table and scraped ash from his pipe into the wash-basin, flushing it away with tap water while he thought. There was a lot missing from Mullet's statement, matters skirted around, and his sensory antennae were telling him that he was again being lied to by the dry and calculating man, if only by deliberate omission. Remaining on his feet, he said slowly, 'Twenty thousand pounds is quite a bit to have stolen from you, isn't it? And I can't for the life of me think of any reason why you shouldn't have lodged a complaint with us. Why didn't you?'

Mullet hesitated, then said, 'We thought he might have the bulk of it hidden away and that we would get it back with less trouble. Nor did we wish to be hard on him.'

'So when you heard that he had been killed and the likelihood of your getting it back was virtually nil,' Rogers mused aloud, 'you still withheld all that and lied to me. Then, apparently, you decided instead that you'd prefer committing a serious crime – it's punishable by up to fourteen years inside, by the way – to saying anything about it.' He hardened his voice, his expression darkly stern as he stared at the wretched man. '*Why?* You're frightened and you're hiding something.' He was trying to read what it was in his face and chanced another guess. 'That's it! He had something on you both and you couldn't. You daren't!'

Either because Mullet assumed the detective had the documents he had failed to find and steal, or he had a below average resistance to interrogation, he suddenly looked shrunken. 'Not me,' he choked out. 'That isn't my responsibility . . . it's always been out of my hands. Hamish . . . Chaffer will tell you that. I had to help. He's my partner and they would never believe I didn't know.'

'Put who "they" are in plain English.' Rogers hadn't a clue what Mullet was admitting.

Committed, he obviously felt there to be no retreat. 'The . . . the Inland R-Revenue,' he stuttered, the words indistinct as if fighting to stay in his throat.

'And the documents Lattimer had would prove it?' Rogers could understand his fear of the consequences of their obvious tax evasion. Even in his own Pay As You Earn situation, the Inland Revenue frightened him with their capacity for extracting sickeningly large amounts of money.

'He . . . he told us he had photocopied them. Chaffer made me do it. He honestly did.'

Rogers felt all the irritation of a hungry man fly-casting for a fat trout and hooking a couple of miserably small minnows. Never seriously having considered either as a suspect for killing off Lattimer, it was still a disappointment that the bits and pieces found in his house, the inferences he had drawn from them, had led only to this relatively tuppeny-ha'penny result. Their employee's possession of damning documents would surely have been an effective insurance against his own fraud being reported to the police, as well as one against his being murdered by the two no doubt anxiously sweating rogues worried about the safety of their own skins. Thus far his logic, accepting that he could be wrong and ultimately shot down in flames; an investigator as incompetent as the inept Mullet had been a housebreaker.

Preparing to leave – the suffering woman had re-started her shrieking and he was anxious to get out of earshot of it – he said, 'I must tell you now that you're going to be charged with burglary, Mr Mullet, and held in police cells at least until tomorrow. When we catch up with your runaway friend I don't think you're going to feel too lonely.'

With Mullet having been taken over by Collins, Rogers climbed wearily into his car, started the engine and pointed her nose in the direction of his flat. Though only three-fifteen in the morning and nothing unusual about that, he had had enough and it was time he called it a day. He was bone-tired, his legs feeling heavier than they should, the blood in his arteries surely deoxygenated and, worst of all, being able to think of Eleanor Caine without any danger of his heart jerking out of its envelope.

Still in possession of enough caution not to forget to creep past Nanoushka's door – the lateness of the night would be no bar to her finding something wrong with her television set – and into his rooms, he flopped into a chair to lift the telephone and dial the number of a sleeping Inspector Hagbourne. When awake, Hagbourne dealt largely with crimes committed on paper, being above average numerate and the only man known to Rogers who could baffle the mind in proving the equation 2×1 to equal three. Putting him in the picture about Mullet, he ordered him to organize an immediate search for Chaffer who, though surely no man to sink in a stream of despairing bubbles, must surely be findable if only on account of the difficulty in disguising his bulk. After making certain that Hagbourne would not call him until late the following morning with any news of Chaffer's arrest – he made no bones about his present disinterest in him – he dropped the receiver back on its cradle and headed for his bed.

His need for food now of secondary importance, but promising himself a trencherman's breakfast, he was asleep before he could begin to fret at a growing realization that after sixteen hours or so of listening to flapping mouths he could be questioning what he had been told from quite the wrong point of view.

19

Lost and anonymous in the vastness of Great Morte Moor, seeing in the inky darkness only the insect eyes of a distant car's headlights moving towards him, the remote sounds of a trilling bell penetrated the silence of his mind. When summoning enough will to open his eyes, a shaft of sunlight through a gap in the window curtains struck blinding gold in them. His awakening consciousness accepted through its stupefaction that he was one George Rogers struggling naked from between his sheets in response to the ringing of his telephone bell. With all the imagined sensations of being a warmed-up corpse, he felt distinctly less than amiable, and ready, figuratively, to screw Hagbourne's bloody neck from his shoulders were he calling about Chaffer's arrest.

Reaching the sitting-room – he saw bleary-eyed the time to be seven-twenty – and managing to lift the receiver before it stopped ringing, he snarled 'Rogers here,' poised to blast Hagbourne's eardrums.

'It's DC Lewis, sir, at Thurnholme,' his caller gabbled breathlessly. 'I tried to get somebody in CID at Headquarters and couldn't, so I was given your number. I've found Mrs Lattimer and I think they're about to go off. I need some instructions because the boat's going out.'

Rogers, struggling with his half-asleep mind, said, 'Slow down, for God's sake. Where is she? Who are "they" and what's this about a boat?'

'Yes, sir, of course.' He sounded as though he thought Rogers an ungrateful sod. 'I was doing some early morning obbo on the fish market when I thought I saw the car you wanted checked being driven by a man. I was in my own car and followed him to the marina where he went on board one of the boats there. She was on the deck and I thought she must be Mrs Lattimer. I had to ask her to make sure and he was chucking his weight about when I did. When she said she was I had to say something so I told her we were looking for her to tell her that her husband was dead. I said he'd been killed in his car, which she took very well considering she must have been shocked, although she did say he always was a rotten driver. But that was all, I didn't mention anything else. When I offered to take her to Headquarters to see you, she refused and said she'd go under her own steam when they got back. I think they're getting ready to leave now and they're quite set on it. I'm watching them now.'

'Where are you?'

'In the kiosk on the quay. It's not far from the boat.'

'Right. Get back on board, hold her up by any means short of arresting her and wait for me. Tell the man his car's on the suspected stolen list or some twaddle like it. How will I know the boat?'

'It's a white motor cruiser called *Snapperjack* and it's moored about halfway along catwalk D on the right.'

'And the man's name?'

'I don't know, sir. He told me it was no concern of mine.'

'Good work, Lewis,' Rogers said before closing down and now verging on being awake in mind, if not in body. 'Don't go and spoil it by losing her. Or him either, if it comes to that.' Lewis, in his opinion, while good for the routine stuff, was far from being the brightest man in the department.

If Rogers had washed, shaved off overnight bristles, dressed and cooked up a cup of instant coffee in a shorter time, he had yet to recall it. While doing it, he deliberately excluded all conjectures about the supposedly preposterous Audrey Lattimer's reappearance, though experiencing an irrational frustration in that she had not been found dead as he had earlier feared or later expected.

It was an increasingly torrid sun and a glittering sea below him along the coast road until he could look down the steep gradient onto Thurnholme. Occupying the two crescents of a hillside, the primary reason for its being lay in the stepped rows of white-painted bed-and-breakfast establishments and guesthouses rising from the harbour between the grander, more exclusive hotels commanding the rocky headlands. Behind the harbour and joined to it by a narrow channel lay the marina, a small tidal basin made civilized by dumping huge stone blocks around it. On its dark-green water floated disciplined rows of tall-masted yachts and motor cruisers tethered at their mooring walkways. Rogers knew without envy that it, and not the small-boat-crowded harbour, was mostly for the filthily rich who used the expensive amenities of the *Club Mouiller l'Ancre* with its blue awnings and sun umbrellas and thickets of tubbed yuccas. His grey suit and white shirt would be conspicuously out of place there.

When he reached it through the uncrowded early morning streets that smelled of baking seaweed and – intolerably – frying bacon, he parked his car in the as yet unattended Club Members Only compound. Easily identifiable among the scattering of cars from the description given him by Eleanor Caine, although she had downgraded it somewhat, he saw a crimson Porsche and, from habit, memorized its registration number.

Finding as easily catwalk D – there were only five of them – he saw along the line of moored boats the top half of Lewis's figure, his arms resting on the deck rail and apparently mesmerised by the water below him. Walking along the planking between the boats he reached the *Snapperjack*. Roped sideways on to the catwalk, she was about thirty feet of glaring white paintwork in the brilliant sunshine and swaying only gently against her fenders. Squat rather than slim and with a square stern, she had a glassed-in wheelhouse superstructure high above the saloon deck. She seemed fitted with a superfluity of stainless steel railings and slender aerials and, for Rogers, unidentifiable and mysterious pieces of electrical equipment. A small pale-blue flag emblazoned with a dolphin and the Gothic letters HT hung limply from a wheelhouse mast. Through the blue-tinted windows of the saloon he could just make out the heads of a man and woman.

Lewis, tall and gangling and looking, despite a blond crew cut, as if he had just left school, detached himself from his glum contemplation of salt water and a floating plastic bottle, and met him as he stepped up on to the deck through a gap in the guard rail. Rogers, about to ask him how the score stood, changed his mind at the boat-owner's sudden emergence from the saloon companionway.

Late middle-aged, burly and balding, he looked excessively fit and was tanned to a deep coffee. His face, decorated with a thick black fighter-pilot's moustache, showed unrepressed vein-engorged anger. He wore blue shorts that showed unlovely woolly legs, a thin tee-shirt through which could be seen the dark shadows of a hairy chest, and white deck shoes. He planted himself solidly in front of Rogers, his blue eyes glaring at him, and growled, 'You took your bloody time in getting here, didn't you! What's all this business about my car being on your damned suspect list?'

Rogers held his glare calmly. 'Would you give me your name first?' he said; pleasantly, he thought, considering. 'And try not to shout at me.'

'It's Thomson if it's any business of yours,' he ground out, his anger still with him. 'And I'll damned well shout as much as I choose to on my own boat.'

Rogers allowed perplexity into his expression and he wagged his head ruefully. 'That's probably it,' he said, about to make it up as he went along. 'It could be a computer error. We're looking for a man named Tomkins who stole a Porsche and somebody could have got it wrong.'

Thomson was far from being mollified. 'Now that you're satisfied that you've buggered things up, we'd like to get on with what we've been stopped from doing.'

'After I've spoken to Mrs Lattimer, you probably shall.' Rogers smiled cheerfully.

'You can't. She doesn't want to be seen until she's over the shock your chap gave her with his damnfool questions.' He scowled at Lewis. 'And it won't be today because we're off to the Isle of Man.'

Rogers considered that poor Lewis was taking a lot of unearned stick. '*I'm* in charge of the investigation into the death of her husband, not DC Lewis,' he said sharply, his hackles up, 'and I don't intend to be obstructed from seeing her when I wish to.' A shortage of sleep, a solitary cup of coffee for his breakfast and uncomfortable heat bouncing up from the decking weren't any-thing to sweeten his temper.

Thomson scowled again and thought about it. 'All right,' he agreed grudgingly, 'but not for long and I insist on being present.'

'And I insist that you won't be,' Rogers said, at his most authoritative and thinking, God preserve me from hairy macho characters of any age. 'Listen to me. Mrs Lattimer's husband was killed by a bomb planted in his car. It was planted . . .'

'I heard about that,' Thomson interrupted him. 'Not that it was her husband though.' He looked hard at Lewis. 'You said it was an accident,' he accused him.

'Who said what is of no consequence now,' Rogers intervened. 'I was about to say that the bomb was planted when the car was in his garage. You were there a few days previously, took his wife away from him and would obviously know about the garage.' He stared at the man from beneath lowered eyebrows. 'There could be implications there that need clearing up. Such as your being so closely associated with the scene of the crime and the possibility that you abducted a married woman against her will with intent to have sexual intercourse.'

Thomson goggled at him, looking shaken for reasons the detective couldn't guess, but wasn't particularly interested in, for he believed nothing of what he had said. 'Against her will?' he echoed. 'For Christ's sake, why don't you ask her!'

'It's what I intend doing once you're off my back. And while I am I know you'll want to let DC Lewis check your car and its documentation against our records. Just to make sure. And while you're at it, to tell him the circumstances of your taking Mrs Lattimer out of the care of her husband.' He jerked his head dismissively at Lewis who, he was hopeful, knowing his senior had been talking near-gibberish, would understand and keep Thomson away long enough.

The balding man, surprisingly malleable and his outrage fled, followed the baffled-looking Lewis off the boat. Rogers waited a few seconds to ensure that they were heading for the quay, then descended the companionway steps, rapped on the partly-opened door and walked in.

The saloon, roughly the size of a small bedroom, had chintzy settees fixed against two sides of its wood-veneered walls. A semi-circular bar, only big enough to accommodate a pair of not-too-thirsty sailors, was squashed in between one of the settees and a bulkhead. The long blue-tinted windows diffused the incoming brassy sunlight to a cool translucency in air that felt humid and heavy with scent.

Audrey Lattimer lay lengthwise on one of the settees, her

shoulders propped against the upright cushioned end, showing no signs of having lost a husband or of wanting sympathy because she had. An open box of chocolates, a flat red packet of cigarettes and a gold lighter rested at her side. 'I told Humphrey I couldn't see anyone,' she snapped at him as he entered. 'And what was all that nonsense about me being abducted, and about a bomb?'

'I'm sorry to bother you, Mrs Lattimer,' he said gravely, 'but it's necessary. I'm Detective Superintendent Rogers from Abbotsburn and I'm investigating the sad death of your husband. May I sit down?' The designers of the boat hadn't reckoned on accommodating seventy-four inches of visiting policeman and, in standing, his neck was being forced to a creaking angle by the low ceiling.

When she made no answer, he sat on the settee opposite to her, then studied her calmly and openly. The photograph of her that he had seen could have been of another woman. She had changed the style and colour of her hair to a lion's mane effect and it narrowed her face to a pallid triangle. Her eyelids were turquoise over the palest of grey eyes, her nose thin and her greedy-looking mouth lipsticked a shiny orange. Smaller than he had imagined, she was neatly bodied with slender arms and legs. Bare-footed, she wore a flounced black-and-white striped dress that would not have looked out of place at a Royal Ascot race meeting, tight enough to show beneath it the tiny prominences of her pointed breasts. Several of her beautifully manicured fingers held rings, two at least set with emeralds, and she smelled as if she had recently bathed in an expensive and therefore dizzying scent.

Giving himself what he thought to be a dispassionate assessment of her, he judged that were she not a monstrously oversexed woman, then she used cold-bloodedly what she possessed in the way of female equipment to feast on the bank accounts of men owning to unsatisfied urges. Being neither well-favoured in face nor visually seductive in body, she yet emanated a powerful carnality. She would possibly attract the type of man who, closing his eyes against graceless make-up on discontented features, could imagine himself ravishing the innocence of a sixth-form schoolgirl.

'Well,' she said, in no way discomfited by his silent scrutiny of her, 'I hope you're satisfied with what you've seen. Is that what you came for?'

'I'm sorry,' he apologized again. 'I thought you were about to say something to me.'

'I asked you what was this nonsense about me being abducted?'

'And the bomb,' he reminded her, feeling that he had lost the initiative. 'I do have to explain that your husband was killed in his car yesterday morning by an explosion. We've been searching for you since then to tell you the sad news.'

'You mean somebody blew him up?' Her frown and the incomprehension in her face might have been genuine, but of grief there was nothing. 'I don't believe it.'

'It's so, nevertheless.' Rogers suspected that if he had told her that a tree had fallen down in her garden, he might have received a more emotional response. And that, possibly, because Lewis had already blunted whatever capability she had in her for showing it. He suggested, in less of an undertaker's tone of voice, 'I think it's possible that you could have some knowledge of who may have done it.'

'I most certainly do not. And if I did, why should I do your work for you?' She took a cigarette from its packet and, scowling, snapped her lighter at it. Having blown smoke through her pursed lips, she suddenly burst out, 'You've got a damned nerve, haven't you? Saying I've been abducted when you should know very well I left him days and days ago. And what's that got to do with you?'

'I do get things wrong occasionally, and I'm not here to accuse you or your friend of anything,' he said amiably. 'Tell me about your leaving your husband if it doesn't embarrass you.' Being so close to her, he chose fancifully to believe that he would be safer with vampire-repellent garlic hung around his neck.

'Why should it embarrass me?' She was smoking her cigarette with nervous jerkings of her hand. 'I had good reasons for leaving him. He was a boring miserable creep, and not less so because he's dead. I was expected to sit at home and listen to him rabbit on and on about his dreary job because that's all he could talk about. That and buttering up those bitchy sisters of his he was always seeing. Spending more time with them than with me, and I wonder why?' If she was posing a question, Rogers wasn't choosing to say anything. Looking at him contemptuously and shrugging her narrow shoulders, she said, 'Up to you, clever dick, but it was after years of that when I told him I was leaving, that I wanted a separation, and I did. *Not* abducted, but doing what I should have done ages ago. Does that satisfy you?'

Lamentations for a dead husband, he thought. She was incredible and he was already beginning to sympathize with Thomson for what he had landed himself with. 'Of course,' he agreed mildly. 'I'm only puzzled now why you didn't leave him for your other friend, Jervaise.'

She slit her eyes at him, her cigarette held motionless in mid-air. 'You are a sneaky bastard, aren't you,' she said, though not too forcefully. 'Have you been giving him the third degree, too?'

'He was most informative,' Rogers assured her. 'Have you seen or heard from him since you left home?'

'No,' she said abruptly. 'He began to think he owned me. But you don't want to know that, do you? You want to know about me leaving my poor pathetic husband who couldn't even be that with me.' Anger showed in her mouth and she tapped a finger viciously on her cigarette, its ash dropping unregarded onto the settee. 'If you must know, he wasn't in any position to give a curse what I did or didn't do.'

'Why? In what position?'

'Mind your own bloody business,' she retorted sharply. 'It's nothing to do with you.'

'If you say so,' he said equably. 'He knew about you and Jervaise?'

'Of course he did. That's what I'm telling you. I used to ring Hodge – that's him – from the house often enough. Oh, he knew all right. *And* that he was to blame for it. He didn't own me either. Not just because I was fool enough to marry him.' Astonishingly, she gave him a thin half-smile. 'Would you believe me if I told you that he wanted to know in detail what went on between me and the high-and-mighty Hodge Jervaise?'

'You'd surprise me, Mrs Lattimer, but it isn't anything I need to know about,' he said, although that didn't mean he believed it.

'No, you wouldn't, of course,' she said mockingly. She drew up her knees slowly, her dress sliding down to expose her thighs. With her widened grey eyes holding his, she held out her

112

unfinished cigarette. 'Will you put that out for me,' she asked him, the tone of her voice suddenly intimate.

He took it from her, unable to avoid a quick pressure from her fingers, and stood, rubbing it to extinction in a glass ashtray on the bar counter. The woman, so bloody-minded at dodging the issue, puzzled him. Even in his long experience of some of the worst of them, he would classify her as being rock bottom in female stony-hearted insensitivity. And irritating him in that, using her lean and dissolute body to distract him, she should believe it could.

As he re-seated himself, she said, 'I've been thinking. What about Hodge Jervaise? I wouldn't put it past him. He could be an awful pig when he wanted to be.'

Rogers raised his eyebrows and said, deliberately off-putting, 'You mean killing your husband? Under what he told me of the circumstances of your leaving him, what possible reason could he have?'

She had read what his words had meant. 'How in the hell would I know?' she snapped, her attempt at a sort of intimacy short-lived. 'I thought you were the detective. You asked me, and I told you.'

'I'll bear it in mind,' he said, even more convinced that this had to be a rejected woman's vindictiveness. 'But say, just say, that you had a suspicion, even a small suspicion, that he would do that, would you have felt concerned enough about it to have warned the police it might happen. You know, such as sending them an anonymous warning letter?' He had watched her closely, seeing nothing in her face suggesting awareness.

'For God's sake!' she spat at him. 'Don't ask me such bloody stupid questions. How do I know what I'd do about something I only suggested to be helpful.'

'And I'm so grateful that you are,' he assured her, holding back his intended sarcasm. 'About your husband again. Did you know that he was away from work for at least a week before his death? Coincidentally, with your leaving him, it seems.'

'Was he?' That, manifestly, hadn't interested her.

'He apparently had a problem over a loan,' he continued as if he hadn't heard her. 'Some twenty thousand pounds' worth that his employers seem to be looking for and intending to get back.' He wished that she would cover her naked thighs. Difficult to avoid looking at even from the corners of his eyes, they and her heady scent were unsettling, calculated to stir the purple worm of lust lurking in the basement of every normal man's brain.

About to eat a chocolate she had taken from the box, it was as though she had read his thoughts, that he had also reached across and slapped her. Furious, she straightened her legs and pulled down her dress, jerking into startled uprightness from her resting postion. 'What are you saying!' she demanded harshly. 'They can't! It's mine and going to stay mine!'

'It's been alleged,' he said cautiously, not certain of the truth of anything Mullet had confessed, 'that your husband obtained the loan by forgery and fraud. If that's found to be true, then your right to keep it is certainly going to be questioned.'

There was a fraught quietness in the saloon in which Rogers could hear the boat's hull creaking on the uneasy water, and the distant crying of gulls. Then, explosively, she yelled 'The bastard! The bloody bastard!', her lips drawn back in a face contorted with raw hatred. Then, staring silently into space for long moments, rigid in her anguish and withdrawn from Rogers, she suddenly turned on him and screamed in a passion of furious despair, her opened mouth an orange-rimmed hole of wet pink tongue and glistening teeth. Her scream exhausted against the momentarily astounded detective, she flung herself sideways to curl little girl-like against her cushion and break into a noisy weeping.

Rogers stood, deciding to leave before her tears did things – he couldn't think what – to his opinion of her as a hard-faced female predator, certain that he had trodden heavy-footed on possibly the only deeply-held feeling she possessed. And that, it occurred to him, remembering the paint-splashed dresses, could have been planned deliberately by Lattimer as a cuckolded husband's revenge. Though there were other questions he needed to put to her, he was happy to go, thankful that Thomson had not re-turned. Overwrought women and angry men could make be-tween them an undignified and troublesome misunderstanding.

Once outside in the sunshine, he used his handkerchief to blow from his nose the erotic scent it had been collecting, seeing the two men at the entrance to the catwalk. Neither had apparently heard the scream and, when he reached them, he said to Lewis – who hadn't apparently made too much of a pig's breakfast of his interviewing – 'You're satisfied about the car and Mr Thomson's

114

collecting of Mrs Lattimer?' It was more of a direction to agree than a question, not needing Lewis's nod of agreement.

To Thomson, set-faced and obviously holding back both his opinion and his dislike of interfering policeman, he said affably, 'I shall probably need to see Mrs Lattimer again at a later date, and you'd better go to her. I think she's rather upset about her financial situation now that she finds herself a widow.' Then, as Thomson brushed past him and strode towards his boat, he managed to call without irony, 'And thank you for your helpful co-operation.' If he wanted to complain about Rogers and Lewis in the future, that would count against whatever malice he used in doing it.

Rogers would, in fact, have liked to have taken him aside for unofficial and friendly words, but knew that a menopausal male set on what he had determined to be his primrose path to a sexual Shangri-La, could rarely be dissuaded from following it by a warning of poison ivy ahead.

20

Determined to eat before leaving Thurnholme, Rogers parked his car near the harbour and, walking the now busy main street, searched unsuccessfully for a restaurant serving breakfasts. Driven by his hollow belly into reluctantly considering the plastic garishness of *Bob's Bacon Sandwich Bar*, he was about to enter it when he saw a patrolling beat constable staring at him in surprise and holding up his arm. Headquarters had, the PC said when joining him, put out a force circulation requiring that if located he was to contact Chief Inspector Stout by telephone as a matter of urgency.

Conscious that in his eagerness to get to Thurnholme he had failed to report his destination before leaving, and wondering if enforced fasting made a man more spiritual, he walked hurriedly to make his call from the Section Station conveniently overlooking the harbour. Stout, a man approaching retirement and not likely to worry overmuch about a senior officer's irritability, answered his call. 'We've been trying to find you since quarter past eight,' he said, his voice implying that Rogers had caused a major upheaval as a result. 'When we couldn't, Mr Lingard was called out and he's been dealing with a dead man he's not satisfied with at all.'

'That's what he's there for,' Rogers said tersely. 'Do we know who he is? And where is he anyway?'

'Mr Lingard says he's the man Jervaise you're already dealing with and he was found dead at the entrance to his estate. And he thinks there's a strong probability he was murdered.'

He swore vividly in his mind. It couldn't be true. Either he was still bloody well dreaming it, or God, for something he must have done, had it in for him. Aloud, the only skin-deep unflappable Rogers said impatiently, 'So? What killed him?'

'He didn't know for sure other than it was a bit peculiar, but he did say he'd anticipated you'd want Dr Twite to examine him at the scene and he's called him out.'

'Tell him I'm on the way,' Rogers said, unaware that he had replaced the receiver and cut short his own words.

Recovering his car from the park and leaving the town by a different route from that by which he had entered, impeded at its junctions by incoming tourist traffic and in having to fill and light his pipe one-handed, he was miles inland before he could curse with an uncluttered mind that his second-in-command had, by his default, been called out when due for court attendance. On top of which, Jervaise's death, too related in time and involvement with the dead Lattimer, threatened the fragile theory to which, since interrogating Mullet, he had provisionally pinned his investigation.

He was damp with unearned sweat when he pulled into the short approach to the massive archway leading to Brigthorpe Hall, crowded already with the department's Major Incident coach, the melancholy Body Van and its attendant coroner's officer, a police patrol car, Lingard's Bentley and Twite's white shark-nosed Citroën. Once out of his car, the first principle he routinely observed, he took in the scene.

Fronting the arch's two huge piers holding the gatekeeper's double lodge were grassed areas merging into shrubbery. The left-hand area was shut off from the view of the passing inquisitive by hopsack fabric screens, its entrance guarded by a uniformed PC. Parked on the other side of the arch and facing the outside road was Jervaise's Ranger Rover, heat waves already shimmering from its roof. The driver's door was fully open and, through the windscreen, he could see Sergeant Magnus doing things to the steering wheel with his fingerprint brushes. Behind the Rover, Jervaise's black-faced sheep made a silent and interested audience in what was going on.

The elegant Lingard, wearing his lightweight dog's-tooth tweed suit, came out from behind the screens at Rogers's approach, flapping snuff grains from his nostrils with a gold silk handkerchief. 'Beaten you to it again, George,' he said flippantly, not at his most diplomatic.

'Aren't you supposed to be at court?' Rogers asked, noting his suit to be wholly inappropriate for it. For himself, he had been conscious in his car that his clothing had smelled powerfully of Mrs Lattimer's scent – a brothel-keeper's cat's smell, he would call it on anybody else – hoping that Lingard would not detect it through his snuffed-up nose, for its presence would admit of no explanation that wouldn't have put him in too close proximity to a woman.

'The defence asked for a last-minute adjournment before the judge rose, and they got around to dewarning me late last night.' He smirked provokingly. 'Just as well, it seems, with you getting yourself lost overnight.'

'Temporarily mislaid this morning, David,' he corrected him, 'and sorry you got yourself lumped with it.' Now at the scene and about to catch up, his calmness of mind had returned. 'Before I go in, give me the details.'

'Right,' Lingard said. 'In the beginning *was* the beginning. Jervaise discovered kaput by a postman at seven-thirty approximately, having spotted his boots sticking out from the shrubbery. His butler character, one Basil Wort, immediately informed by postman and apparently came here in the postman's van, identifying his boss and then returning to the house to dial 999 for help. Since seen by Sergeant Llewellyn and says that Jervaise left the house in his Rover at ten-ish last night for unspecified parts. That, very roughly, approaches the time Wilfred is hazarding a guess he was clobbered. The postman – quite agitated, I'm told – left before we arrived, the delivery of Her Majesty's mails being apparently of more importance to him than the odd dead body floating about on his round. And I must say that he has a point

117

there. Two women from the village arrived on bikes about an hour ago, they said to do the housework. Names and addresses taken and told to have a day off. Magnus has done his photography stint and I've put five bods out to cover the village and odd houses in case anybody passed by here last night and saw something. I've another looking for the postman, and one keeping sentry-go outside the Hall in case the butler did it . . .' – he grinned to show that he was joking – '. . . and then there are six idling their time away in the coach waiting to scratch through the undergrowth when you and Wilfred have finished with the body.'

'And the Rover?' Rogers was walking towards the screens, Lingard keeping up with him.

'Ah, yes. Key in ignition and the door believed to be open as you see it now. Until we catch up with the postman, that's not a certainty. The sidelights were on and I've had them switched off. The engine's cold, of course, and there's nothing inside to indicate where he was going or why. Nothing but the usual stuff in his pockets, but there is the mystery of the right-hand glove that doesn't appear to be his. As for the body itself?' Lingard pulled a face. 'I think it's even got Wilfred wondering what the hell.'

The amiably fat pathologist, sweating copiously in his fawn safari suit, open-neck shirt and gaudy silk cravat, was squatting on his hams at the side of Jervaise's body, still obviously puzzling out the how of it. An unashamed gourmand, his tightly-waved black hair, long side whiskers and the incongruity of a Mexican-style moustache gave him the appearance of an over-nourished Latin just happened to be wearing clear plastic gloves. He said, 'I see they've managed to find you, old George,' to Rogers, but otherwise maintaining his brooding.

Standing on the comfortably spongy turf, Rogers filled and lit his pipe without knowing he was doing it while his brain recorded what his eyes could fathom from dead flesh. Jervaise lay on his back in a smother of broken bush foliage, appearing larger in his bigness than when he had been standing on his own two feet. Wearing the tweed jacket and twill trousers in which Rogers had seen him the previous evening, his arms were crooked rigid across the chest as if frozen in a dying effort to reach his throat. His face gave the picture of his death. The eyes were bulging, dulled and devoid of expression, his ears tinged a deep mauve.

118

The mouth and nostrils were surrounded by what appeared to be a ragged mass of greyish-white shaving lather which, on a closer inspection, was seen to be a silky fine-grained powder. A hole sunk in it showed the dried tip of the tongue and the front teeth, a packed bolus of the stuff filling the open mouth behind them. A smaller hole exposed the two cavities of the nostrils, similarly plugged. The once powerful hands were clawed into hooked fingers, their ends powdered white. Close to his side, palm upwards and partly folded, rested a woollen and leather driving glove.

Rogers took the pipe from his mouth. 'You made the holes, Wilfred?'

'I improved them,' Twite replied, standing with a grunting sound of extreme effort, pulling off the plastic gloves and dropping them on the body. 'It needed doing to confirm that he died from obstructive asphyxia – which is what he did.'

'And the stuff that did it?'

'That's what I don't know.' With an unprofessional disregard of the General Medical Council's proscription against it, Twite lit one of the scented cigarettes he favoured in between over-eating. 'It's a powder, obviously, that seems to have partially solidified inside his mouth. Whatever it is, he managed to swallow it and it's probably filled up his pharynx and blocked the nose enough for a complete occlusion of the air passages.' He wagged his head glumly. 'The poor bugger would've had a nasty going; he's showing all the signs of acute respiratory distress. Not just difficulty in breathing, but an impossibility to do so.'

'He kicked his heels somewhat while he was trying to,' Lingard said to Rogers. 'Can you see the marks?'

Rogers crouched at Jervaise's feet. Close to them were ragged tears in the turf showing disturbed earth beneath them. On the backs of the well-polished shoes were smears of soil and fragments of grass. He straightened his legs and stood as Twite remarked, 'Caused in paroxysmal spasms. I said that he'd had a hard going. It does rather tend to happen when you're struggling to breathe,' he added drily as if they should know, but didn't.

'And he'd die in minutes?' Rogers asked. 'Or is that too impossible a question?' He and Twite were friends of many years and not averse to implying ineptitude in each other without offence.

'It is rather, but I think two, three or even four minutes at the most. Not any longer with a complete obstruction, although the heart could go on pumping for quite a bit longer.'

'And that powder would have to be forced in – obviously. Any ideas about that?'

Flapping his hand and carelessly dropping ash down the front of his shirt, Twite said, 'An aerosol? It'd need a fair bit of pressure behind it, but who in the devil puts powder in aerosols?'

'The same people who put hair lacquer, pesticides and air fresheners in them, I imagine,' Rogers suggested. 'Why not talc under pressure for armpits and suchlike? And isn't there a starch-based spray around for doing shirt collars? Might that not dry to a powder?' When neither Twite nor Lingard said anything, he answered his own question. 'It must do, I suppose, although there seems to be too much there to be that. Anyway, it shouldn't be too difficult for us to find out if you can tell me what powder it is.'

Twite snorted. 'That's a laboratory job I haven't the staff to cope with. And it would take a day or more even if they hadn't anything else to do.'

'You're a miserable sod, Wilfred,' Rogers said cheerfully. 'So when you do your examination pack some in a jar for me to send off. When are you proposing to do it, incidentally?'

Twite flipped his cigarette end over the screens and looked frowning at his wristwatch. 'Ten o'clock? It needs to be that early, or not until very late tonight. I've pressing matters on my plate that can't be put off.'

'I'm sure they can't and it suits me fine.' Rogers was straight-faced, knowing that the most pressing matters in Twite's life were lengthy lunches at the town's four-star French restaurant and a late fellow medico's rather fetching widow with long legs and a reputation for *cordon bleu* cooking. 'I've pressing matters too, so David will stand in for me when you do. Before that, what sort of a gap does your estimate of time of death cover?'

'Two hours, possibly three.' Twite pushed out his bottom lip, indicating some doubt. 'The warm weather doesn't help, but say provisionally between nine last night and eleven o'clock.' He bent his legs to pick up his black bag of instruments and, Rogers suspected, the smoked salmon sandwiches wrapped in foil he was prone to carry as stand-by rations. 'I can't do any more here, so if your transport does manage to find where the mortuary is I'll see our dead friend later.'

With Twite gone, sounding true to form in reversing his Citroën at speed on to the the main road and probably without looking, Rogers picked up the glove from near Jervaise's side and examined it. 'I won't try it on,' he said, 'but it's a gent's large and well-worn. You've looked under the body for the other?'

'First thing,' Lingard assured him as if pained that it should be doubted. 'And in the Rover. It could be his if he drives one-handed, but I'd be a fool to believe it.'

'He certainly wasn't wearing gloves when I saw him last evening. So, if not, it was dropped by the character who didn't like Jervaise all that much. Careless of him, wasn't it? Particularly in wearing it in the summer when few do. And when they do, wearing them thin with air-holes punched all over.' He shook his head. 'I'm not happy, David, so have it examined at the laboratory for the usual dusts and debris to see if it tells us anything.'

Taking the glove from him, Lingard said tactfully, 'I expect you've already noticed the other marks, George?'

Pegged with small white plant labels, it would have been difficult not to. About six feet from the soles of Jervaise's shoes and between them and the wall of the arch pier, the grass had been crushed in two barely discernible parallel lines, each bifurcating in a curve where they joined the asphalt surface of the entrance approach. Obviously wheel tracks, they each had in them two spaced-out oval indentations. Midway between the tracks the grass was stained with a small glistening black patch of oil.

'A car,' Rogers said. 'A smallish one. Possibly an elderly one, driven onto the grass, or reversed on it. Then staying in place long enough to leak engine oil and for the tyres to sink in a little and make the marks.'

'On the button,' Lingard told him. 'Magnus has measured the wheelbase as six feet eight inches, give or take an inch either side. And it's been reversed in, I'm sure, because Jervaise has to be lying on what would be the driver's side of the car for me to make my point. It suggests that when he was driving out to wherever he was going, he spotted the car hidden away and on his property. He'd get out because he'd certainly be suspicious about trespass or sheep-stealing or anything else he'd be concerned with, go to the car, poke his face down to the driver's window and bellow something like "What the hell are you doing here!" Then sssssshhhhhaa! through the window from whoever it was wanted him dead and he'd stagger back to fall in the bushes with his mouth full of talcum powder or what have you, choking to death while chummy in the car drives away and leaves him to it.' Lingard fed snuff into his nose, his vivid blue eyes watching for Rogers's reaction.

Rogers had been looking down at the man he had so disliked in life and, although admitting it wouldn't do much good, finding it easy to feel sorry for him; accepting that so many provocations and resentments were trivialized at the sight of their instigator as a corpse. 'You could be right, David,' he said. 'I've only one thing against it. The Rover's been left the other side of the arch and we can't see it from here. That being so, he wouldn't have seen a car parked here until he was well through the arch and passing it. And possibly not even then.'

'But if he had, he could have stopped and then reversed back through the arch. It's only a few yards and he might have intended using his headlights to see who it was.'

Rogers shook his head. 'That doesn't sound right to me. One, it was bright moonlight last night. Two, they'd have been found switched on this morning. And Jervaise, being the extremely aggressive man I know he was, would have reversed back in front of the car to stop it from being driven out.'

'So he might,' the not-to-be-beaten Lingard persisted. 'Then, once he'd been killed, whoever it was moved the Rover back so that he could get his own car out.'

'Magnus will find his fingerprints in it if he did, but I think it's far more likely he'd arranged to meet somebody here. Don't ask me why he should, but that's how I read it at the moment. And it does point to a somebody who had the spray all ready for him, knowing he would be coming out. Which would mean pre-meditation and murderous malice aforethought.' He lifted his leg, standing like a stork as he knocked ash from his pipe against the heel of his shoe. Beginning to refill it, he said smiling, 'You can get him moved now and I'll see you back at the office and update you on Mullet's arrest and my risking the scented menace of Mrs Lattimer while you slept through it all. And while you're in the mortuary, you might give her a bit of serious thought.

Though I don't begin to believe that she could be directly responsible, she does seem to have a fairly lethal habit of leaving dead in her wake a couple of husbands and a lover.'

He took a last look at a man who, now to be subjected to Twite's scalpel and dissecting knives, would soon resemble something similar to a carved-up side of beef on a butcher's block. Uncomfortably, he saw in Jervaise a confirmation of his belief that the human reproductive apparatus, used indiscriminately for free-wheeling fornication, had in it the too frequent threat of a retributive violence. Moving out of the screens to his car, intending to have words with the dead man's butler, he half-heartedly promised himself that he would try and remember it.

21

Driving on the estate road between undulating parkland at a crawling thirty miles an hour took Rogers just over two minutes to reach the trees surrounding the hall, a time and distance assessment that suggested it would prove to be of no great significance. Before entering them, he stopped the car and looked in the rear-view mirror to confirm that from there the arch was out of sight in a fold in the ground.

Drawing his car up alongside the foot of the parapeted steps of the Hall, its stone façade an unusual warmish-grey in the strong sunlight, the curtains drawn closed behind the ground-floor windows, he got out and looked about him for the man Lingard had detailed to keep watch on it. He had heard the car's approach and came around the corner of the building, recognizable behind impenetrable dark glasses, of which Rogers disapproved on his staff, as DC Clayburn.

'All correct, sir,' Clayburn reported to him, having snatched off his glasses before doing so. 'The butler's looked out the door on two occasions, that's all. I think he's been drinking. The first time he asked me where his cleaning women were and I couldn't tell him. The second time he was waving a bottle about and wanted me to go in and drink with him. He called me an officious little prick when I said no thanks, I was on duty. Then he told me I'd better let in the cook when she came because he still had to eat.'

'Not very butler-like and I'm sure he'll survive without her,' Rogers told him. 'You stay on here until I say otherwise. I may want the place looked over later on. And in future don't go around looking like a bloody mafioso doing it,' he added with reasonable geniality, although Clayburn didn't look as if he thought so.

Climbing the steps, considering ringing the bell and deciding against it, he opened the door and walked in. The butler wasn't going to be difficult to find for he could hear a male voice, talking non-stop in a monologue, coming from the direction of the room in which he had interviewed Jervaise. Passing by the suit of black armour, which now had a tweed deerstalker hat fitted jauntily on its helmet, he entered the room and, finding it empty of the talker, walked its length and through the open door at its far end.

Darkened to gloom with its windows curtained against daylight, it was a smaller room, its walls hidden behind shelved books. Otherwise it was almost empty, containing a huge dark-oak table with a Spanish-style studded leather chair behind it and two similar chairs handy to the book shelves. A green-shaded reading lamp illuminated the surface of the table and the figure of the portly and fallen silent Basil Wort seated behind it with his back to the window curtains. His grey hair was tousled, his tie hanging out from behind his jacket and, with a green luminosity reflected on his face from the lamp, looking even more lugubrious than when Rogers had seen him before. A dusty black port bottle stood in front of him and he held a filled crystal goblet in unsteady plump fingers. A very long cigar smouldered on the edge of the table. It needed no blowing through the crystals of a breathalyser for the detective to know that he had had more than a few.

Focusing his eyes on Rogers, he said thickly, 'You're the m-man I saw yesterday. I didn't hear y'ring.'

'I'm Detective Superintendent Rogers, Mr Wort, needing a few words with you.' He dragged one of the spare chairs to the side of the table and sat, well within the sweet smell of wine surrounding the butler. 'There are one or two points I'd like clarified about Mr Jervaise's movements last night.' Having drawn the curtains, presumably as a mark of respect for death having visited the house, then getting himself drunk, Wort would seem to be taking

124

his employer's dying badly, and Rogers kept his expression suitably grave.

Wort drank from the goblet, made a visible effort to pull himself together and said, 'W-What's that chap doing hanging around outside? What's he want?'

'Wanting only to speak to me,' Rogers told him. He started again. 'You're the butler here and . . .'

'No!' Wort interrupted him, jerking his hand and slopping port from the goblet onto the table. 'P-Please get it c'rectly. I'm a g-gentleman's gentleman.' He spoke with difficulty but without antipathy. 'No, I mean I *was* a gentleman's gentleman who's n-now about to fall on hard t-times. For a m-man just made redundant, I'm in a right b-bloody mood.' He picked up the cigar with an elaborate flourish, looked at it in doubt and replaced it, its ash dropping unheeded onto the carpet. He beamed foolishly. 'I took a drop of the vintage to g-get over the shock you understand. As a . . . as a sedative.' There was a sudden flash of anger. 'Stupid b-bugger! . . . getting himself killed . . .' Tears brimmed in his eyes and he took out a large white handkerchief, dabbing it at them. 'Sorry about that,' he muttered. ''S the drink.' He folded the handkerchief neatly, tucking it carefully into his pocket, then placing his hands flat on the table and pushing himself upstanding. 'P-Pardon my behaviour,' he said with great dignity. 'I need to do something about it if . . . if you'll excuse me for a few minutes.'

Rogers said, 'Certainly,' moving his legs aside to allow him, taking carefully measured steps, to pass him on his way to the door.

With the rich aroma of the burning cigar – he judged it to be one of the £5-plus Havanas – prompting him to fill and light his pipe, he was left to take in the room while waiting for Wort to recover the aloof aplomb he felt sure a self-styled gentleman's gentleman needed for the job. The uncountable and mostly unreachable books, the majority leather-bound and ancient, were tiered up to the dull yellow stucco ceiling moulded in arabesques heavy on a boar's head motif with Tudor roses. The patterned carpet was threadbare in places and looked old enough, had she ever visited Brigthorpe, to have been trodden on by the shoes of the virgin Queen Elizabeth. The table held only the reading lamp, a saucer-sized magnifying lens, the port bottle – Rogers held it against the lamp, seeing it to be nearly empty – and the goblet. It seemed to be an odd room in which to drown a grief or to rage against the loss of a job. His mind had changed tack to a hungering after coffee and a breakfast with, alternately, some pleasant thinking about the fascinating Eleanor Caine, when the door opened and Wort came in. Rogers estimated that he had been away for some ten, possibly fraught, minutes.

While miles away from moving briskly, his gait was steady for a man who had probably been vomiting up vintage port. His hair, darkly wet at its edges, had been combed, his face reset from drunken looseness to a sober gravity by the cold water into which he had undoubtedly plunged it, and his tie had been returned to inside his jacket. He went directly to the windows and pulled on cords, drawing back the curtains and admitting a flood of sunshine.

Not returning to his seat at the table, he sat himself near Rogers in the second chair, then rested his plump hands on his thighs and said, 'Forgive my unseemly lapse in good manners, Mr Rogers. You wished to know about Mr Jervaise's last movements?' He was painfully careful with his speaking.

'They might help.' Rogers thought him an agreeable sort of man, worthy of friendly respect. 'I'd be grateful if, under the circumstances of his death, you'd be frank and open in answering my questions. Tell me about his movements from yesterday afternoon when I left him.'

'I understand and, of course, I shall be,' Wort said, his face bilious in the sun's light, his shirt collar now showing damp stains on it. 'There's been nothing unusual that I've noticed. After you left, Mr Jervaise returned to his office for a while, going out later to the farm, which was his routine. I served tea at four-thirty when he came back, after which he worked in his office again. He was visited by Mr Abernethy, the farm manager, who had been out somewhere, and that was routine too. Later in the evening he told me that he would be going out and that cook should prepare and put by a light supper for him when he returned. That wasn't unusual either, for he normally had a cooked lunch, disliking a heavy meal late in the evening.' He stopped to clear his throat. Despite an occasional hesitation, he was controlling his voice well, and Rogers had noticed how deliberately he had avoided even glancing in the direction of the goblet still half-filled with port. 'He left the house at about a quarter past seven,' he continued, 'and remained out until nine, which was a little unusual as he nearly always returned between half-past ten and eleven. He didn't ask for his supper and later – it would be shortly after ten – said he was going out for a few minutes and that I could retire to my rooms. Which I did and never saw him again until this morning.'

'Very succinct,' Rogers said amiably, 'but not, I'm afraid, very informative when I suspect he was going out to meet the person who was to kill him. Did you notice whether he was wearing his driving gloves?'

Wort looked at him blankly. 'Driving gloves?' he echoed. 'He never wears them. I don't . . . Ah! I see what you mean. That glove near his body. I did notice it and it wouldn't be his. Not that sort, and I'd have recognized it immediately.'

'I'm sure you're right,' Rogers encouraged him. 'When he went out, did he happen to say where he was going? Or why?'

'He hadn't any need to. It would be to meet a lady and bring her back here. It was understood that when I was dismissed to my rooms it was because he wished complete privacy in this wing for . . .' – he gave Rogers a half-smile – '. . . for the purpose of what I might call cross-pollination. That meant making myself scarce and staying like it until rung for, to know nothing of what was going on. I have my rooms in the east wing,' he explained, 'and I think he may have been ashamed about entertaining some of them.'

'Often enough for the understanding to be necessary?'

'I've been with him seven months and the occasion has arisen three or four times a month. He was, I believe, attractive to the ladies, and he had money and position.'

'I know where he was going when he left here after seven,' Rogers said. 'Do you?'

Wort was unsurprised. 'He's well-known there. I take it he was seen in the bar of the Minster Hotel? That's why it was unusual for him to be back so early. He sometimes ate there, too.'

Rogers was digging unknown ground here, requiring him to think it out. 'It's no great secret that I spoke to him at the hotel,' he said. 'He told me that he had an engagement there. Had it been with a woman, wouldn't he have brought her back with him?'

'When he did, he would phone me beforehand so that I would be in my rooms before he arrived here.'

'Would you know, or could you guess, that he made a habit of meeting women or anybody else where he was found this morning?'

'No, I can't see that he'd have any need to.'

'You've never at any time seen a woman he's brought here? Or who's visited him?' It was dificult for Rogers to believe that he hadn't.

'My rooms are at the rear of the house and his orders in that respect were very strict. He would have dismissed me quite summarily – he said so – had I disobeyed them. So I saw nobody, heard nobody and was told nothing.' Wort sounded defeated. 'And a lot of good it did me. I'm not getting any younger, Mr Rogers.'

Nor, Rogers thought, were he himself and several billion others, but nobody had been able to do anything useful about it. 'You wouldn't have seen or heard of a Mrs Lattimer then?' he persisted. 'She visited here several times, usually in a taxi.'

Shaking his head a little impatiently, he said, 'I took one or two phone calls from her, but not recently. And I never saw her if she did come here.' He frowned. 'There was a phone call yesterd . . . no, the day before. In the morning. It mightn't be connected, but he said his name was Lattimer and he wanted to speak to Mr Gervaise. He said it was important, so I called him and he spoke to him. Afterwards he told me that if the man called again he was to be informed that Mr Jervaise was out. I rather believe he was annoyed at him phoning.'

'And did he? Call again, I mean.'

'Not so far as I know.' This time, Wort did look at his abandoned port and bite at his bottom lip. But it was a momentary lapse and he returned his gaze to the detective.

'Have there been any other calls you think might be relevant?'

'A Mrs Conway? She phoned yesterday afternoon from a public call box asking for him, and he spoke to her.'

'She'd telephoned before?' The name rang a bell, though not loud enough for Rogers to place it.

'Mr Jervaise said "Who?" when I told him her name, so I'm sure she hadn't. Or that he knew her because when I answered her call she asked me if it was Mr Jervaise speaking.'

'Could you tell from her voice what sort of a woman she was? Young or old?'

'She sounded youngish, but I can't be sure. A nice voice, though. Well-spoken, but a trifle on the . . .' – he searched for the words he wanted – '. . . on the bossy side?'

'Were there any others?'

'Yes, but from people we both knew. Men, and mostly concerning his farming.'

Other than the snippet about the woman caller, Rogers didn't think he was getting very far; that Wort was grossly lacking in the kind of nosiness he needed in a source of information. 'Would the rest of the staff know anything about Mr Jervaise's women friends?' he asked.

'If they do it would be village gossip. There are only two part-time cleaners and bedmakers, and a cook who normally finishes at six each evening. They all live in the village and couldn't possibly know what goes on here after they'd finished.'

Rogers considered Wort to be something of an innocent were he not to know that a bed could only too clearly reveal the signs of a night's carnality to any woman making it. He sighed inwardly, his expectations had envisaged a bigger trawl. 'Who is his closest relative, Mr Wort? His wife? We'll have to notify her or somebody of his death.'

'I've been told that they've been separated for many years. She's certainly never been here so far as I'm aware. Nor do I know where she is, or anyone else who may be a relative. I phoned his London solicitor this morning and told him and he said he'd be here as soon as he could tomorrow.'

Rogers stood. 'I'll get Sergeant Llewellyn who saw you this morning to take a statement from you later on,' he said. Then casually, 'Did you like Mr Jervaise?'

Wort stared at him, surprised, and Rogers thought he saw in his eyes that he hadn't. He hesitated, shaking his head. 'He wasn't ever a man to be too friendly with his staff. He kept us at more than arm's length, and certainly wasn't averse to some quiet sort of bullying. Particularly with the farm workers.' He hesitated again, uncertain of whether he should say what he was about to. 'I think you would be interested to know that while he never told me you were a policeman, he did instruct me that should you phone again, or call, I was to say that he was unavailable,

129

that I didn't know where he was or when he would be back.'

'It's a sad thing to be so unloved,' Rogers said sardonically, 'but I expect he feels differently now that he has me looking for whoever killed him.' He made his voice sound helpful, careful not to give offence. 'Because I understand how you feel about all this, I'll give you some friendly advice before I go. I wouldn't, were I you, let Mr Jervaise's solicitor find you digging into his port and best cigars, or anything else not necessary for your subsistence while you're here. He might have a somewhat stuffy opinion about whose property they remain, dead though the owner might now be.'

22

When Rogers switched off his car's engine and climbed out at the arch, it was to a scene of dismantled screens, the disappearance of Jervaise's body, and the sight of six detectives searching on hands and knees the flattened grass and shrubbery where it had lain. Only the Major Incident coach and patrol car remained, attended by a uniformed sergeant and PC ordered to apply constabulary authority on the few square yards of ground made sacrosanct to a justice yet to be enforced until Rogers decided that it had been stripped bare of any information it held.

The ginger-haired Sergeant Magnus, whose eye for the microscopic was such that he could trip unaware over an oversized dustbin, yet fall triumphantly on a fibre not a lot more visible than a detached eyelash, had finished his lot with camera and fingerprint powder and was waiting to be dismissed back to his darkroom. Rogers, affecting not to notice his packed equipment, said, 'I'm glad you haven't finished yet, sergeant. There's a house back up there that needs your attention. While I don't think you'll find them there, prove me wrong by doing a search of the garages, the stables and outhouses for any signs that Jervaise could have been making the pipe-bomb you found in Lattimer's car yesterday. And check on his gun room if he has one to see what shotgun cartridges he's holding. Tie up with the butler, only don't call him that to his face – he prefers to be a gentleman's gentleman – and have him go round with you.' He smiled, guessing that Wort would by now be finishing off the port and the cigar. 'Be gentle with him, sergeant. He's sad and badly hung-over and quite a nice chap when you get to know him.'

Driving back to Abbotsburn and beginning to grill in the contained heat of the car, Rogers was well aware that he had put Magnus onto confirming a negative – a probably negative, he qualified to himself – in case he had been thinking along entirely the wrong track. In truth, he was more concerned at his inability to put a face to the owner of the name Conway; not the 'Mrs Conway' named by Wort, but having a strong feeling that it had been mentioned in a male connotation, or that he had seen it written down as such.

He suspected the reason for its refusing an identification to be his lack of a full night's sleep and its consequent shortfall of replacements for the millions of brain cells he understood were shed like autumn leaves during an active day. Or, a sobering thought – he peered anxiously at what he considered to be a hag-ridden reflection in the rear-view mirror – he was already on the downward slope towards senile amnesia. Doing what he had done before, he stopped fighting it, pushing it into his brain's pending tray to brood in darkness while awaiting a stimulus to revelation. Concentrating now on more pressing matters such as traffic lights, halt signs and other bloody-minded motorists wanting to use the same driving lane entering the town, he headed for what he was determined would be a more than ample working breakfast.

'Here yesterday and gone today, and never mind who has to clear up the bloody chaos behind you,' he muttered ungenerously on leaving his car in the yard of the Minster Hotel, being reminded that Jervaise, his heart still beating and his mind set on his appointment with somebody, had parked his Range Rover there the previous evening. Sweat dampening the back of his shirt, his socks feeling as if knitted from steel wool, were not adding to his bodily comfort.

Urquhart, the manager of the hotel, shared Rogers's voracious notion of what was a decent breakfast, although it was now a late eleven o'clock. Giving him the occupancy of a small ante-room reserved for wedding and funeral gatherings, he had sent into him a huge serving of bacon, kidney, eggs and potato cakes with toast and a tall jug of dark-brown coffee, promising him the attendance of Joseph McGuffey, one of his long-serving barmen.

McGuffey knocked on the door and came in when a distended and more genial Rogers was finishing his third cup of coffee and feeling that life might probably be worth living after all. White jacketed and smelling strongly of shaving lotion, he was an undersized elderly man, cock-sparrow chirpy and wearing incongruously for his age, a black nylon toupee. The detective, who knew him well, believed him to have been born a ready-made bar-tender because he possessed an unflappable cheerfulness, small neat hands that made a single whisky look bigger than it actually was, and never drank any of the stuff himself.

'Sit down, Joseph,' Rogers said. 'I've finished and I've things to ask you. Mr Urquhart's told you why? About Mr Jervaise?'

McGuffey took a chair, looking suitably serious. 'That he did, the poor man,' he answered, crossing himself with a quick pass of his hand. 'God rest his soul and I only saw him last night.'

'Which is why I want words with you. You knew him, naturally?'

'I did indeed. Two or three times in a week and himself as regular as clockwork.'

'Tell me about last night,' Rogers asked him. 'The time he came in, what he did, who he was with – if he was – and when he left.'

McGuffey looked up at the ceiling – probably, Rogers guessed, asking for divine approval – then said formally and with little trace of his Irishness, 'Mr Jervaise came into the bar at half after seven as close by as I can remember. He looked about himself like for a friend there and then went to one of the snugs where the lady was sitting. He stayed with her for the serving of three brandies and two medium-dry white wines, then left the bar about an hour or maybe more after he came in. On the way out he stopped to speak to Mr Norton who was with another man sitting two tables away from the snug. That's as close as I can remember, Mr Rogers.'

Rogers, accepting that McGuffey was patently not as garrulous as his nationality might suggest, prompted him. 'You know the woman he was drinking with, of course?'

He shook his head vigorously. 'That I doubt. I saw her when she came in and I swear she had not been in before.'

'Describe her, Joseph. From her toes to the top of her head.'

He looked at the ceiling again, scratching at his chin. 'You have me there. I saw her but I misremember that. A dress? She had to, I'm telling myself. White?' He was screwing his face into creases in his efforts to remember. 'She was pretty, that's for sure. And young. And sure, wasn't she wearing a ribbon in her hair?'

'She was? What colour was the hair?'

'Dark. Dark as Satan I think she was, the ribbon showing so I'd remember it.'

'I know you'd be a busy man behind the bar, but was there anything special about her you'd remember?' Rogers persisted, deciding not to suggest too much for fear of prompting him into his misremembering.

'Not a thing.' It obviously worried him that he was proving so unhelpful. 'I wouldn't see her being in the snug as she was. Charlie who waited on them would, but he's away until tonight. I never saw the lady again until she went out.'

'I take it that she stayed behind after Mr Jervaise had left?'

McGuffey nodded happily at being able to answer positively. 'That she did, her not leaving for a few minutes after. One or the other do that more often in the snugs.'

'You mean they don't like it to be obvious they've been there together? Philandering husbands and deceiving wives sort of thing?'

'It's a wicked world we live in, Mr Rogers,' McGuffey said piously.

'Disgusting,' Rogers agreed, attempting piety himself. 'You said he spoke to Mr Norton on his way out. Was that Waldo Norton? The falconer chap with the beard?'

'It would be, yes it would.'

'I suppose you'd be too far away, too busy, to hear what was being said?'

'I was for sure, but I don't think it was friendly. Mr Jervaise looked angry and, sure, Mr Norton was still sitting down and looking to be baiting him. It was only a minute or two and Mr Norton was laughing about it afterwards with his friend.'

'And you know him? His friend, I mean.'

'No. Not being a regular I can't put a name to him.'

'Did Mr Norton speak to the woman?'

'Not at all that I saw. He stayed in the bar a long time after she had gone.'

Rogers was thoughtfully pushing tobacco into his pipe. A part of his mind not engaged with the barman had just thrown up inconsequentially a disagreeable picture of Jervaise's powder-covered face and, from that, its possible cause. Thinking of it as an adjunct to a car made it sense. It wasn't anything to yell 'Eureka!' about, but something to suggest that he might have at least a few brain cells left. Pushing it aside for later consideration, he said, 'Did Mr Jervaise meet other women in the hotel?'

'That he did,' McGuffey said promptly and disapprovingly, apparently quite willing to consign the dead man to the burning pit. 'Off and on, you understand. Sometimes I was sure he had picked up some of them in the bar. They come here, you know. Respectable ladies who should be at home with their husbands, not being out for a bit of a fling. But I'm thinking I'm not to be the judge of them.' He was suddenly a man with ethics concerning his imperfect and fallible customers. 'You wouldn't be asking me who they are, would you? I would misremember for sure?'

Rogers knew what he meant and, in a way selfishly, agreed with and respected his discretion. He had, on an occasion or two a few months earlier, been himself in one of the snugs with a woman who could reasonably have been judged married had she not been celebrating with him her decree absolute. Not suspecting that any of Jervaise's other women could be connected with his death, he said standing from his table, 'It doesn't matter all that much, Joseph, so I won't be asking you. I think I'd rather you showed me exactly where these people were doing their drinking.'

The Wellington Bar was already occupied by a few drinkers. They were necessarily quiet because the manager was an unwelcoming host to the gregariously loud-voiced, the excessively unconventionally dressed, or to those who would wince audibly at its up-market charges. It was a spacious room with ceiling beams, two massive smoke-blackened brick fireplaces, tables and chairs a glossy black from a couple of centuries of polishing and standing on dark-crimson carpeting, and glass cases of stuffed pike, perch and trout on tobacco-coloured walls. At each end of the panelled mahogany bar counter was a snug, a windowless alcove screened from the unduly inquisitive by tall-backed black-

134

wood pews. The one pointed out by McGuffey as that occupied by Jervaise and the unknown woman had at its rear a long fish tank. Illuminated by a light in its metal lid it bubbled green with swaying plants and inch-long scarlet and electric-blue exotic fish, provoking an identifying comparison in Rogers's mind.

The table which had been occupied by Waldo Norton and his companion would provide a partial view into the snug. It convinced Rogers that the bearded falconer was a man to be seen not too long after he had satisfied himself about the powder he had seen on the dead Jervaise's features.

Releasing the obliging McGuffey to his bar and settling with the manager for his breakfast – he did have to restrain a wince at what he was charged – he drove from the hotel yard to the Fire Brigade Headquarters. There, he spent a useful fifteen minutes or so being lectured at by Willie Edmunds, its Station Officer who had attended at the scene of Andrew Lattimer's fiery death.

23

Rogers, having taken off his jacket and opened the windows of his office to the sounds of traffic and the stench of its mephitic fumes as not too bearable alternatives to stifling heat, sat at his desk and wrote up his evidential notes – always a delaying chore – while they were still fresh in what he now accepted to be a somewhat unreliable mind.

When finished, he skimped through a few waiting message forms of unimportance, put a ten-inch stack of unread crime files in his pending tray, and then read and initialled a report from Hagbourne detailing the wholly anticlimactic arrest of a frantic Chaffer in his bedroom at home, his being charged as an accessory to Mullet's burglary and his lodgment in a cell. Statements of admission had been made by both men and he, Hagbourne, was then arranging for a conference with a representative from the Inland Revenue's Investigation Department. It left Rogers deciding that, excepting the matter of Lattimer's alleged fraudulent loan, he could happily dismiss any concern with the rough road the two pettifogging rogues would now be travelling.

He was on the telephone to Waldo Norton and achieving an appointment against a forcefully expressed wish to leave for the moor to fly one of his birds, when Lingard walked into the office. Replacing the receiver, Rogers said, 'Sit down, David. If I don't get you up to date now I don't think I ever will.'

It took him nearly ten minutes, a few of which were expended in lighting and relighting a refractory pipe, to programme the weary-looking chief inspector. When he had finished, he said casually, 'You did mention that name Conway, I know. Shame on me, but I've forgotten in what connection.'

Lingard regarded him curiously. 'You must have. I wondered why you left the mysterious Mrs Conway unexplained. *You* mentioned him to *me*, remember?'

'Agh!' Rogers was still in the dark. 'So I did. I've mislaid the reason for it.'

Lingard was amused. 'Mrs Lattimer's first husband. The one who broke his neck watering flowers.'

'That's it!' Rogers had covering-up to do. 'At the time it wasn't important enough for me to file away. Norman Conway, deceased. I thought it might be, but wasn't certain until you confirmed it.'

'A subterfuge for Mrs Lattimer to get to speak to Jervaise?' Lingard suggested, side-stepping any suggestion that his senior had been waffling. 'He probably wouldn't have otherwise.'

'Not if what they both told me was the truth. But he'd know as soon as he spoke to her, wouldn't he?' He answered his own question. 'Which he might have, of course. Wort wouldn't know what was said between them.'

'So she could have been the woman he was drinking with last night?'

'With dark hair? I think not, unless McGuffey's colour blind. I don't suppose it means all that much, but she was an orangy-yellow when I saw her this morning.' Rogers was clearly irritated and he looked at his watch. 'I'd say she'll be about halfway to the Isle of Man by now, if that's where they were actually going. And, anyway, I don't think she's fond enough of me to be in a mood to give an answer one way or the other.' He shrugged. 'Leave her for the time being. I'll brood on what we can do after I've seen Norton. What happened at the mortuary?'

Lingard, with a second-in-command's privilege of sprawling

136

rather than sitting in his chair, tugged down his shirt cuffs. 'Much as Wilfred prognosticated at the scene,' he said. 'Lungs badly congested, confirming air-starvation from major clogging of the breathing passages. Other symptoms too, of course, such as acute failure of the pump and purple lips, but otherwise minor indications. Nail scratches on the face suggesting violent reaction to being unable to suck in air, and skin scrapings under his nails to confirm the scratches were made by him. Wilfred hooked the powder out from his throat and nose and weighed it.' His own patrician nose wrinkled. 'Think of it in passing as a thickish porridge, George. Altogether it weighed a little over five ounces – damp of course – and Wilfred reckons that with what was sprayed around the mouth and into thin air there could have been a lot more of it. He's sticking by his estimated time of choking to between nine and eleven, but insists that because of the high temperatures we're enjoying it could extend to something more on the eleven side.' He pinched snuff from the tiny ivory box he held ready in his hand and inhaled it. 'Clever stuff, and Wilfred's not positive about this, but he believes that the powder was sprayed at poor old Jervaise's face from below.'

'I'm sure he's right,' Rogers said. 'That'd fit in with its being used from the window of a small car.' He reached down to a drawer in his deak, opened it and retrieved a small glaringly-red cylinder, standing it upright on his blotting pad. 'The possible murder weapon,' he said, affecting a casual nonchalance. 'Agreed?'

'A fire extinguisher,' Lingard said, refusing to express surprise. 'It's been found?'

'No,' Rogers admitted. 'This is a new one I've borrowed and I'm doing, I hope, some inspired guessing with it. It's the midget version designed for use on small fires in kitchens and for any petrol or ignition fires you might be unfortunate enough to have in a car. It contains just over a pound of sodium bicarbonate powder which is sprayed out under pressure. I'm told by Willie Edmunds that its reaction to heat is to form an air-excluding crust which douses the flames. More significantly for us, he tells me that it would tend to cake together on contact with moisture. And, I'm sure, there'd be a sufficiency of that in the nose and throat.' He smiled. 'It'd probably turn into that thickish porridge you mentioned so revoltingly. If you know what a good old choke

137

you can have when an aspirin tablet powders in your throat, consider what a mouthful of this . . .' – he tapped on the extinguisher with his finger – '. . . would do to you.'

'A more likely bet than your aerosol of talcum powder for sweaty armpits,' Lingard conceded, though pointedly.

'A tossed off suggestion,' Rogers said blandly. 'Willie also told me that firing off the spray at anything from two to three feet away would widen it only to about a couple of inches in diameter. That would fit what we saw, given a shaking of the hand that'd put some of the powder over his chin and cheeks. He showed me a box of the stuff they keep for refills; a white silky dust that slopped around almost like water. It has to be it, David.'

Rogers found much to agree with in Lingard's earlier reconstruction of what had happened, found it easy to picture it in his mind. The car with its murderously-inclined driver waiting in the shadow of the moonlit arch, the tall figure of Jervaise stooping to peer into the driver's window and the person he must have been expecting to see looking up at him. Words spoken or not, the sudden uplifting of the concealed extinguisher, a snake's hiss of expelled powder into a startled face and Jervaise staggering back to collapse in the violent convulsions brought on by lungs bursting for air.

He said, 'There's one thing Willie didn't have to tell me, and that was that Philip Lattimer is a sub-officer at his station and would know what's what about powder-filled extinguishers. They use them routinely, only they're very much bigger than this little chap and not the kind you'd carry around with you in a car.'

'You're dying to tell me now that he wasn't on duty last night,' Lingard suggested.

'I don't know. It wasn't the time for asking. But I do know this. On top of being a nasty-tempered sod, he drives a Spitfire sports job and that's low enough to the ground to be a small car in anybody's language.'

'You're not suggesting he also killed his own brother, are you?' Lingard said doubtfully.

'A fratricidal character called Cain apparently did,' Rogers reminded him. 'And more than a fair number of others have since. Especially when there were large amounts of money to be had. And there was.' He shook his head. 'For all that, I'm sure not. In any case, we've no evidence to connect the two deaths to one person and the *modus operandi* couldn't be more different.' He put irony in his voice. 'I might be slandering an honest and worthy citizen, but it could be that brother Philip was driven to killing Jervaise out of an imagined revenge for the death of Andrew. Or even . . .' – he gave a short laugh at the thought – '. . . for the debauching of his sister-in-law's virtue. A joke,' he added quickly, before Lingard could take him up on it. 'Still, I don't think I'd put either past him if his thinking was cocked up. In fact the number one nail in his coffin, if he's destined for one, could be the wheelbase measurement of his car. That's something for you. When we've finished, you can get it for me from the Reference Library or from one of your friendly car dealers.'

'I can hardly contain my excitement,' Lingard murmured. Louder, in his secondary role as a floater of theories, in none of which he need seriously believe, he said, 'Devil's advocate and all that nonsense, and rather hackneyed I'm afraid, but say that Jervaise knew more about the killing of Lattimer than he let on to you? Say he knew the identity of the villain he suspected of doing it. And if he did, and silencing him was the motive, you'd have to agree that he was struck dumb extremely effectively. Taking it a little further, couldn't he have been the writer of the anonymous note?'

'And been frightened in doing it?' Rogers was sceptical. 'He wasn't a man to be intimidated by anyone.'

'That could have been meant to mislead, even to suggest that a woman wrote it.'

Rogers grimaced. 'It could at that, I suppose.' He rose from his chair and began to put on his jacket. 'I'll have Norton breathing fire at me if I don't go,' he said. 'I'll see you back here when you've so excitingly checked on the Spitfire.' He smiled a lot of teeth. 'That's one of my failings, David; always keeping the dull and dangerous jobs for myself.'

Getting into his car, he felt that matters were going well for his investigation, that he was getting a grip on the hitherto imponderables. And that worried him, knowing from experience that Whoever it was up aloft had the distressing habit of clouting the overconfident, the man who thought he had things satisfactorily buttoned up, back into a properly humbled frame of mind.

24

Were Norton to be the subject of an entry in the *Police Gazette*, Rogers would expect to read his name and description as Waldo Ralph Norton, bn 1948; 5′ 4″; bld sinewy; c. weatherbeaten; hair, beard & moustache black; e. grey; nose aquiline; educated speech; self-employed falconer. No pre cons.

That official description, while not misleading, would show only the bare bones of the whole man. Rogers, should he exercise an imagination of words, would describe him as a bantam-sized, dark-skinned obsessive with a small pointed beard and eyes the colour of wet roof slates. Characteristically damn-and-blast-you quarrelsome, arrogant and insolent, he had a notably short-fused temper. With no interests outside his birds, he was particularly scornful of anyone ignorant of the differences between a falcon and a hawk. Usually dressed as if about to crawl into a muddy badger's sett, Rogers could yet see him in sixteenth-century doublet, breeches and hose with a rapier hanging at his waist, itching to slice somebody's guts with it. Despite the sum of these traits he could be likeable and was, unless poked in the chest with an aggressive finger, reasonably harmless. He and the detective met seldom enough for each to be able to have a more or less congenial scorn for the other's occupation.

Norton had moved since Rogers had first met him, now living in a redundant farmhouse adjacent to a few cottages collectively called Mockbeggar, too few to own to a civilizing pub or a church. Interestingly for Rogers, Mockbeggar was only five miles or so across a spur of the moor from Brigthorpe.

Leaving his car in a lane rutted with hard-baked mud, he had to walk sweatily the gauntlet of a few dozen circling horse-flies, a shaggy pony, two donkeys, several white goats and a large red pig, all apparently believing that he was carrying food for them, before reaching the house. At one side of it were large wire-netting compounds holding hawks and an owl tethered to wooden blocks, a form of captivity not meeting with his approval.

Jane Norton, answering the door, delicately attractive, gentle and – in Rogers's opinion – necessarily long-suffering, seemed nervous about a policeman's visit. Which, he accepted, was understandable when, like a croaking raven, he was so often the precursor of trouble. She led him through the house to what had once been a front parlour and was now her husband's workroom. Norton, standing at a bench under an open wire-meshed window and concentrating on sewing a miniature scarlet plume to a leather hawk's hood, said without turning his head, 'Shut the door, cock, and wait until I've finished this.'

Rogers did so and, having noted that Norton, wearing scruffy thorn-proof khaki trousers with a pocketed plum-coloured shirt and ankle boots, was kitted out for the hawking he had delayed, looked around him. Apart from the bench cluttered with leather-working tools, pieces of animal skin and green baize, and a collection of tiny bells and swivels, there was only a rough pole perch wedged across a wall angle with a canvas screen nailed to its underside. On it, secured by a leash, stood an unhooded peregrine tiercel, his haughty unblinking black eyes watching him. Behind his tail feathers, probably to Jane Norton's helpless despair, the plastered wall was spattered liberally with stale and fresh squirted faeces; what Norton would always bluntly call hawkshit. Beneath the bench lay a snoring liver-and-white setter bitch, grey in the muzzle and gaunt.

When Norton had finished his fiddling chore, he turned and faced Rogers. 'All right, cock, what's this you're telling me about that bastard being dead? And don't raise your voice doing it.' He jerked his beard at the tiercel. 'Coz is barefaced and likely to bate at coppers shouting the bloody odds.'

'He was murdered, Waldo,' Rogers said as though such a happening was his daily fare. 'I'm interviewing the neighbourhood's shady characters, and naturally you're the first on the list. I'm not telling you how or when yet, but it was committed at about ten last night.'

'Always the secretive bugger, weren't you.' Norton was amused. 'It wasn't a moment too soon. I only regret I didn't do the swine in myself.' He raised his eyebrows. 'You didn't want me to say I did, did you? I could've after that business with Emmie.' He cocked his head at Rogers, challenging him to ask what he was talking about.

'You're a wicked sod, Waldo,' Rogers said equably, willing to go along with him. 'But not that wicked. Who's Emmie?'

Norton was suddenly dark-faced. 'Coz's sister. The bastard shot her. He'd accused me of poaching grouse from his bit of the moor because she'd downed one once when I'd flown her at a rock and she'd raked away. I loved that bird. *And* she was worth every bit of a couple of thousand.'

'He'd seen her do it?' Rogers suspected that Jervaise could have been right about the poaching of his grouse.

'No. But one of his hirelings obviously did. He phoned me and told me to keep my birds off his ground, or else.'

'And you didn't?'

'Christ, cock, don't you coppers know anything? He doesn't own the whole bloody moor and I'm not up there with her once she's been thrown off. She can fly onto a quarry of her own picking and there's sod-all I can do about it. On the day I lost her and I'd released her to a rook, I wasn't on his piddling piece of ground. So, sure as fate she raked away after a woodie – a wood pigeon to you – and stooped, putting it into cover in his bloody trees. That's when I heard the shot. I couldn't find her when I got there, I couldn't find any bugger and I never saw her again. I saw him later that day and all he'd say was "Really? You don't say? Do you have any proof?"; rabbit-turd words like that until he told his bloody butler to show me the door.' Norton scratched savagely at his beard, scowling at the remembrance of it.

'I suppose you'd threatened him with doom and disaster?'

'That I had. I'm only sorry some sensible bugger beat me to it.'

'How long ago was this, Waldo?' Rogers asked, neither of his sensory antennae stirring even slightly.

'Last summer, and I've not been able to replace her yet.'

'Is all this why you had a go at him in the Minster last night?'

'The nub, eh cock?' Norton bared small discoloured teeth in a grin. 'Do I come quietly?'

'Why not? I told you that you're number one suspect.' Rogers smiled briefly back at him. 'What was it about?'

Norton made a dismissive gesture. 'Nothing at all. When he was on his way out I said – quite courteously, considering – "Shot any good birds lately?", just to remind him I hadn't forgotten. He got bloody snotty and said I'd better watch what I was saying or I'd have his solicitor on my tail. That's all, except that he wasn't

142

very mannerly about it. He's a touchy bastard – or was, I should say.'

'Not the only one,' Rogers said drily, 'but I'm more interested in the woman he was with. Do you know who she is?' Despite the open window it was hot in the room and smelling pungently of elderly dog and birds' faeces, his shoulders already beginning to sweat.

'No, but I think I've seen her before. I don't know where or when so don't start pushing me. I'll tell you this, though, she was a looker.' Norton sounded almost enthusiastic.

'Describe her, Waldo. Everything, right down to any moles she might have.' He took out his notebook and pen. 'It's really important.'

'I'm sure it must be, cock. You're being too bloody polite for a copper.' Norton was silent in thought for a time. 'Right,' he said, 'I've got her. Twenty-five to thirty years for a start. Not too tall and a good-looking figure. Hair down to here . . .' – he touched the side of his chin – '. . . a reddish-brown, auburn I think. She had a bandeau round it as if she'd been playing tennis. A very, very attractive face. Lipstick. That was a lightish red, not too conspicuous. A lovely mouth and I wouldn't think any other make-up. She had a pale skin, kind of sallow, but it suited her. Made her look foreign and interesting. Dark eyes; brown I suppose.' He was silent again, looking down at his feet, then said, 'That's it, and not bad at all. You can toddle off now and see about finding her.'

'She was naked then? Not wearing any clothes?'

'A bright bastard, eh?' Norton poked two fingers ceilingwards in mock derision. 'Yellow. A plain yellow tunic over a skirt. That was black or dark-blue, I didn't see it until she walked out. And I think she had on a belt to match the dress, though I'm not too sure about that.'

'Tell me if they came in together or not, what happened between them and – if you noticed – his attitude towards her and vice versa.'

Norton raised his arm, looking pointedly at his wristwatch. 'You've another five minutes, cock, and then I'm going. She was already in one of the nookeries when I came in, drinking wine I think. He came in later and went straight to her. They shook hands – odd that, don't you think? – and then he sat down with

143

her. He ordered drinks and there was lots of cosy chat between them. I wouldn't say exactly gay and animated, but they were getting on well together. I wasn't peering at them too much because I was with a friend, but later on I saw she was coming the female on the make with him. Fluttering eyelashes, pushing the old titties at him and so forth.' He made a kissing noise with his mouth. 'If she'd looked at me like it I'd have been steaming from my trousers. Perhaps it was the wine she'd drunk, or just as likely the size of his wallet he wasn't shy in waving about when he paid for the drinks. You could see him lapping it up, not even trying to keep his eyes off her bosom. At one point, she was showing him a magazine of some kind, not that I think the ignorant sod can read, mind you. It stuck out a mile he was persuading her to go somewhere and then I think she started to cool herself down a bit, play a little hard to get. You know? Biting her lip as if she had a problem on board. Whatever it was, he got up and said something to her and left her, and it wasn't to go to the gents either. No hand-shaking this time and after he'd been gone some minutes she left too, giving me the old hard eye as she passed. I expect she noticed him giving me a bit of stick on his way out. Which is where you're going too, cock.' He pushed himself away from the bench and pointed a thumb at the tiercel which had straightened his legs and lifted his wings as if about to take off. 'His flying's a bloody sight more important to me than your yacking about Jervaise is, so come back tonight if you think I've more to offer. And bring a bottle with you.'

Leaving the room, the setter ploddingly following, Norton said, 'I suppose you're teed up about him being cock-happy? That he'd bonk anything female?' He pushed out his cheek with his tongue, his eyes wicked. 'Do you know he put the wife of one of his farm-workers in the family way and had to pay him and her off?'

'That'd be anathema to us celibates, wouldn't it,' Rogers said with sarcasm, not impressed or willing to believe him wholly. 'If you can put names to any of them I'd be interested.' They were outside in the dazzling sun and he could see quivering heat waves rising from the sea-blue enamel of his car. Norton wanted to be rid of him, but no more than he wanted to get away from his unforgiving antagonisms towards a dead man, useful though any spin-off from it might prove to be.

144

Norton shook his head. 'I'd have liked to have got something on him. Somebody did, I guess, and beat me to it.' He waited until Rogers was unlocking the door of his car. 'When is he getting buried?'

'God knows,' Rogers grunted, stripping off his jacket and climbing into the interior oven. 'He hasn't been dead five minutes. Why?'

Norton's expression showed that had he been the type to spit his contempt, he would have. 'Because I'd like to go there afterwards and piss on his grave,' he said, leaving the detective not knowing whether he had meant it seriously or not. He was a man Rogers had once seen – unanticipated and to his horror – split with a knife the head of a not-quite-dead rook and feed its brain to the hawk that had downed it. If he could do that, urinating on a hated man's grave would be nothing to him.

Bumping down the lane with all the windows wound down and cursing the heat, Rogers tried to convince himself that he had obtained something more from Norton than the certainty that the woman in yellow had definitely not been Audrey Lattimer. Were she the woman telephoning Jervaise and calling herself Mrs Conway, then he had a finger already poised to put an identity to her.

25

There had been an unfathomably something female about Jane Norton that had resurrected in Rogers the temporarily buried-alive emotions he had attached to Eleanor Caine. Seated jacket-less at his desk and waiting for Lingard's return, he was experiencing all the inner compulsions of a vigorous male's breeding cycle. Eliminated as a suspect – had she ever been one – or as a source of further useful information, she was threatening to haunt him with her new-found availability for some favoured man. Her beautiful image, her elegant sexuality – he was sure that her mouth would taste of summer flowers – and her compatible persona had crept into his system as addictively as the nicotine from the tobacco he smoked. Had he been the fifteen-

145

years younger Detective Constable Rogers, had there been a moon outside instead of a torrid sun, he would probably have stood on his hind legs and howled his need at it. He was recollecting with approval the self-styled gentleman's gentleman's euphemism of cross-pollination for what he was so pleasurably imagining in fairish detail when Lingard, the equivalent of a deflating cold shower to his fantasizing, entered the office.

'Ah, David,' he said, trying to look as if he had been puzzling out legal abstrusenesses, 'sit down. I've been working things out. I only want your Spitfire measurements and your agreement about the female seen with Jervaise at the Minster last night and I think we'll be on the home stretch.'

Lingard flopped into his chair, his narrow features flushed. 'You couldn't start to guess how many hot pavements I've tramped to find out a simple thing like the wheelbase of an out-of-production car,' he complained. 'And you're not going to like it either. According to the manufacturer's specifications for all Spitfire variants, the wheel base is fixed unalterably at six feet, eleven inches. And if my memory's still in working order, we're talking about the marks at the scene being six feet, eight inches.'

'Give or take an inch on either side,' Rogers reminded him. 'But sod it, just the same. It wouldn't wash as evidence against him, would it? You can't shrink wheelbases.'

'Sergeant Magnus could have made a mistake,' Lingard said, his expression showing it to be a forlorn improbability.

'His middle name is Infallibility or somesuch, David.' It was Rogers's only comment on an absurdity. 'Still, it won't stop me believing that brother Philip is in this up to his neck.'

'I knew I'd be wasting my time,' Lingard murmured. He pinched snuff from its box and charged his nostrils with it, the scent of attar of roses carrying across the desk to Rogers. 'What about the woman?'

'Norton gave me what appears to be a good description of her. That and her probable use of the name Conway to arrange a meeting must mean something.' He opened his notebook and smiled. 'I've already written down the name I'm expecting you to give me. She's aged twenty-five to thirty, chin-length reddish-brown hair with a bandeau tied round it, dark-brown eyes, sallow skin, light make-up and possibly a foreign appearance. She was wearing a plain yellow dress with a matching belt – it's possibly one of those tunic things – over a black or dark-blue skirt.'

'Apart from the screamingly unlikely Mrs Gullick, I've only seen one woman on your behalf,' Lingard drawled flippantly. 'So you're obviously expecting me to say she's Kirstin Lattimer. And so she must be.' He was silent for a moment or two, his blue eyes veiled in thought. 'She wasn't wearing a bandeau when I saw her, but she did have on a yellow dress and black trousers. Not a skirt, but she'd likely change into that for the evening. I'm surprised that her eyebrows weren't mentioned, being very conspicuous. And, I suppose at a stretch, she could give one the impression that she was a signorina or a senorita.'

Rogers held out his notebook for Lingard to read *Kirstin Lattimer*, the name he had written down. 'Who else?' he said. 'And who else locally would know of Mrs Lattimer's former married name but one of the family? And of two sisters, one eliminated because of her disfigurement.'

'And you think she killed Jervaise?'

'I don't know, I haven't got that far yet. You saw her – would you consider her capable?'

'She impressed me as a woman of some determination.' Lingard was reliving his interview with her, his finger and thumb pulling at his lower lip. 'A forceful character, probably a paid-up member of fem-lib. I wouldn't care to be married to her, that's for sure. Very soft on her dead brother though – unbeatified saint and all that – and conversely hard as nails on whoever she'd believe had blown him up. To wit, evidently one Roger Jervaise.' He stared hard at Rogers. 'We're tolerably sure, are we, George? Sure that he didn't?'

'When I'm sure about something, I'll pass it on,' Rogers assured him, conscious that he had been short of apportioning anything but undisputable facts. 'I don't want your thinking blinkered by what may prove to be half-witted theories.' He scratched with apparent perplexity at the emerging stubble on his chin. 'There is one aspect of your forceful character that strikes me as being odd. You told me that when you saw her she'd obviously been crying over the death of her brother. Well, she should, shouldn't she?'

'She had been,' Lingard said. 'Not broken up, but it was

hurting. Eyes watering and so forth whenever he was mentioned – that sort of thing.'

'Think on it, David. A couple of hours later and, if Norton's to be believed, she's drinking with Jervaise and as he says fluttering her eyelashes and pushing out her titties at him.' He shook his head, grimacing. 'Even for somebody as hard as nails that's a bit cold-blooded, isn't it?'

He lifted his telephone receiver and dialled the number of the fire station, speaking to Station Officer Edmunds. When he had finished and closed down, he stood, shrugging himself into his jacket. 'That's all right then,' he said to Lingard. 'While I'm jumping on brother Philip, you're for Love Lane and Kirstin. When you've satisfied yourself that she was the woman with Jervaise, bring her in. Don't take it any further than that, but let her sit in your office and sweat it out until I get back. I might have some useful information from her brother to confound her, if she needs confounding. While you're at it, check her Mini to see if it's got a bracket fitted in it for holding a fire extinguisher. I don't think she'd be that daft, but you never know. And if there's a driver's handbook in it, see what the wheelbase measurement is.' He grinned mockingly. 'Exciting stuff, isn't it?'

On the way out to his car, he was thinking that if she had used her hated sister-in-law's former name to lure Jervaise to his death, there had to be a certain irony to it.

26

'Although he's what you'd call my second dickey, George,' the uniformed and cadaverous Edmunds said to Rogers, 'I don't like the bugger. He's a trouble-maker and I'd be glad to see the back of him.' He tapped a bony forefinger on his temple. 'And I think he's a bit touched up here.'

Rogers, sitting with Edmunds in his office and drinking with him a mug of nauseatingly sugared canteen tea – more from politeness than because he liked it – had told him merely that there was a suspicion of a relationship between Lattimer and the dead Jervaise which, although slight, needing clearing. Though he hadn't chosen to question it, it had been obvious to the fire officer, as it would have been to anyone short of being *non compos mentis*, that there was considerably more to it than that.

'In what way, Willie?' he asked. 'When I had him at his brother's house he struck me as being just ordinary bloody-minded and unhelpful.'

'That too,' Edmunds said feelingly, darkly saturnine. 'He's a pain in the arse. A pain in mine in particular, and a bloody nuisance. Since his promotion – and God forgive me for ever recommending him for it which I did – he's been a work-to-rule man who I'm damned certain sleeps with the service regulations under his pillow. Normal married men don't do that, do they?'

'Is that why you think he's touched?'

'Not only. He talks to himself. I've sometimes passed his office and seen him in there chuntering away to himself like nobody's business. I think he's a chapel man too,' he added, as if that made it even worse.

'He didn't sound like it when he was yelling off about his brother's wife,' Rogers told him, then silently rebuking himself for being too forthcoming. He wasn't usually so gabby.

'I'm not surprised.' Edmunds must have read the detective's expression for he left it at that. 'Mind, I'll say this for him. When he's dealing with a fire, he's good. No nerves at all and the first one inside when it's necessary.' He looked Rogers straight in the eyes over the mug of tea he had lifted to his mouth. 'I know you won't tell me how or why, you being such a close-mouthed bugger, but he's got to be connected with the sodium bicarbonate I showed you this morning, hasn't he?'

'He could be,' Rogers conceded, giving away that much. 'I'll tell you all when it's been straightened out.'

'And his brother? The one we dealt with yesterday?'

'I shouldn't think so,' Rogers said ambiguously, only guessed at what Edmunds was asking. He pushed back shirt cuff from his wristwatch. 'Could I see him now? I'm on a pretty tight schedule and they're queueing up to see me back at the office.'

Edmunds stood and reached out a lanky arm for his cap resting on the top of a filing cabinet. 'Which reminds me. I've business with the Borough Surveyor, so I'll have Lattimer sent in. Use my office like your own . . .' – his expression was mocking – '. . . but don't get splashing blood on my walls, there's a good chap.'

When the door closed behind him, Rogers took over his chair, a bright green concoction of plastic and aluminium tubing, and, waiting, began stuffing tobacco into his pipe. He was conscious that he had nothing against Lattimer but an intuitive feeling that he had been involved in the killing of Jervaise. And intuitive feelings, hauled out in daylight from the back of the brain and called hunches, were as infuriatingly difficult to grasp as wind-blown soap bubbles. Should an unco-operative Lattimer tell him to get stuffed, then he would have to accept it. At least for the time being, he qualified, and certainly not too good-temperedly.

Lattimer, in uniform and with his cap set square and uncompromisingly over a scowling face, came in without knocking. Moving no further than inside the door he left open, he thrust his bearded chin at Rogers and said angrily, 'Whatever you've got to say to me, say it quick. I've a situation drill coming up and you've no right to ask to see me when I'm on duty.'

Rogers, hardened to a society over-populated with angry and hectoring males resentful at being questioned by policemen, spoke without raising his voice. 'I don't particularly mind myself, but unless you want the rest of the station to hear what I've to say, you'd better shut the door and sit down.' He held Lattimer's angry grey-eyed stare, willing him to submission.

It succeeded only partly, Lattimer banging the door shut, but remaining where he stood. 'You've made me curious, Mr Lattimer,' Rogers said, putting perplexity in his words. 'And you've hurt my feelings. Wouldn't you expect me to come and see you at any time about the investigation into your brother's death? Is that anything to be so angry about?'

Lattimer was silent for long seconds, his anger dying to an apparently habitual surliness. 'You didn't say,' he muttered. 'But I still think you could have waited and not made my watch wonder what was going on with me being sent for by the police. What was it you wanted to tell me?'

Rogers was convinced that his anger had been the pre-emptive response of a man against something he feared, a defence against an attack that hadn't been given a chance to materialize. But which was about to. He said, 'This isn't anything directly concerned with your brother, but interesting enough for you, I imagine. It seems that last night we had one of your sister-in-law's lovers murdered at Brigthorpe. A chap called Jervaise.' He

150

had watched Lattimer closely as he spoke, seeing a tensing of his body, an exaggerated surprise that hadn't been reflected in his eyes.

'Who? Jervaise?' he asked, frowning his incomprehension excessively. 'I don't know him. Never have.'

'Oh.' Rogers managed to look disappointed. 'You did say yesterday that you were going to find out, and I thought you were going to say that you had.' He was now puzzled. 'But surely you'd have heard of him? He was a magistrate here for years, well known in the town and all that.'

Lattimer was shaking his head violently. 'Not me,' he ground out. 'I've never heard his name mentioned and if that's all you wanted to ask me, I'm going.' He turned his back on the detective to push down on the handle of the door.

'Do that,' Rogers said, unmoving in his chair, his voice forbiddingly hard, 'and I'll be forced to think you're running away, and I'll do something about it you won't like. As it is, I'm beginning to wonder what you've got to hide.'

That there was anger, possibly fear, going on in the face turned from him, Rogers had little doubt. He waited while Lattimer made up his mind what to do about it. Then, releasing his hold on the door handle, he faced Rogers and folded his arms, his hostility unconcealed. 'Ask what you have to and hurry it up,' he growled. 'I don't have time for playing games.'

From somewhere in the building Rogers was picking up the echoing sounds of clashing metal and men's voices, of loud scraping noises and muffled hammering. 'They seem to be getting on all right without you,' he pointed out to him, 'and that's just as well, for I know you'll be interested in this. The Mr Jervaise you appear not to know was choked to death by somebody forcing powder – it's probably sodium bicarbonate, by the way – down his mouth and into his nose. Quite an unusual way of killing a man, wouldn't you say? I mean,' he said as if it were an afterthought just striking him, 'as a fireman you'd know about sodium bicarbonate and what it could do to a man's breathing.' That had brought nothing to his face that Rogers could read.

'Most anybody would know that,' he said with angry scorn. 'They're sold in shops.'

Rogers raised his eyebrows. 'Really? What are?' He thought

that he had been given a prepared answer to an anticipated question, although it hadn't yet been put to him.

'Fire extinguishers. Isn't that what you're talking about?'

'So I must have been,' Rogers conceded drily, accepting that the man was a fool. 'You do have one in your car, I suppose? Being a fireman and setting a good example to us all?'

'No, I don't. I never have.' His mouth was working oddly. 'I know what you're suggesting, and you'd better be careful.'

Rogers considered that he was being underestimated and that suited him. Particularly so when his instinct was confirming that Lattimer's anger was a poor mask for his fear. 'Do you mean my mentioning your connection with fire extinguishers and sodium bicarbonate,' he asked, putting on an expression of bafflement. 'You could have had one with fluid BCF in it and not had to worry at my asking you. That's too late now though, isn't it?'

Lattimer's thick throat had shown him swallowing hard at that. 'You don't know what you're talking about,' he grated. 'You're accusing me of knowing about that man being killed, and I don't. That's what you're getting at, isn't it?'

'Was I now?' Rogers stared at him up and down, deliberately thoughtful. So far, Lattimer hadn't given out quite the smell of a man charged with talking aloud to himself, but he was definitely an oddball. 'I hadn't thought so,' he said, 'but since you've brought the matter up, perhaps you'd better satisfy me that you don't. The easiest way for that would be for you to detail your movements last night.' He beamed his encouragement at him. 'Yes? Say from the early evening?'

'That's as good as saying that I did have something to do with it, which I didn't.' Lattimer, apparently only simmering now, had unfolded his arms and put his hands in his trouser pockets. 'So why should I?'

'I only wish to save you a lot of personal embarrassment,' Rogers said amiably. 'You know, having my chaps calling on your friends and associates – anybody who might be able to give us information about where you were, or were not. If you've nothing to hide, it's all so much easier to tell me.'

Even for a policeman used to being disliked and feared as the nemesis of those he dragged to their downfall, hatred, even impotent hatred, could be an unsettling emotion to face. And it

152

lay naked in Lattimer's eyes, though neither in his expression nor in his voice. 'I've nothing to hide,' he said. 'I don't know why you're stupid enough to think I have. I spent the first part of the evening at home with my wife like anyone else who'd just finished work. After the nine o'clock news headlines I visited my sister, arriving there at quarter past nine. She was also watching the news and I joined her until it was over at half-past. Then we just talked, mainly of what to do about our brother's funeral, and she made me a cup of coffee. I left her at eleven o'clock when she said she wanted to go to bed. I went home, had the supper my wife had left for me and went to bed about quarter to twelve.' He pushed his beard out aggressively. 'Is that what you wanted? Or do you want to know what I had for supper as well?'

Rogers felt that after his unabated hostility, that had come too easily. It jarred on his level of acceptability. It was only intuition again, but it sounded rehearsed, held back for release to the right question. The times he had given covered the period estimated by Twite for Jervaise's death and little more, when he, Rogers, had said only that Jervaise had been murdered last night. It allowed him to change his attitude towards Lattimer, and he asked him with much less amiability, 'Which sister were you visiting?'

'Drusilla, and you'd better leave her alone. She's a sick woman and you've already upset her with your stupid questions.'

'It's a fact of life you'll have to bear with that this being elsewhere business needs corroboration by the second party. In this case, your sister who, of course, would also be an emotionally related party.' He cocked an eyebrow at him. 'I take it there'll be no difficulty there?'

Surprisingly, Lattimer said, 'You do what you have to do. I can't stop you, can I?'

'I don't intend that you should,' Rogers told him tersely. 'You drove your car there? The Spitfire sports I saw you in?'

'I wouldn't walk, would I? Not that far.' He hesitated a moment, then said, 'I parked it in Pennyfarthing Street.'

'You would, wouldn't you? Being next door to Love Lane.' Rogers, wondering why he had been offered that, chose not to question it but to consider it later. The Spitfire's unaccommodating wheelbase measurements were proving an awkward inhibition. 'Apart from an understandable brotherly affection and

153

your brother's funeral,' he said, 'was there any other reason for visiting her?'

'I visit her regularly. Wouldn't you?' His unfriendly eyes, shadowed under the peak of his cap, searched the detective's face for whatever it was he needed from him.

'Certainly I would,' Rogers agreed urbanely. 'Was your other sister – Kirstin, isn't it? – there too?'

'No, she wasn't.' Too quickly, reacting like a nerve being pricked.

'You didn't see her at all?' Rogers implied doubt in his question.

'No. I would have said so, wouldn't I?'

And that, Rogers accepted, promised to be a fair specimen of what he would get in asking more questions for which he had no background information. Staring at the glowering Lattimer, he knew it to be decision-making time. He unstuck himself from his chair and moved to stand facing him. 'One more thing,' he said, choosing his words carefully, 'and then it's possible we're finished. Whoever killed Jervaise did so from a car parked outside his property. We know that because there were tyre-marks at the scene. It's no problem for you, I imagine, but I shall have to look at your car to satisfy myself officially that it's not the one.' He thought that he had read sudden unease in Lattimer's eyes. 'It's here, of course?'

'You've seen it already!' he exploded. 'You said so yourself just now.' He glared his erupted anger at the impassive Rogers, spittle flecking his beard. 'You'll be sorry about this. I'll see what a solicitor says about it, just you wait.'

'That's been said to me a few times before, so there's no need to shout it.' Rogers had rarely questioned a man more difficult, more capable of sustaining angry hostility. He had to be guilty of something, if only of owning to excessive bile. He said shortly, 'I'm going to look at it either with you or without, so please yourself. Shall we go?'

Lattimer's mouth framed inaudible words as he turned and pulled open the door, not waiting but stalking stiff-legged along the corridor outside. Though Rogers was having doubts about his intentions, they were stilled when he went through a rear door, allowing it to swing back in Rogers's face as he stepped out to an open hard-standing. Among the few cars parked there,

154

quivering heat waves in the sun, he recognized the yellow Spitfire. Lattimer, taking up a position with his back to the driver's door, waited, his lips clamped shut in determination.

With the small car's roof not quite reaching the middle button of his jacket, Rogers gave its exterior and tyres a cursory inspection. He grunted 'H'm' and walked to its rear. 'The spare in the boot, please,' he said. Lattimer took keys from his trouser pocket and opened it, watching silently while Rogers checked its contents, none of which interested him, and examined its inner shell. Closing the lid he moved quickly to the passenger door, saying, 'Better do the inside, hadn't I?' and opening it.

Lattimer's reaction was a too-late strangled 'No!' as Rogers, ignoring it, stooped his head and shoulders into the hot interior. In semi-darkness after the outside dazzle, he closed his eyes for three or four seconds, feeling the start of sweat on his face and trusting that Lattimer wouldn't be hauling him out with violence in his mind. When he thought he could cope he lowered his chest on to the seat, focusing his eyes onto the body linings beneath the instrument panel. On the side wall nearest to him were two small holes, he guessed eight inches apart, with one at an angle above the other. They were enough for what were called reasonable grounds for arresting a suspect and he said 'Agh!' with satisfaction, loud enough for Lattimer to hear. Had he been a religious man, he would have promised to light a candle, or whatever it was one did when there arrived unexpected good luck. And having it, he wondered whether the normally meticulous Magnus hadn't made a cock-up of his wheelbase measurements.

Levering himself out backwards from the confining cockpit, he stood and brushed down his jacket with the flat of his hand. Lattimer, his anger gone, looked as though something calamitously heavy had fallen on him. Rogers, his expression stern, said, 'Telling me that you'd never carried a fire extinguisher in your car wasn't exactly the truth, was it?'

Lattimer shook his head despairingly. 'Somebody else . . . the man I bought it from . . . three years ago.' With little resistance left in him, he searched Rogers's face for some sign that he was being believed. 'I wouldn't know, would I? I didn't look . . .'

The man was coming to pieces and that Rogers didn't want, for he would get no sense from a distraught mind. 'Lock your car and give me the keys,' he ordered him. 'I've grounds for believing you to have been concerned in the death of Roger Jervaise, and I'm taking you into custody.'

'No.' Lattimer looked jerkingly around him, then back at Rogers, his mouth shaking. 'You can't do it, I'm on watch,' he said, his voice strained to hoarseness. 'If there's a fire call I have to be there.'

'I *can* do it,' Rogers said patiently. 'It's what I'm doing now. Lock your car or I'll do it for you.'

Lattimer, still with the keys in his hand and submitting without further protest, more tamely than Rogers had anticipated, locked the doors and then handed over the keys. Escorting him back through the corridor and outside to where he had parked his car, Rogers hoped that he wasn't about to make one of the bigger errors of judgment in his career. Though Lattimer's reactions to his questions, to his finding of the revealing screw-holes, had all been clear manifestations of a guilty knowledge, without further evidence they would count for less than nothing in the brief of a defending counsel.

27

Lattimer now occupied a cell; adjacent, had he cared or was even aware of it, to those containing Chaffer and Mullet, soon to be released on bail. Suffering from what appeared to be a form of mental paralysis at the enormity of what was happening to him, he had shaken his head, dumbly unhappy, when told formally by the Duty Chief Inspector that, on the complaint of Detective Superintendent Rogers, he would be detained as a suspect to a serious arrestable offence, that is, the unlawful killing of one Roger Loring Jervaise. Stripped of unessential items of clothing and searched, advised of his right to free legal advice, he had been escorted from the Charge Room, leaving Rogers with an initial twenty-four hours to prove with hard evidence why he was a suspect at all.

Deigning not to use the lift to the second floor as a matter of masculine pride, he took the stairs to his office. Lingard was waiting for him in the corridor outside it. 'I saw you bringing chummy in,' he said flippantly. 'We can all go home now?'

Rogers pulled a not-too-happy face. 'I haven't got much, David, other than what the hell was I talking about and that he was somewhere else when whatever it was happened. With his sister Drusilla, so he says. And God strike him down dead but he'd never had a fire extinguisher in the car in his life. The couple of screw holes I found under the dash belonged to someone else, but of course.' He wagged his head. 'He's in shock at the moment so he won't be amenable to more questioning for an hour or two. It's just as well, it'll give me time to check his story with Drusilla.' He strode into his office with Lingard following him. 'What about Kirstin?' he asked.

'She's in my office with a WDC,' Lingard said, 'and you'd better hear about her before you have her in.'

Rogers, slipping off his jacket and loosening his tie, slumped into his chair, sweating damply and wishing he had taken the lift. 'You'd think the mean sods would have come up with a fan or two for us, wouldn't you,' he complained inconsequentially. 'Tell me while I try to cool off.'

Lingard, remaining standing and not hiding his amusement, said, 'The worst is yet. I don't think we've a dog's chance of getting anything out of her that doesn't mean get lost. She already had a touch of girding her loins for battle when she answered the door and saw who it was. I dived in straight away – investigating the messy death of a Mr Jervaise, understood she was with him at the Minster last night, possibly last to see him alive et cetera, that it was possible she could help us with our enquiries. Basilisk glare meant to cause sudden death. Had met a man there if any of my business, so what would his death have to do with her? Grateful, I told her, if she'd come with me for chat with anxiously waiting Superintendent Rogers. Not bloody likely, she said, or words to that effect. Pointed out not convenient for unknowing, uncaring woman with other things to do, getting very cross with quite inoffensive Chief Inspector.' Lingard took out his snuff box, tapping a fingernail on its lid. 'Pointed out duty of honest citizens to help further cause of justice, that being under most stringent of instructions I must insist. Egad, George, definitely not one of your admirers. Gave me another of her glares, but conceded defeat and said she'd come under protest. Checked her Mini next door in Pennyfarthing Street, but no bracket for fire extinguisher.'

He had stopped tapping on his box, a habit irritating to Rogers depending on his mood, opened it, took a generous pinch of snuff and inhaled it. 'However,' he said, reverting to his normal drawl, 'I think we're onto something. Her Mini's fairly elderly, does leak oil and its wheelbase is given as six feet, eight and a quarter inches. That could be significant whichever way you look at it.'

'It'd be a damned sight more if there weren't dozens of other elderly Minis in the area.' Rogers was exaggerating his pessimism. 'Apart from not being overwilling to talk, what's your opinion of her attitude?'

'As I said, loins already girded for an expected battle. Not liking it, naturally, but ready for it.'

'The same with her brother, and something that gives me hope.' He stood and began putting his jacket back on. 'Give me five minutes, then bring her in and I'll go for bust.'

Waiting, he resumed his seat, tightened his tie and re-lit the tobacco ash in his pipe for a quick fix of nicotine, inclined to smoking it economically since recently calculating that it was costing him a horrifying £2375 a hundredweight. He was mentally uncomfortable for no reason he could put a finger on, but suspecting that a flawed intuition might be letting him down. Nothing of what he had heard sounded quite right and, having confidence in his second-in-command's assessments, if he got anything useful from Kirstin Lattimer he was going to be a very surprised and grateful man.

When she was ushered in by Lingard, he stood and said, 'Good afternoon, Miss Lattimer, please sit down.' As Lingard – a fraction over-attentive, he thought – led her to the visitors' chair, he took in her physical characteristics. Slim and below an average woman's height, her bobbed hair a deep auburn, she wore a featherweight cream jacket and skirt with a chocolate-coloured shirt. Her eyes, beneath strongly marked eyebrows, were a dark brown just short of being a luminous black, her skin a smooth olive, a first impression being given of a warm and attractive brownness. None of it showed in her eyes, in the set of her unspeaking mouth or in the air of positive self-assertion emanating from her. She held a clutch-bag in a hand undecorated with rings and was, Roger's unusually sensitive nose told him, un-scented. He had now seen the three of them and a photograph of the dead fourth. But for their hair colour they had no discernible similarities, and he thought that they might share only an out-going auburn haired mother with a randomness of odd fathers.

He sat and clasped his hands together on his blotting-pad. 'I understand that Mr Lingard has told you of the death of Mr Jervaise,' he said expressionlessly, 'and that we are investigating what appears to be his murder. I also understand that you were with him in the bar of the Minster Hotel last evening. The circumstances of that could, of course, be of interest to us.'

'Is that why I've been forced against my will to come here?' Her voice was cold with a controlled bite to it. 'To tell you something you already know and which can have nothing to do with that man's death?'

Rogers sighed inwardly. The Lattimers were proving a difficult lot and she sounded as if about to follow the pattern of her brother's hostility. But it could promise well, innocence under interrogation being less aggressive and more accommodating, of which she was neither. 'Mr Jervaise was one of your sister-in-law's lovers, Miss Lattimer. Out of all the men in the Abbotsburn district, your seeing him socially would be surprisingly in-appropriate. Furthermore, outside the staff at his house, you appear to be the last known person with whom he spent time.'

She was sitting stiffly in her chair, girded, as Lingard had said, for battle. And being no mean adversary, Rogers judged, for unsettlingly attractive as she was, her strength of will seemed sufficient enough to numb to discomfiture any faltering of male purpose. 'If you are assuming that I knew him to have been that woman's lover,' she retorted, her dark gaze fighting his, 'you are assuming in ignorance. As for him being called Jervaise, I wouldn't know. He didn't tell me and there was no reason why he should.'

Rogers could see Lingard leaning against the wall behind her, a barely concealed smile on his narrow features. 'Perhaps you'll lighten my ignorance,' he said to her, 'and tell me how you came to meet Jervaise. Certainly the details of what you were talking about.'

'I intend to tell you,' she said precisely, 'and, because I've no reason to hide anything, I shall expect to be taken home as soon as

159

I have.' She lifted her chin at him. 'I was in the bar when this man came in and immediately approached where I was sitting. I didn't know him, I'd never seen him before, but he said that if he wasn't mistaken we had met on one of the flights to Gatwick. That was possible, although I wouldn't have remembered him from the hundreds of others. I made some off-putting remark to him that I wished to be left alone, but he ignored that and said that if I wasn't waiting for anyone might he get me a drink in return for those I'd brought to him. Without being terribly rude I could hardly refuse, and I was feeling so dreadfully depressed that it seemed a relief at the time. I had an hour to spare anyway and he was a friendly and superior kind of man, unlikely to be much of a nuisance in a public bar.'

She stopped abruptly, opening her clutch-bag and retrieving from it a slim orange packet. She said tartly, 'I presume I shall be permitted to smoke?', taking out a long brown cigarette and snapping an enamelled lighter at it as if underlining the completion of what she had told him.

'There's more, of course? What you talked about?' Rogers had the same feeling about what she was saying as he had had with her brother; she accepting this questioning of her activities as though anticipated.

'Is there?' she said, her eyebrows down. 'I thought I'd already told you. I talked about what I did, and he talked about his house, about his shooting and his sheep farming; nothing in which I was particularly interested. He said that he was eating later at the *Provençal* and would I care to be his guest. Which I refused, partly because I obviously wouldn't be able to and partly because he wasn't a man I wished to become involved with.' She appeared to be trying to browbeat him with her stare as she inhaled at her cigarette, then tapping its ash on to the rubber flooring.

'Do you recall the man with the small beard sitting a couple of tables away from you?' Rogers asked.

'Yes, I do.' That had been a guarded answer.

'He had the impression that you and Jerviase were meeting by arrangement, that you shook hands as if expecting each other.'

'Then he's either a fool or a liar,' she replied contemptuously. 'Is he the man who said something to him when he went out?'

'I imagine so,' Rogers said, dismissing Norton as a tool unlikely to prise anything but denials from her. 'Mr Jervaise received a phone call yesterday afternoon from a woman calling herself Mrs Conway, apparently arranging a meeting later that evening. Could he have taken you for her?' That, he was certain, had done something to her expression, but it was gone before he could read it.

'If he did – and I've only your word for it – he didn't say so.'

'But the name Conway does mean something to you, doesn't it?'

'It's a common enough name. It's not one I like or am prepared to discuss.'

Lingard, out of her vision, was raising his eyes to the ceiling in a parody of amused despair. Rogers said, 'You told me just now, Miss Lattimer, that when Jervaise asked you out for a meal, you obviously wouldn't have been able to go. Why was that?' There had been a slight emphasis in her words and the thought had lodged in his mind that she had angled for him to ask that particular question.

'Because I had work to go to,' she said, her lipsticked mouth scornful. 'Surely you knew that?'

'Apparently not,' Rogers admitted, deciding that a little un-comprehending amiability might promote forthcomingness, and giving it the help of a half-smile. 'What do you do?' He had already guessed what.

'I'm a hostess with NorAuk Air, this week on the night shuttle flight to Edinburgh and Inverness.' She almost spat that at him.

'From Chudlow Airport, naturally,' he commented, knowing that she was about to tell him the time she was on duty. He had suspected that she would be lighting a fuse under him when opportune. 'You left the Minster at about eight-thirty; surely that's early for a night flight?'

One of his office flies had settled on her forehead and she slapped at it impatiently. 'It's not early at all,' she contradicted him sharply. 'We're airborne at five-past ten and we're required to be in Flight Operations Room for briefing at nine-thirty. That means I have to leave here at about half an hour beforehand to have time to change into uniform and be ready for it. Which is exactly what I did,' she said, holding his regard of her challengingly.

'I'm sure you're right,' he told her. 'It's twelve miles to the airport, so do you get picked up by the authority, or make your own way there?' When for a brief moment her eyes were away from his, he stared hard at Lingard and jerked his head to signal an unspoken instruction to get out and do some checking. He thought irritably that the three surviving members of the Lattimer family were something like a bloody domestic Mafia.

'I drove there,' she answered him. 'As I always do.' She had shown the first sign of unease, and that barely perceptible, in saying it.

'Ah,' he said, deciding to turn on the screw, 'your blue Mini. It's a remarkable coincidence, but where Mr Jervaise was found dead – outside the entrance to his house, by the way – there were tyre marks which could only have been made by a Mini.' He rubbed at his chin with thumb and fingers as though in deep thought. 'Mentioning that, perhaps I should have told you earlier that your brother Philip's in custody downstairs.'

She had gone rigid at that, dismay paling her face, shaking her head forcefully in refusing acceptance. 'No!' she cried. 'You can't! He hasn't done anything! What are you . . . ?' She trailed off into silence, struggling away from an outburst she had been surprised into and must now be regretting, gradually attaining a composure which, though stricken, showed her unsubdued. Straight-backed, she demanded, 'I want to see him.'

Rogers had watched her carefully, against his commonsense approving the indomitability of her spirit, a different mettle from that of her brother. 'Possibly you may when I get the truth from you,' he said, his amiability withdrawn and intending to abandon any subtlety he may have been using. 'First, there are some facts that I want you to know. After leaving you at the Minster, Mr Jervaise returned to his home, arriving at nine o'clock. That, for a start, gave him no time for eating at the *Provençal*, or precious little for meeting anyone else. He remained at home, telling his butler that he was going out at ten o'clock and would return in a few minutes. We can accept, as did the butler, that he was intending to meet a woman and to return with her to his home. Wherever he had arranged to meet this woman, it was only minutes away but still far enough for him to drive there. The entrance arch to his property fits that, and that's where he was found dead the following morning. *This* morning in fact, Miss Lattimer, and a happening in which you appear to have no interest whatsoever.'

Lingard had referred – he had thought exaggeratedly – to her basilisk glare. Rogers, receiving a baleful briefness of it, knew it to have been no exaggeration. 'Well,' he went on, 'I don't suppose you'd know him intimately enough to want to shed tears for him, especially a man who'd been cuckolding your dead brother. You'd know that, I'm sure.' If a brief licking of her mouth was an answer, then he'd had it. 'The post-mortem examination on Mr Jervaise,' he said. 'That confirmed he'd died near enough to ten o'clock, the time of his intended meeting with this woman Mrs Conway, or whoever she was. Of course, if you're telling the truth about being at the airport then, or already on your way to Inverness, you couldn't possibly have been involved in that, could you?' He shook his head, turning down the corners of his mouth. 'Don't imagine that lets you off the hook. I still believe you were a party to the meeting.'

He let his words hang in the silence of the room, never taking his eyes from her. The only movement she had made while he talked had been to drop her cigarette onto the floor and put her foot on it. Otherwise, apart from the licking of her mouth, she had sat tight-lipped and hard-faced, intending a stubborn refusal to acknowledge hearing his words. Accepting that he had used most of his ammunition without visible success, he said, 'Let me go on from there, Miss Lattimer, and consider how Mr Jervaise could be persuaded to be where he was found dead, so late at night, without having eaten and so short a distance from his house. I suppose that for a man with a known reputation for womanizing, the obvious form of decoy would be female. Necessarily an attractive one who promises much; possibly, if posing as a married woman, urging a need for discretion in a meeting she knew she would never need to make, but which someone else would.' She was looking past him now, her dark eyes fixed trance-like on the window at his back as though she were not listening. 'Someone who intended to kill him . . .' – he heard the sharp hiss of indrawn breath – '. . . and did so by choking him to death with a fire extinguisher. I imagine that's a reasonable assumption of what happened, don't you?'

He didn't expect an answer and he got none. Whatever iron control she was imposing on her tongue wasn't doing anything for the restless fingers working on her clutch-bag. That he had spelled out correctly what had happened was, he considered, reasonably confirmed by her refusal to deny it. Or, unreasonably, not. 'There is a further point to make,' he said. 'Brigthorpe Hall – where I'm sure you know he lived – is a fair distance from here and needs a car to get there. Not, I'm sure, an easily described small yellow sports job that'd stick out in moonlight like a sore thumb. But say something like a blue Mini that'd be virtually as unnoticeable as a dark shadow. Yours, Miss Lattimer? You using your brother's car to get to the airport; he taking over yours for Brigthorpe?'

Her continued muteness scratched irritated frustration in him although, professionally, it should not. Wanting to fling his bloody telephone through the window at which she was still staring, he thought that might seem a bit of selfish overkill, bottling it up for taking it out on his waste paper bin when he was alone. A testy question about her brother was forming in his mind when the door opened and Lingard came in. He pulled a doleful face and nodded in the direction of the silent woman. It decided Rogers and he said to her, 'I don't think there's any point in taking this any further at the moment, and it means that you'll be held in custody pending any further enquiries into the death of Roger Jervaise.' He spoke to Lingard. 'Take Miss Lattimer down, will you, and see that she's made comfortable. But not, and pass it on to the duty officer, to be allowed to speak to her brother.'

She rose from her chair and faced him. 'You must know that you are making a dreadful mistake,' she said, her expression either one of guilt defending itself to the last gasp, or innocence going to unjustified disaster; he could take his choice.

Rogers said nothing and, filling his pipe for a much-needed smoke after she had gone, sat and tried to work out which it might be.

28

Rogers felt bird-broody, sitting on eggs that weren't hatching as he might have expected them to, and, mixing his metaphors, he had put his few cards on the table to little effect. A policeman being convinced of the guilt of a suspect was worth nothing, being as inadmissible in evidence as would be a divine thunderbolt striking dead an unconfessed adulterer. Not escaping him as a pointer to their guilt had been the two belligerent Lattimers' new-born disinterest in what he had done, or was doing, about the death of their brother; indicating, he was certain, that they were now satisfied that their idea of justice had been done.

When Lingard returned to the office, he was wondering whether *intransigent* was the appropriate word to describe Kirstin Lattimer's attitude in his official notes. 'You're going to be sued for wrongful arrest and false imprisonment, George,' Lingard said with all the affability of the uninvolved. 'So Kirstin told the Duty Chief Inspector before he had her locked up.'

'Nothing very original there,' Rogers grunted, 'and I'll try and bear up under it. I take it you meant that she was in the clear for being somewhere else?'

'As far as I could check on the phone she is. NorAuk's a small concern and there was no senior bod available. Nor, of course, any of the night staff. However,' he said, shaking his head, 'there's no record in Flight Operations of her being absent with or without leave. As, I'm told, there would be. Plus all kinds of hoo-ha to boot in having to find a replacement. Without committing himself too rashly, my chap was sure that if she said she was, then she was on the flight. So you'll want me to pop over there and do a check?'

'You're on the way, David. And while you're there, find out whether she was using her brother's Spitfire. It's a bright yellow hard-top incidentally and it'd probably be noticed. I'm sure she was, leaving her Mini for him to do his dirty work. I'm for Love Lane,' he said without any noticeable optimism, 'to persuade Drusilla, a sad case already, that she'll be sadder still and doing herself no good at all if she's set on committing perjury to protect that bloody brother of hers.' He grimaced. 'And how in the hell can I lean hard on a woman in her condition?'

With Lingard gone, he telephoned for an available policewoman to nanny him. Anticipating the probabiilty that he could be embarrassingly cried on, be subjected to a distraught woman's unmanageable hysteria, he was unwilling to suffer it on his own. He was unlucky, none being handily available and he being too impatient to wait until one was.

The sun was about to drop behind the town's backdrop of purple moor when he turned into Pennyfarthing Street and parked his car. Walking towards Love Lane, he pased an Oxford-blue Mini, the only Mini in the street, with a seven-years' old index plate and certain to be Kirstin Lattimer's. Though it looked most unlike a car from which murder had been committed, it and the upwards-looking face must have been the last earthly impressions the unfortunate Jervaise had taken with him to wherever he had gone.

Pressing the bell-tit of number thirty-one, he waited. Expecting it, he saw a lightening of shadow in the door's tiny viewing lens, then heard her voice, low and tense. 'What do you want?'

'A few words with you, Miss Lattimer,' he said. 'But not from standing out here.'

'What have you done with my sister?' The disembodied voice was agitated. 'You must tell me.'

'If you'll let me in I will,' Rogers said firmly, feeling ridiculously exposed talking to a violet-coloured door. 'And not until you do.'

He could sense her long drawn out hesitation before he heard the clinking of the door's safety chain and the turning of a key. She was already walking away from him towards her chair when he pushed open the door and entered. Seeing her sit and receiving no demand that he should keep his distance, he moved to a wooden-armed chair close to her.

As if neither he nor his sensibilities to facial mutilation were of importance any more she was confronting him, and he could see clearly the reddish striations running from beneath the patch over her missing eye and the mottled discolouration of the skin. She wore a loose coffee-coloured dress and the dying sunlight filtering through the closed parchment louvres gave her the sepia tint of a Victorian photograph. Only her dog was missing from what he had seen the previous evening.

She waited for Rogers to speak and he cleared his throat. 'I apologize for bothering you again,' he said, 'but it is important and does concern your sister and brother. They're both at my office helping us in connection with the death last night of a man named Jervaise.' Her pale mouth had tightened and her eye had widened at his words. 'You know him?' he asked.

'No,' she said. 'Who is he?' Then agitatedly, without waiting for an answer, 'Why do you think they can help you?' The shiny pink patch over her eye socket – Rogers could imagine the red emptiness behind it – was turned to him only when she spoke

166

and it was disconcerting him. Otherwise, she was now obviously intent that he should see only the uninjured side of her face.

'I'm specifically interested in your brother's whereabouts last night,' he told her. 'I have to tell you that he's suspected of being at or near the scene of Mr Jervaise's death. His movements need checking and it's thought that you could help.'

'Are you saying that this Mr Jervaise was killed? That you suspect my brother and sister of doing it?' She was showing the edge of what he had already accepted as a typically Lattimer hostility.

'I'm saying that he was murdered; that and your brother being questioned about where he was at the time.'

'He was with me for most of the evening. Is that what you want?' There had been the slightest signs of shakiness in her voice.

'I'd like to know what time and for how long he was here.'

She had bowed her head, her hands resting on her lap and formed into what seemed a submissive steeple of slim fingers. 'I don't know when Mr Jervaise is supposed to have died,' she said in a low voice without looking up, 'but I know that it's unlikely my brother had anything to do with it. He was here, as he often is, from close to nine o'clock until he left at about eleven.' She lifted her head, her eye staring resolutely at him. 'I can't say where he was before or after, but I'm sure that his wife will be able to. Did he tell you that?'

She was lying as he had expected she would, guessing that she could never be shaken from defending her brother down to the last scrap of made-up conversation. 'Was your sister here when he was?' he asked.

'No. She had already left for work.'

'In her Mini, of course?' he said agreeably as if it mattered little.

There was a moment's indrawn silence before she replied. 'Of course. How else would she get there?'

'How else indeed?' Rogers echoed her, his instinct telling him strongly that badgering her to change her story would result only in her re-affirming it. While they both sat unspeaking in the hushed room, he sought in what he called the compost heap of his mind for straws with which to poke truth from her. She had bowed her head again, this time at fingers rubbing slowly together, and, while he kept his gaze unmoving on her, he

167

detached his mind to visualize again his reconstruction of Jervaise's death.

He saw the massive arch, livid in the moonlight, the dense shadow thrown by its pier and, in it, the soft glimmering darkness of the Mini with a paleness of bearded features showing through its open window. The arrival of the Range Rover on the other side of the arch, its stopping short of going through it and the big figure of Jervaise leaving it to approach the car he had to expect to be there. Then, his bending down to speak to the woman he was to meet, his probable angry surprise at who he saw and the lethal spray of powder in his face, his staggering back and falling in the bushes. His murderer, possibly waiting to satisfy himself of the onset of death, then starting up the engine of the car and driving back on the road and . . . *no!* He was forgetting the man's glove, dropped or thrown down to rest close to the body. Worn to guard against leaving fingerprints and carelessly dropped from the car? Possible, but not probable, for where else but in the car could fingerprints be left? Thrown down as a misdirection? Much more likely, but as a misdirection from what? *You stupid bugger, Rogers*, he swore in his mind. He hadn't given that enough thought. Inept as it was proving to be, it had to be a misdirection from the sex of the killer. Were that so, then it *had* been a woman in the car.

He stared at her sombrely, finding it difficult to believe it of so pathetic a wreck of a beautiful woman; as difficult to believe that a frail butterfly could savage to death a lumbering beetle. He had allowed pity to blind him to what her mutilation and love for her dead brother had done to her mind, and now he hoped that the brutality of what he had to say would be justified . . .

Breaking the silence, he said, 'I've given some thought to what you said about your brother, Miss Lattimer, and I see no reason not to accept that he was here.' He paused as she gave him a quick upward glance of her eye. 'It seems that I made the mistake of accepting that you were giving him an alibi,' he said with more confidence than he felt and wishing that he had a policewoman with him. 'I see now that he was giving *you* one. That it was you who kept the meeting with Mr Jervaise that your sister had arranged. You who killed him.'

He knew its truth immediately from the paling of her face that made more conspicuous the tracery of her scars, from her eye

168

staring aghast at him and the terrible fraught silence that filled the room. She had lifted her hands from her lap, knotting tormented fingers together, fighting for steadiness. He said gently, 'And I think I know why you did it.'

'My brother,' she whispered, her eye sparkling with brimming tears. 'He killed my brother.'

'And you killed him because of it?'

'I didn't mean to.'

'But you did.' She had come so easily that Rogers's expected interrogation had been scattered. 'Tell me about it. And why you didn't mean to.'

She had control of her agitation now, her face turned towards the window. 'He told Andrew he would, and he did. His wife was living with him and she wanted a divorce. Andrew said that he refused, that he would fight it, and he was threatened. Threatened that he would be killed. Which he was.'

Rogers tried to read in her face any sign of disbelief in what was patently incredible and saw nothing. 'You do mean Jervaise and Andrew's wife?'

'Yes. Andrew said Jervaise kept telephoning after she left him and there was talk of money which I didn't understand. Several times he came to the house late at night when Andrew refused to answer the door. He said he was frightened to go to the police because that would make it worse for him and they couldn't stop what was happening even if he did. He told me that if anything happened I would know and then I could. Report it to the police, he meant.' Tears glistened on her cheek. 'When I was told he had been killed I knew Jervaise had done it . . . that it had happened as Andrew said it would.'

'And you decided between you to do something about it.' He spoke softly, keeping as motionless and as inconspicuous as he could, feeling that he was acting more the surrogate priest behind the grille of the confessional rather than an interrogator.

'I wanted to hurt him, to make him pay for what he had done to Andrew. I went there last night . . . when it was done and I saw that he was dead I was terrified. I didn't know what I could do, so I . . .' She trailed off, then burst out, 'I'm not sorry the filthy beast's dead, even if you think I am! He was a brute and he should have been hanged. I don't care what you do to me, my life's nothing now. It hasn't been since this happened to me.' She drew

169

in deeply a shuddering breath, her face tragic. 'I wish I could have died with Andrew. That would have been a blessing . . . so frightening for him . . . now so lonely for me.' Her head was bowed and she was crying, her hands held over her face.

Rogers waited patiently. He needed to ask questions about the involvement of her sister and brother, but not to a sobbing woman, certain anyway that she would refuse to compromise them. They could come later, but there was one that he was certain she would answer, and truthfully. When her sobbing had lessened to a fluttering breathiness, he said, 'Believing that Andrew's life was threatened, did you write an anonymous note to that effect and send it to the Chief Constable?'

Taking her hands slowly from her face but still not looking at him, she shook her head. 'I don't know what you mean,' she whispered shakily, drained to a dull apathy and threatening, Rogers believed, to collapse on him.

Distasteful jobs were part of Rogers's lot and the inevitability of imprisonment for this pathetic woman was nothing in which he could take the pleasure of accomplishment. He stood and said, 'I'm sorry, Miss Lattimer, but I'm now going to call for a police-woman and you'll be taken into custody on a charge of murdering Roger Jervaise.' He recited the formal caution to her unresponsiveness, not sure that she was understanding him. That, and her forlorn condition, persuaded him from telling her that he knew beyond any reasonable doubt that Jervaise had not killed her brother, that she had murdered an innocent man. It was something she would later have to live with and, should she possess a normal woman's sensibilities, to have haunt her to her grave.

29

With a sultry darkness outside his office and a moon hanging invisibly somewhere above its ceiling, Rogers, stubble-chinned, short on sleep and hungry again, was tape-recording his Progress Report that an over-optimistic Chief Constable would expect to be on his desk at nine the next morning.

Having finished with the evidence against the three co-conspiring Lattimers, he had recapitulated the circumstances of Andrew Lattimer's death. Sucking at his freshly-filled pipe, he switched alive the microphone he held. 'There are indicative actions with some resulting incongruities on Lattimer's part,' he said into it, 'but all, I suggest, persuasive of only one conclusion. The planting of the explosive device in his car could only have been done after seven o'clock when Mrs Caine heard him return and garage the car. He did not, so far as she could hear, take it out again until the following morning. Any intruder opening or closing what is an extremely noisy metal door between those times would almost certainly have been heard by Lattimer and, possibly, by Mrs Caine. There remains in my view a distinct improbability of entry to the garage by any person other than Lattimer. The metal and glass case I saw on the front window sill of the house – used as a miniature greenhouse for plants – has since been identified as a tropical fish tank. This, theoretically, put Lattimer in possession of the type of thermostat used in the explosive device or having, at least, a knowledge of its function. The smokeless gunpowder used was almost certainly extracted from shotgun cartridges, these readily purchased without licence from any gun dealer.'

He thumbed the microphone dead, relighting his pipe and reflecting that mental certainties never sounded quite so convincing when reduced to commonplace words. He said 'Bugger it!' amiably enough and switched on again. 'The evidence of Mr and Mrs Gullick that Lattimer accelerated excessively the engine of his car, that he reversed it unnecessarily, suggests that he was deliberately increasing engine heat in order to effect a closing of the thermostat's contact points and expedite the resulting explosion. On leaving the house that morning he left the door key on the hall table, not being found in possession of a duplicate when his body and his car were searched. This, admittedly, could have been an oversight though, as likely, it could be a subconscious recognition that he would not need it again. The impression on the reminder pad reading "Meet 10.00", being the only legible writing in a mass of scribble, suggests a deliberate pointer to his meeting someone at the time of his expected death, and meant to be read in any resulting police investigation. His seeming attempt to blackmail Jervaise (who, within limits, I believe to

171

have been truthful with me) and his seeking a face-to-face discussion with him was, if meant to be carried out, an unbelievable and potentially dangerous departure from a blackmailer's norm. It was, in my opinion, a contrived manoeuvre to persuade Jervaise to visit his house, possibly for him and his distinctive Range Rover to be seen and identified by one or more of the neighbours. This, if successful – and it was – would add substance to those alleged threats from Jervaise he had already complained of to his sister Drusilla. I believe these to have been wholly fictitious and motivated by malice and a desire for revenge. His allegations to his sister of Jervaise's wish to marry his wife, and the threats to kill him should he not agree to a divorce, are nonsensical in the extreme. Given what the situation actually was between Jervaise and his wife, as a motive for murder it is unbelievable by any standard of common sense. Lattimer, clearly emotionally under the influence of his wife, had fraudulently obtained a loan of twenty thousand pounds from his employers, the bulk of which it seems he transferred to her. Despite this, or because it gave her the financial freedom she needed, she decided to leave him to join her lover Jervaise. In this, although Lattimer would not necessarily know it, she failed, transferring her choice to another man with whom it seems clear she was already associating.'

Rogers switched off to rest his voice for a few moments. Poor Jervaise, he reflected, forgetting that he hadn't liked him overmuch in life. Not only had he thrown away five hundred pounds on a worthless trollop, but his life as well. And, taking it back to its beginnings, probably all because he had been left wifeless by a cuckolding hairdresser. Looked at in that way, it made lusting after another man's wife something of a misfortune. He shut that uncomfortable train of thought off and continued with his recording. 'Lattimer's known mental condition shortly before his death needs, I suggest, a psychological review and interpretation for the information of the coroner. So far as I can discover, he was a man of weak character. He had certainly suffered the loss of his job and any future he might have had in that particular field, and, although he had apparently insured himself against prosecution by Chaffer and Mullet by his possession of evidence of their tax evasion offences, he could never be certain that they would not in some way still exact retribution. Coincident with this, he lost his definitely unloving wife with whom he was by most accounts inexplicably besotted, and who, it is certain, had no intention of returning either herself or the stolen money to him. His resulting deterioration has been remarked upon by those who knew him and I have no doubt that in this condition he canalized the blame for it, and his hatreds, on Jervaise. Everything he did in relation to him points to a design to entangle him as his murderer in the death he himself sought and eventually found. This, to the extent of predetermining what would appear as his murder in the anonymous note he must surely have written. With its printing unidentifiable as it stands, he may yet be proved its author by a laboratory examination of the writing materials at his house.'

He hoped that it would, for he had believed Drusilla when she said she knew nothing about it, and he could think of nobody else who would be likely to. The complexity of Lattimer's malice had underlined for him how twisted and fundamentally evil he had been; a man who, though unwittingly, had led his sister into murdering a man guilty of little more than promiscuity. He thought that he had said enough to prove his point and he dictated his conclusion. 'If the foregoing facts are put to HM Coroner, I feel that he will have no hesitation in directing a jury to find a verdict of suicide against Lattimer, probably with a rider that it was committed while the balance of his mind was disturbed.'

As whose wouldn't be, he thought as he switched off and replaced the microphone on its hook. He would have liked to have added a rider himself about Audrey Lattimer; mentioning that, not too wildly, he believed her to be a woman who, in the giving of her corrupt body, inevitably brought violent death to any man using it. It made him hope that when a certain Humphrey Thomson, owner of the motor cruiser *Snapperjack*, was reported as having fallen accidentally overboard and drowned, that it would be reported to a force not his own.

For himself, given a quick mowing of his stubble, a re-invigorating wash and a discreet absence from his flat, he could be his own man until the following morning. According to some pessimistic character he couldn't recall, all flesh was grass, destined one day to wither like the grass in a field. That was true enough, and it led him to remembering the more robust character who had said something about after the battle one should seek the anodyne of embracing arms. If Eleanor Caine did possess an irresistible bent towards post-separation adultery, he thought he could persuade her that it would be better she should commit it with a freshly-scrubbed, clean shaven and crammed with red corpuscles Crown servant than with somebody of whose occupation her gone-away husband might not approve. Getting her number from his desk directory and reaching for the telephone, he prayed that she would be civilized enough to first offer him a coffee and a sandwich or two.